BUFFALO BILL'S DEAD NOW

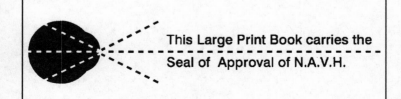

This Large Print Book carries the
Seal of Approval of N.A.V.H.

BUFFALO BILL'S DEAD NOW

MARGARET COEL

THORNDIKE PRESS
A part of Gale, Cengage Learning

GALE
CENGAGE Learning·

Detroit • New York • San Francisco • New Haven, Conn • Waterville, Maine • London

LIBRARY OF CONGRESS CATALOGING-IN-PUBLICATION DATA

Coel, Margaret, 1937–
    Buffalo Bill's dead now / by Margaret Coel.
        pages ; cm. — (Thorndike Press large print core) (A wind river mystery)
    ISBN 978-1-4104-5355-6 (hardcover) — ISBN 1-4104-5355-3 (hardcover)
    1. Arapaho Indians—Fiction. 2. Large type books. I. Title.
    PS3553.O347B84 2012b
    813'.54—dc23   2012034536

Published in 2012 by arrangement with The Berkley Publishing Group,
a member of Penguin Group (USA) Inc.

Printed in the United States of America
1 2 3 4 5 6 7 16 15 14 13 12

For Luther Wilson who, as director of the University of Oklahoma Press, took an enormous chance on an unknown writer by publishing my first book, *Chief Left Hand*; and who, as director of the University Press of Colorado, published in hardback my first attempt at fiction, *The Eagle Catcher*. Which made all the rest of it possible.

I circle around
I circle around
The boundaries of the Earth —
Wearing the long wing feathers as I fly.
Wearing the long wing feathers as I fly.
As I fly.
— Arapaho song from the 1890s

PROLOGUE

"I hear you're calling yourself Trevor these days." The big man with bushy, steel gray hair and big hands with stubby fingers folded himself into the booth across from Trevor Pratt. A skinny guy, Hispanic, black hair slicked back from a horselike face, took the edge of the bench. The skinny guy looked familiar. Trevor bit off a chunk of hamburger and took his time washing it down with beer. Music had started thumping from the speakers tacked up on the walls of the Empire Lounge and two or three couples sauntered out onto the dance floor and began gyrating. Lights from traffic on Federal Boulevard flashed in the pane glass window alongside the booth.

Trevor set the beer bottle on the table, leaned back, and stared at the big man. Hol Chambers hadn't changed much in the last dozen years. A little paunch, a few extra pounds, the vein-traced nose and leathery look of a drinker, but not the kind of change that mattered, that went to the heart of things, not a change in character. Trevor could see it in the man's eyes.

"Do I know your friend?"

"Raphael here? Raphael Luna. We partnered up a few times since you took that trip to jail. Tried to catch up with you that one time in Colorado."

"How'd you find me here?"

The big man emitted a laugh that sounded like a truck motor starting up. "Come on, Trevor. You know the network keeps track of business associates. Let's just say you were spotted at an auction, going by the name of Pratt. I started following your success." He shook his head, as if he had thought of a tragedy that might have been avoided. "Nothing compared to what might've been yours."

"What do you want?"

"Thought it was time to pay you a little visit. For old times' sake. Cowboy at the ranch said you were dining out at the Empire Lounge." Hol shrugged a shoulder in the direction of the skinny guy beside him. "Figured we'd join you. Have a little chat."

"Nothing to chat about." Trevor pushed his plate into the middle of the table, swallowed the last of the beer and signaled the waitress for the check. The lounge was stuffy. Cigarette smoke swirled about the rafters and odors of burned tobacco, beer, and fried potatoes clogged the air. He felt old suddenly, and weary, as if the weight of the past had crashed onto his shoulders. He would never escape the past. He had come so far, built a new, legitimate life. The Bar Z Ranch, a couple hundred head of cattle, three cowboys on the payroll, pastures and meadows that wound into the foothills of the Wind River range. A house filled with museum-quality parfleches, pipes, bows and arrows, beaded moccasins, vests, tanned deerskin ceremonial dresses. He had never lost the passion for Indian artifacts, with their mystical connection to the past. Each item belonged to him, and he had the sales receipts and other documents to prove their provenance. That was the biggest change from the past. He was a dealer now, collector and dealer. He bought American Indian artifacts from around the world — the quantity of artifacts in Japan, the Middle East, and Europe never ceased to amaze him. He never shipped a package to a foreign address without a dull sense of regret that the artifacts were leaving the place where they belonged. And yet, all of it

11

tenuous, hanging by a thin thread. Mortgages on the ranch and stock that he scrambled to meet every month. He'd even borrowed to purchase artifacts, but the market had slowed. Museums and wealthy collectors were holding onto their money.

"We have a chance to do some real business," Hol said. The waitress slid a check onto the table, and he told her to bring three more beers. "Arapaho artifacts from Buffalo Bill's Wild West Show. Due to arrive in Riverton any day now, thanks to the generosity of an anonymous donor. Raphael here sent me the newspaper article. Had Trevor Pratt written all over it. Raphael thought I might be interested in how you bought the collection in Berlin and was donating it to a third-rate museum at an Indian mission. I was interested, all right. I got a client nuts about Buffalo Bill stuff. Original Indian artifacts from the Wild West Show — you know how rare they are? Museums have grabbed most of it. Hasn't been a collection on the market like this in years." He gave a quick nod. "My client will write a check that'll put us both out of the game. No more hustling, looking for the big score. You can retire on your ranch, buy all the artifacts you want."

"I'm not in the game," Trevor said. "I paid

my dues." He set some bills on top of the check and started sliding across the booth.

"Hold on," Hol said. "You can't be serious! Donating a collection like that to a museum at some Indian mission nobody ever heard of? That's not the Tom Plink I used to know. Tom would never let a score like that get away."

Trevor reached the end of the bench and stopped. "It's Trevor Pratt," he said. "The artifacts are going home where they belong."

"You said you could talk to him," Raphael said.

"Shut up." Hol spoke out of the corner of his mouth. "I'll tell you where the collection belongs. Real nice house, lots of windows, three, four stories, high up in the Spring Mountains, lights of Vegas in the distance, and the whole place a museum filled with stuff to knock you cold. Like I said, the client is nuts over Buffalo Bill and the Show Indians. He'll pay any price. He wants the Arapaho collection." He leaned back and waited while the waitress delivered three glasses of beer. Then he took a long drink, set the glass down and said, "You're the new owner. You can make the collection go wherever you say."

"What's in it for you?"

"Finder's fee, thirty percent of what the

client pays. Don't be a fool. Tom Plink would jump at this."

"Tom Plink has debts to pay." Trevor started to his feet, then sank back. The idea of a windfall shook him to his core, enough to pay off the mortgages, hold on until the collectors and museums wanted to buy again. A last score. He felt a ripple of excitement slice through him.

"You think you can give back what you stole fifteen, twenty years ago?" Hol said. "The artifacts we dealt with are gone. In the houses of collectors that appreciate them. You can't bring them back to the tribes."

"I can bring back some things."

Raphael let out a giggle and Hol told him to stifle it. The music throbbed and thumped. The dance floor was full — a swaying motion of blue jeans, boots, and flowing skirts. A cowboy spun a girl who lurched sideways toward the booth. Trevor reached out to steady her, but the girl righted herself and headed back to the dance floor, hugging herself, giggling.

"You haven't changed," Hol said. The words, low and distinct, sliced through the beat of the music. "Always the gentleman. What happened between you and Kim?"

Trevor leaned over the table and brought

his face close to the man. "You bastard! You should have gone to jail with me."

"You, being a gentleman, didn't snitch on your friends. Good man. In case you want to know . . ." He took a long drink of beer. "Kim didn't stick around. Evidently I wasn't her type. Heard she got married. Somewhere in California. New name, new life, just like you. Water over the dam. I seen you had yourself a new gal in Colorado."

"This chat is over." Trevor got to his feet.

"Hold on." Hol stood up beside him and moved in close, as if the conversation were just beginning. "All we need is information, and we'll take it from there. I'll see that you get your cut. Nothing will be traced to you. You can collect a million dollars in insurance." He paused, but Trevor didn't say anything. "I guessed right then." Hol broke into a grin. "The collection is worth a million easy, even though an old horse trader like you paid the dealer — what? Half million?" He put up the palm of his hand before Trevor could say anything. "Don't forget, we're in the same business. Maybe on different sides, but the same. We saw in the newspapers how the Arapaho collection turned up in Berlin after a hundred and twenty years. Some dealer bought the whole collection from a developer that found it in

15

the basement of a building he was about to bulldoze. We would've paid the dealer a couple hundred grand more than what you paid, but the fool had already signed a contract with you."

"I paid what he asked," Trevor said. He was thinking that he had paid all he could borrow by mortgaging the rest of his own collection. "The artifacts are going back to the Arapahos."

"Oh, yeah. Still full of high-minded ideals."

"You're crazy if you think I'm going to help you steal Arapaho artifacts," Trevor said, but Hol wasn't listening. He was going on about a win-win proposition, how the artifacts would be preserved in a climate-controlled environment, enjoyed by generations of well-heeled and appreciative owners. Who knew how the artifacts might be preserved in a two-bit museum? He was only thinking of the artifacts, what was best for them. Hol Chambers could have been a politician.

Now Hol was talking about a time schedule, and Trevor tried to concentrate on the man's words. "All I need from you is shipping information. Flight numbers, schedule for when the artifacts leave Berlin and reach Denver. Flight number from Denver to Riverton and arrival time. You got all that information. All you gotta do is arrange to store the artifacts in an airport warehouse overnight, before they can be trucked out to the mission. That'll give us our chance."

Trevor could feel the stiff smile cracking his face. Simple. In return for the schedule in his desk drawer and a telephone call with instructions to house the artifacts in a warehouse for a few hours, he could collect a million dollars in insurance money, another two thirds of a mil from Hol, and the ranch would be free and clear, his own collection secure. It surprised him, the way temptation could rise up like an old, familiar hunger and start to gnaw at his insides, take him over, push him off balance.

"Get outta my face." Trevor could feel his fists clenching, the nails biting into his palms. "If anything happens to the artifacts, I'll . . ."

"You'll do nothing," Hol said. Raphael was also on his feet. Both men leaned in close. "We'll swear you were in on it. You gave us the information."

Trevor slammed a fist into Hol's jaw, then dodged Raphael's fist and caught the man in the throat with his elbow. The music was still pounding, but the swaying on the dance floor had stopped, and out of the corner of his eye, Trevor saw three cowboys heading for the booth. Raphael bent over, coughing and sputtering. Hol had collapsed into the booth. Trevor could feel the man's eyes fixed on him like laser beams.

"You're a dead man." Hol mouthed the words.

"Little business taken care of," Trevor told the cowboys as he shouldered past. The waitress was huddled across the lounge, but she jumped forward and pushed the door open for him. He strode out into the chilly Wyoming autumn.

1

The pickup rumbling past the administration building sent a tremor through the old walls. Father John O'Malley set his pen down and pushed the notes he'd been making into a neat stack. Topics for next month's sermons, ideas for the men's club he'd started this fall, agenda for the social committee meeting this week. Five parishioners in the hospital, six new mothers who needed help with diapers, blankets, and baby food, a dozen elders who might run short of food this winter. Plus notes he'd written on the budget, never his strong point. What was it the provincial said? He ran St. Francis Mission on a hope and a prayer? Some truth in it. His business plan was to make lists of what the mission needed and pray for miracles. The donations always arrived, checks for five, ten, even a hundred dollars from people he had never heard of. *Help the Arapahos on the reservation* the scribbled notes said.

He hurried outside and down the concrete steps. The black pickup slowed in front of the Arapaho Museum at the far curve of Circle Drive. He broke into a jog along the drive, past the turnoff to Eagle Hall and the guest house, past the white stucco church decorated in the blue, red, and yellow geometric symbols of the Arapaho people. It was the third Tuesday in September, the Moon of the Drying Grass, as Arapahos kept time, and the sun was hot, the sky crystal blue. Gravel crunched under his boots and wild grasses in the center of the drive swayed in the wind. He liked autumn best, the trees and brush, the earth itself, engulfed in flames of red, orange, and gold.

St. Francis Mission on the Wind River Reservation had been home for almost ten years. Still a surprise, when he thought about it. A Boston Irishman, a Jesuit priest on the fast track to an academic career teaching American history at Boston College or Marquette University, at home in the middle of Wyoming on an Indian reservation with a Plains Indian tribe he had only read about in the footnotes of history texts. One day he would be assigned somewhere else, but he was here today.

The driver's door swung open just as he

reached the pickup in front of the old gray stone building, the mission school once. The school had closed decades ago, with not enough Jesuits or money to keep it going. A few years ago he had turned the building into a museum of Arapaho history and culture. The wind whistled in the banner stretched over the front porch. Printed in black on a red background were the words: "Arapaho Artifacts from Buffalo Bill's Wild West. September 21 to January 10."

Father John leaned down to steady the old man starting to climb out of the pickup. Scuffed boots swung forward and planted themselves on the ground. "How are you, Grandfather," he said, using the term of respect for elders.

Bernard Tallman pushed his Stetson back with the knuckle of an index finger and blinked up at him. He had been tall once, Father John suspected. Bent forward now, shoulders pulled in around him. A hollowed look to his chest. At six feet four, Father John loomed over him as the old man steadied himself. "*Ni isini*," he said. "It is a good day. Black Heart's stuff has come home."

Father John nodded. He held onto the old man's elbow and guided him up the steps and across the porch. An hour ago, he had

21

stood at the window in his office and watched the last delivery truck back up to the porch. Delivery trucks had been arriving all summer, bringing items borrowed from other museums for the Wild West exhibition. This was the most important delivery. Chief Black Heart's regalia that he had worn in the Wild West Show. Two men had unloaded cartons and carried them into the museum, cradling them as if they knew the contents were precious. The phone had rung as the truck headed back out to Seventeen-Mile Road. "Artifacts arrived." It was Eldon White Elk, the museum director. "I'll call Grandfather."

The over-sized wooden door, a remnant from the past, like the building itself, swung open. Eldon motioned them inside, nodding and grinning. A row of white teeth flashed against his dark skin. Part Arapaho, part Lakota, the director was at least six feet tall with thick shoulders and arms and a little pouch that hung over his silver belt buckle. He had on blue jeans and a red plaid shirt, cuffs rolled up partway. His hair was black, slicked back into a long ponytail that emphasized his high forehead, sharp cheekbones and hooked nose, the kind of sculptured features that had appeared on posters for the Wild West Show or the

Indian nickel.

"Cartons in my office," Eldon said, tilting his head toward the end of the corridor that bisected the building. Rows of doors led into what had once been classrooms but now served as offices and small exhibition areas. Directly across the corridor was the large exhibition hall. "Got here just in time. School kids are coming for a preview later today. Let me show you what we've prepared." He motioned them past the staircase that wound upward to another corridor and still more rooms. Another staircase, Father John knew, had taken students to the third floor dormitory for Arapaho kids who had lived too far out on the rez to walk or ride ponies into school each day. Items from that time were still stored in the basement, he suspected.

Father John followed Eldon and Bernard into the exhibition hall. Plexiglas display cases wrapped around the walls, a row of low cases ran down the center. The glass surfaces reflected little flares of light. For an instant, Father John felt as if he had stepped back in time and wandered into the Wild West Show itself. A kaleidoscope of colors and motion burst from the display cases. Red, yellow, blue, and black posters of Buffalo Bill leading a charge of cowboys and

Indians, horses galloping, dust flying beneath the hooves. The red-printed banners across the top of each poster said Buffalo Bill's Wild West. Along the bottom edges were the printed words: "Colonel William F. Cody, 'Buffalo Bill.'" There were posters of the performers: "Johnnie Baker, The Marvelous Marksman," printed in black letters beneath the illustration of a teenaged boy holding a rifle. Another poster illustrated a dark-haired young woman in a fitted jacket filled with medals, one hand on the muzzle of a rifle, the barrel planted on the ground. Black letters said, "Miss Annie Oakley, The Peerless Lady Wing-Shot."

Alongside the posters were buckskin shirts with beaded designs, feathered headdresses, beaded vests, and worn cowboy boots with the toes curled up. Bows and arrows, Winchester rifles, silver spurs and belt buckles had been laid out in the middle cases. Arranged around the displays were black-and-white photos of Indians. Show Indians, they had been called. Photos of Indians posing in front of tipis outside an arena, visitors strolling past. A photo of a cavernous canvas tent with "Dining Tent" scrawled across the bottom and the Wild West train standing on tracks in the background. Another photo of Buffalo Bill himself in a gondola with a group of Indians. "Venice," neatly printed along the bottom edge.

Father John recognized the man and woman on the far side of the hall, peering at what looked like half-empty cases. Sandra Dorris, black-haired and pretty with quick dark eyes, a student at Wyoming Central College who had started working part-time at the museum last spring to help Eldon with the Wild West Show exhibit. Trevor Pratt, stocky, average height with thin, light colored hair that revealed patches of pink scalp as he leaned closer to the display case. Father John knew very little about the man. Two months ago Trevor had walked into his office. Rancher outside Lander, he said. Collector of Indian artifacts. Rare Arapaho artifacts from the Wild West Show that belonged to Chief Black Heart had become available in Berlin, he'd said, and he had arranged to purchase the collection. He'd heard the museum was planning an exhibit on the Show Indians in Buffalo Bill's Wild West. The Arapaho artifacts could be part of the exhibit. He wanted to donate the artifacts to the museum.

For a moment, Father John hadn't known what to say. It was like the checks that spilled out of envelopes when he most needed them. A little miracle. Arapaho artifacts would be the centerpiece of the exhibit.

Trevor and Sandra spun around in unison, then Trevor hurried over and took Bernard's hand. "Your grandfather's regalia are safe," he said.

The old man was grinning. "We're grateful," he said.

Father John shook Trevor's hand. The man had insisted on remaining anonymous. It was the only condition he had put on the donation.

"Dealer could've gotten more money," Eldon said, placing a hand on Trevor's shoulder, "but Trevor here convinced him the artifacts belonged with the people. The display case is ready." He nodded toward the Plexiglas cases where Trevor and Sandra had been standing. "Unbreakable glass, solid locks. Take a bulldozer to remove anything."

"How'd you know?" Trevor said.

Eldon stared at the man, as if he could pull the meaning from the words.

"That the dealer could've gotten more money."

"Museum gossip." Eldon shrugged. "You've been a collector long enough to know there aren't many secrets. Show them what we've planned," he said, facing the young woman.

Sandra Dorris squared her shoulders, walked back to the display cases and trailed her fingertips over the glass. She had a slight build, almost like a teenager who hadn't yet turned into a woman. Father John followed Bernard over to where she stood. "All the other things," she said, gesturing around the hall with one hand, "are borrowed from the Cody and other museums. We want to convey a sense of the Wild West Show."

"Posters are original lithographs," Eldon said, and Father John realized the man was at his shoulder. Trevor Pratt was waiting near the door, arms folded across his chest. "Gorgeous, vivid colors. Buffalo Bill knew how to promote a show. Sent people ahead to plaster posters on walls and fences of every city the show visited. Thousands packed the arenas for every performance."

"We want to showcase the Arapahos in the 1889–1890 season in Europe," Sandra said, tossing Eldon a searching glance for approval. "Black Heart's regalia are the highlight, of course." She stopped a moment, as if she had been drawn in by the large, bronze-tinted photograph on the back wall of one of the unfinished display cases. Black Heart staring into the camera with solemn black eyes, dressed in a bone breastplate and eagle-feathered headdress, hands folded in his lap, the dignified pose of a chief.

Bernard Tallman curled himself closer to the case and gave a respectful nod toward the photo. "My father said that Buffalo Bill himself went to the agent in Oklahoma and asked permission to take Arapahos to Europe." He might have been talking to himself, drawing out a memory. "Some of the Indians was scared the big ship would fall off the earth at the edge of the water. Grandfather" — he nodded again toward the photo — "had gone to England with Buffalo Bill three years before. They put on a show for Queen Victoria herself. He told the other Indians not to be afraid. They'd make twenty dollars every month, a lot of money. They'd get to see new places and meet different people. They could bring their wives and children. So a lot of Arapahos showed up at the agency, and Buffalo Bill came out and stood on the porch. Didn't say anything, just looked over the faces."

Bernard straightened up and turned toward Father John. "He'd been a scout on the plains, you know. He just stood there, like he was waiting for the buffalo to show up. Then he nodded to the Indians he wanted in the show. Put Black Heart in charge because he had experience."

Scattered on the floor of the display case were smaller black-and-white photos of Indians looking nervous and uncomfortable in front of the camera, as if they were staring into a new and unfathomable world. "I'll arrange these photos around the regalia," Sandra said. Then she gestured toward the program opened on the floor of the case. Across the top of the right page, in bold, black letters were the words: "The Wild West of Buffalo Bill. 1890." "This was the show they put on, day after day for almost two years," she said.

Father John leaned down and scanned the program. *Entry led by Arrapahoe Indians, their Chief Black Heart. Ogallala Sioux Indians under Chief Rocky Bear, and Cheyennes under Chief Eagle Horn. Horse races. Pony-Express Rider. Indians racing bareback. Buffalo hunt. Shooting exhibitions featuring Annie Oakley and Little Johnnie Baker. Indian camp and dances and foot races. Surprise Indian attack on immigrant wagon train. Indian attack on the Deadwood stagecoach and frontier villages. Buffalo Bill riding to the rescue, galloping and shooting at the same time, cowboys racing alongside.*

"We'll display Black Heart's eagle-

29

feathered headdress here." Sandra waved toward the back of the display case next to the chief's photograph. Father John saw that the elder hadn't taken his eyes from the photograph.

"The other items will go here," Sandra said, nodding toward the adjacent cases. "Black Heart's beaded vest and moccasins and armlets, bone breastplate, wrist guards, his red, white, and blue shirt that looks like a flag, beaded leggings, painted pouch and belt and medicine bag. Lance decorated with wrapped cloth and feathers." She tapped at the glass above the clear plastic stands. "A dozen pieces altogether."

"Every one of them documented by photographs." Eldon stepped forward and put up a hand, like a professor who had been observing a particularly gifted student, but felt there was something he had to add. He rapped the glass above the photos on the display case floor. "Here you see Black Heart wearing both the headdress and breastplate. Over here, he has on the moccasins, leggings, and the flag shirt. Here he is on horseback wearing the beaded vest, with pouch and medicine bag attached to his belt. In this photo, he's in the Indian camp next to the arena, and his wristbands are clearly visible."

Eldon took a couple of steps toward the end of the display case and nodded toward a photo of several Indians standing around Buffalo Bill. "That's Black Heart on the left, holding his spear. Notice the right wristband. Two rows of beads missing. The wristband in the collection is missing the same two rows." He looked around, the wide grin of achievement creasing his face. "The photographs prove not only that the regalia belonged to Black Heart but that he wore them in the Wild West Show."

"Most things belonged to my grandfather's father," Bernard Tallman said. "My ancestor earned every eagle feather in the headdress. Fought the enemy, protected the village. Broke Black Heart's heart, my father told me, when he learned the headdress and all the rest had gone missing."

The room went quiet a moment, then Eldon said, "Your ancestor's possessions are in my office, Grandfather." He nodded the old man into the corridor, and Sandra and Trevor filed out. Father John followed. The director's office was small. Windows framed a view of the Little Wind River and the buffalo herd in a nearby pasture. Cartons stood against the wall below the window. Eldon had already moved a carton to the top of the desk. "Please do us the honor,

Grandfather," he said, handing the old man a box cutter.

Bernard Tallman looked shaky, a little off balance as he stepped closer. Father John stayed behind the old man until Bernard had propped himself against the edge of the desk. For a moment he stared at the mass of postage and insurance stickers, the thick brown tape crisscrossing the top, as if the carton were a buffalo he had just brought down and he was about to make the first cut. Finally he ran the box cutter down the middle and separated the flaps. Then he set the box cutter down and pulled the flaps apart with the determination of a man used to roping calves.

He was holding his breath. No one said anything. Father John was aware of the sounds of the old building creaking around them. Finally Bernard began pulling out the bubble wrap, iridescent, shimmering in the light. He dropped each sheet on the floor before he pulled out the next one.

The carton was half empty now, hardly enough room left for any artifacts. Father John leaned closer, unable to look away from the bubble wrap deep within. Trevor had moved in beside him, and Father John could sense the barely suppressed anxiety in the man. It was the same with Eldon who crowded alongside the elder, boots snapping the bubble wrap.

Bernard lifted out the remaining wrap and let it fall to the floor. The carton was empty.

"There must be some mistake," Eldon said. It sounded like a wail. Sandra stood at the end of the desk, hands clasped over her mouth as Eldon took the box cutter and swiped at the tape on another carton. He yanked out the bubble wrap and flung it onto the floor, then upended the empty carton and started ripping at another. Father John moved around the desk, tore back the tape on a carton and pulled out an armload of bubble wrap. Trevor did the same, until all the cartons had been emptied, bubble wrap foaming like waves at their feet.

"Gone," Bernard said. "Gone. Gone. Gone."

2

Vicky Holden spotted Adam the minute she turned the corner onto Main Street. Across the street, in front of the restaurant, tall and black-haired, hands at his sides, squinting into the sun as he looked up and down the sidewalk. She would know him anywhere. Handsome, confident, self-assured, a Lakota with the bearing of his ancestors who had ruled the plains. Her own people had tried to maintain friendly relations, trade with them, and stay out of their way. She waited for a break in the traffic before crossing. Adam had called the office this morning. Not long ago, the law firm had been "Holden and Lone Eagle, Attorneys at Law." Now it was just "Vicky Holden, Attorney at Law." He was in Lander for a few days, he'd said, and he needed to see her. She had agreed to meet him for lunch, twelve o'clock sharp, at what had once been their favorite restaurant, but the telephone had rung all morning and two Arapahos from the rez had unexpectedly shown up. Dolly House, needing a restraining order filed today against her husband, Mervin. Basil Weed, hoping to delay the foreclosure of his auto repair shop in Riverton. It had been ten minutes after twelve before she had finally gotten away, leaving Annie Bosey, her secretary, with instructions to call her cell if anything came up. She had walked the three blocks to Main, the weather gorgeous with cottonwoods tinged in gold and crimson, and the September sun warm on her back, the breeze warm, too, pressing her skirt against her legs.

Adam had seen her now. He was walking toward the corner as she stood in the middle of the street, waiting for a truck to pass before she darted to the curb. His hands were strong on her shoulders, pulling her close as he leaned down. She turned her head, feeling the softness of his lips brush her cheek. "It's been too long, Vicky," he said. Then he stepped back, still holding her shoulders and taking her in. She had the sense that he was checking for anything different, the kind of change he didn't want to find. For a moment, she pictured herself in his appraisal. Hair, black and straight, strands blowing across her face. She tried to push them back, and wondered if she had remembered to put on any lipstick. She wore a dark skirt, blue silk blouse, and dangling silver earrings.

They started down the sidewalk, Adam's hand firm against her back. Mums, petunias, and geraniums cascaded from the flowerpots next to the curb. A large basket of yellow and pumpkin mums hung beside the door to the restaurant. After they slid into a booth next to the window that looked out over Main, Vicky said, "What brought you to town?"

"You want the truth?"

Vicky was quiet. She wasn't sure of the answer.

"I wanted to see you," he said.

"How are things in Montana?" She avoided his eyes. Adam had spent most of the year working for the Crow tribe, handling the legal issues of opening the reservation to coal mining. It was what he did best — protect tribal resources, make certain that the days when big oil and gas and coal companies could take advantage of inexperienced tribal officials were over. No one took advantage of Adam Lone Eagle. He had earned a national reputation as a top natural resources lawyer for Indian tribes, and for a while, it had been their dream —

Adam's dream, she thought — to have the best natural resources law firm in the country.

The waitress materialized. Smiling up at her, Adam said a hamburger, fries, and iced tea sounded good. Vicky ordered a chicken salad.

"Everything is on target," he said, when the waitress moved away. "The mine is about to open, and the tribe will have a nice, steady income. That's what I wanted to talk to you about. I don't have to be in Montana every minute. The agreements are in place, and I can monitor the situation from anywhere. I'm moving back to Lander."

Vicky felt her heart take a little jump. Adam Lone Eagle was part of the past, out of her life now for a year and, if she was honest, longer than that. Even when they were practicing law together, sleeping together, and trying to make some sort of relationship work — even then he had moved out of her life. She tried to get hold of this new plan. Adam back in town, and she knew from the way he was observing her, the same way he had looked at her when he had first come into her life, that she was part of his plan.

"You'll be setting up a law office?" She tried for a neutral tone.

"What about us?" Adam said.

"We practice different kinds of law, Adam." She could see Basil Weed seated in the chair in front of her desk in his red plaid shirt and blue jeans, brown, worn hands gripping his knees, struggling to keep back the tears that swam in his black eyes. Warriors didn't cry, she knew, but he was telling her how the shop was all he had to feed his kids. And Dolly, traces of blue bruises under her eyes, not crying now, as if there were no more tears, and saying she was worried about the kids. Not herself. I can take it, she said. But the kids . . .

Vicky shook her head at the images. When she and Adam had practiced together, Adam would have sent Basil and Dolly to Roger Hurst, the attorney they had hired to handle what Adam called the little cases. Cases that any first-year law student could handle. They would concentrate on the big cases that mattered. Indian rights to the minerals and water on Indian lands that corporations had been stealing for a hundred years. Adam would have dismissed even her most recent case for a client who had arranged with a dealer in Berlin to purchase Arapaho artifacts that had been in Buffalo Bill's Wild West Show. She had handled the transaction with a bank in

Cheyenne, arranged for insurance and filed the necessary forms with the U.S. Fish and Wildlife Service. The client had donated the artifacts to the museum at St. Francis Mission. They would arrive today, and this afternoon, she intended to drive over to the mission to see them. The thought of artifacts like that coming home had given her a sense of excitement, of things being right.

Adam stared out the window at the pickups and SUVs moving along Main Street as the waitress delivered the order. Then he leaned over the table. "I've given this a lot of thought," he said. "You can practice your kind of law and help your people."

Vicky flinched at the dismissal in his tone, or had she imagined it?

"I'll continue with natural resources law." He took a bite of hamburger. After a moment, he went on. "We can still work together in the same firm."

"The office isn't big enough," Vicky said. "Besides, we tried this before, and it didn't work." She picked at the chicken and a piece of lettuce. They had given up the spacious office on the second floor of a building two blocks away and she had moved back into the bungalow where she had practiced before Adam came along.

"What is the real objection?"

Vicky took another bite of chicken. She looked away, watching a couple walking arm in arm, heads thrown back, laughing, wind whipping at their jackets. "It won't work, Adam."

"You talking about the law firm or about us?"

"All of it."

"I don't believe you," Adam said. "Don't tell me you don't have feelings for me, that everything's gone, because it isn't true. I feel the same about you. No. Let me take that back. These months without you have only made my feelings stronger. The sense of what we lost is . . ." He hesitated. "As big as the outdoors. We can't let it go, Vicky. We have to get it back."

"Oh, Adam." Vicky set her face in her hands and rubbed at her eyes. If she could have willed things to work out between them in the past, they would have worked out. She had tried so hard. She had wanted everything to be perfect. He was a good man, and he loved her. She dropped her hands and pushed her plate to the side. She was no longer hungry. "My life is going along fine now."

"Your life is fine? There's someone else? That priest?"

"Please, Adam. John O'Malley and I are

40

friends. You know that. We work together."

"You both help people," he said, the dismissive note working through his tone again. "Well, I help people, too. I help them to get a fair return for leasing their mineral rights. I help them to have jobs and put food on the table for their kids." He was quiet a moment, sucking in his breath. "I'm not giving up," he said, placing both hands over hers and holding them steady and warm against the table. "I'm not giving up because I think you feel the same way about me as I feel about you. We can't lose what might be our last chance."

The muffled sound of a cell phone ringing cut through the air. Vicky pulled her hands free, dug into her bag, and checked the readout. Annie, calling to say someone else had wandered in needing a restraining order or a divorce, or help with a DUI. She snapped the cell open. "This is Vicky," she said.

"Trevor Pratt called," Annie said. "He's at the mission."

"I'm on my way after lunch."

"Now, he said. It's an emergency. The artifacts didn't arrive."

"What do you mean, didn't arrive?"

"The cartons were empty," Annie said. "Somebody stole the artifacts."

In front of the museum, a lineup of vehicles. The SUV that Ted Gianelli, the local FBI agent, drove. A couple of silver Wind River police cars. The solemnity of the parked vehicles, as if they had arrived for a funeral service, sent a cold sense of foreboding through Vicky as she drove around Circle Drive. Everything about the mission had a photographic stillness. The administration building with John's office in the corner of the first floor, the white stucco church, the redbrick priest's residence, the old stone museum building where she had gone to school. A banner flapped over the porch: "Arapaho Artifacts from Buffalo Bill's Wild West Show. September 21 to January 10."

She got out of the Jeep, slamming the door behind her, and hurried up the steps. Her black leather bag with the file folder inside banged against her side. Before heading to the mission, she had stopped at the office to pick up copies of the financial, insurance, and transportation documents she had drawn up for Trevor Pratt. The museum door resisted her efforts; she had to jam a hip against the oak to push the door open. The corridor was empty and airless, the main exhibition hall ahead silent. She stepped inside. Everything was ready. Posters from the Wild West Show, an array of regalia and clothing displayed behind Plexiglas. There were black-and-white photographs of Show Indians — her own people who had gone with Buffalo Bill to faraway lands and come home changed, she imagined. How could they not have been? She stared at the large photograph of Chief Black Heart in a case on the far wall. Empty spaces around the photograph, waiting for the chief's regalia.

"Thought it might be you."

Vicky swung around. John O'Malley stood in the doorway, as tall as she remembered, red-headed, flecks of gray at the temples, smiling past the sadness in his expression, eyes as blue as the sky.

"It's true then," she said. "The artifacts are missing."

"I'm afraid so," he said. "Gianelli's here." He motioned her into the corridor, and Vicky stayed with him as they headed toward the drone of voices, like a hive of bees, in the far corner of the building. The syncopated tapping sounds of his boots and her heels rose around her.

"Funny the way losses accumulate."

Thinking out loud, she realized. "They get heavier and heavier."

3

A scarred oak desk — a teacher's desk from
the past — occupied most of an office not
much larger than a storage closet. Ted Gianelli, FBI agent, sat at the swivel chair
behind the desk, scratching something on a
small notebook opened in front of him.
Seated a few feet away was Eldon White Elk,
chair tipped back so far that his head
brushed the plastered wall. Trevor Pratt
stood beside him. Vicky could sense that
she and John O'Malley had interrupted
something because the conversation had
stopped, and yet the words seemed to hover
soundlessly over the desk.

"Let's start over," Gianelli said, nodding a
hello to Vicky. "What are we certain of?"

"Bottom line?" Trevor said in a tight voice.
Vicky could feel the rush of anger in the
man. He gripped his arms across his chest
and stared into the middle distance. "The
artifacts were hijacked. Unless we move fast,

45

chances of getting them back are zero."

A charged quiet dropped over the office. Vicky shot a sideways glance at John O'Malley. They were thinking the same thing, she knew. Black Heart's headdress, breastplate, vest, moccasins, cuffs, all of his ancestor's things that he had worn in the Wild West Show. Gone. Another part of her people's history lost.

"What makes you so sure?" Gianelli, rolling a ballpoint between his fingers, clicking the end with his thumb. Twenty years ago, he had played for the New England Patriots. He still had the broad, hardened shoulders, muscular look, and determined stare of an athlete. Except for the black hair gone gray, he looked as if he could still tackle anyone. Vicky had worked with him — and against him — on more cases than she wanted to remember. Murder, rape, burglary, fraud, assault. The major crimes that fell in the FBI's jurisdiction on any Indian reservation, crimes her clients had happened to get mixed up in. The fed was fair and hardworking, stubborn as a dog digging up a bone.

"I'm a collector," Trevor said. "I know the Indian artifacts business, and the kind of thieves that go after them. Nothing is left to chance. We're not dealing with thugs and amateur burglars that leave a trail of evidence to their front doors. They've already got a buyer, or they wouldn't have gone to the trouble." He jabbed a fist at the air. "The artifacts will disappear into thin air."

"When did the artifacts leave Berlin?" Gianelli said.

"I talked to the dealer, Jens Heuter, before I came to the museum," Trevor said. "Packing, shipping, everything done as usual. The cartons left Berlin yesterday morning en route to New York, Denver, and finally Riverton. Arrived here last evening."

"Moved from plane to plane, and a lot of time on docks." Eldon slammed the front legs of his chair to the floor. "Four cities, two countries. Makes me sick to think about the opportunities."

"One thing we can be sure of," Gianelli said. "This wasn't a lone thief. There had to be a number of people involved."

"How can we know for sure that the artifacts were in the cartons when they left Germany?" Father John said.

"Look, I know Jens," Trevor said. "I've bought dozens of artifacts from him. He uses a company that specializes in transporting art and artifacts. Never been any problem with items disappearing."

Gianelli glanced over at Vicky. "Any documents that might help?"

47

Vicky reached into the bag at her feet and pulled out the file folder. She thumbed through the pages Annie had copied, then handed several across the desk. "Here are copies of the U.S. Fish and Wildlife documents we arranged to have attached to the cartons. It isn't easy transporting any parts from an endangered species into or out of this country. We used the photo of Black Heart wearing the eagle-feathered headdress in 1890 to prove the feathers were more than a hundred years old. We had Trevor's affidavit that the headdress dated to the nineteenth century."

Gianelli skimmed through the pages. "I'll check with U.S. Fish and Wildlife. They'll know whether the artifacts were in the cartons when they came through New York." He threw a glance at Trevor. "I assume the collection was insured."

Trevor gave a dismissive and impatient grunt. "Only a fool would ship valuable artifacts without insurance."

"Purchased by the museum?"

"My client purchased both the artifacts and the insurance," Vicky said. She handed him several other documents. "No amount of insurance can replace the artifacts. We want them found."

Gianelli was leafing through the pages.

"How much did you say you paid the dealer in Berlin?" he said.

"Half million," Trevor said.

"You bought insurance for a million." Gianelli kept his head down, but he was looking up at her client.

"We purchased insurance that covered the value of the artifacts," Vicky said. "Standard procedure."

"Maybe so, but you'll make a tidy profit if the artifacts aren't recovered." Gianelli lifted his head and stared straight on at Trevor. "Why would the dealer sell artifacts below their value?"

"Jens needed the cash," Trevor said. "Takes time to locate buyers. Europe, U.S., Asia, Middle East — collectors of memorabilia from the American West are everywhere. Dealers have to search them out. Museums and even collectors demand documents to prove provenance. It can take months, years to pull everything together and negotiate the best price on each piece. I offered to purchase the entire collection. I'd already done the research. Located photos and Wild West posters and programs that proved the artifacts belonged to Black Heart. The deal was worth the time and trouble I saved Jens, and like I said, he needed the cash."

"I thought he wanted the artifacts back with the people," Eldon said.

Trevor shook his head. "This is about money."

"But some European museums and collectors have returned items to other tribes at no cost to the tribes," Father John said.

"Trust me," Trevor said, and Vicky could hear the angry impatience bubbling beneath the words. "Jens isn't the altruistic type. Last couple years have been tough, with the economy going south."

Gianelli was stacking the sheets of paper and notebook inside a black leather case. After a moment he got to his feet. "There's a chance the thieves will demand a ransom." He glanced around the table. "If you hear anything, call me immediately. Understood?"

"We want the artifacts returned," Trevor said.

"If you want them back, do as I say." Gianelli tucked the black case under one arm, eased his way between the chairs and the wall, and headed into the corridor.

No one said anything until the sound of the door slamming reverberated through the walls. Then Trevor turned to Eldon, and Vicky held her breath. She knew what was coming.

"If you had kept quiet about the artifacts until they were safely here," Trevor said, "this wouldn't have happened. TV. Radio. Newspapers. Everybody talking about the Wild West Show Arapaho artifacts coming home. Every thief between here and Berlin heard the news. What did you expect would happen?"

"We kept your name out of it." Eldon got to his feet, and by the way he clenched his fists, Vicky understood that he and Trevor had argued before over the publicity. For the last couple of months, ever since Trevor had offered the artifacts to the museum, there had been a steady stream of newspaper articles, radio shows, and blog posts. She had heard Eldon going on about the artifacts on three different radio shows, advertising the Arapaho artifacts that would be in the Wild West exhibit. School buses should have been drawing up out front this afternoon, kids tumbling out for a preview.

"You damn fool." Trevor spit out the words. "You gave the thieves everything they needed. Told them who the dealer was, when the artifacts were expected to arrive, where to find the photographs and posters that authenticate the items. Everything."

"I have a museum to run here," Eldon said, his lips barely moving. "We're building

51

this museum into one of the best small museums in the West. We have to keep the public in the loop. Rare Arapaho artifacts from the Wild West Show are a top draw. People have never lost interest in Buffalo Bill. We expected visitors from across the country. Even without the Arapaho artifacts, the show was gonna be a big draw. The artifacts would have made it a truly important exhibit. Why would I keep it secret? And another thing" — the director advanced a few feet along the front of the desk — "we needed funds to mount the exhibit, cover shipping and insurance costs for items we borrowed from the Cody Museum, print exhibit brochures, pay Sandra's salary. The publicity made the exhibit happen."

Trevor spun toward the man. "Some exhibit!"

John O'Malley stepped over, shouldering between Trevor and the director. "This won't bring the artifacts back," he said. "You both know the world of artifacts, collectors, and dealers. Who could have taken them? How will the thieves dispose of them?"

Trevor gave his head a hard shake. "None of you get it. There's no time to stand around asking questions. The artifacts are on their way to the kind of people that never ask questions. They don't care where the artifacts came from. What they want is wall power, something on their walls that is more unusual and rare than anything on the walls of their friends. Thanks to Eldon here" — he shifted his gaze toward the director — "the thieves had all the time in the world to find suitable buyers."

Nobody spoke for a moment, then Eldon said, "I'll check the internet sites for lost and missing art items. I'll post the list of artifacts and photos right away. Maybe we'll get lucky and scare off the buyers. They might not like having their friends know the artifacts on their wall were stolen."

Trevor let out a rough guffaw, then, head down like a bull, charged into the corridor.

Vicky caught up with him before he reached the front door. "We have to file the insurance claim," she said.

"Not yet." He kept walking, flung open the door and went outside.

Vicky was still behind him. "These things take time. Insurance companies drag out settlements as long as possible. We should get started."

He yanked open the door of a black SUV and dropped behind the steering wheel. "I said, not yet." The door slammed and the engine roared into life. Vicky had to step sideways as the SUV jumped back, spilling bits of gravel over her. There was the hard, grating noise of shifting gears as the SUV spun forward and sped around Circle Drive.

She sensed someone behind her and swung around. John O'Malley was coming down the steps. "How well do you know him?" he said, squinting in the sun, worry lines creasing his forehead.

She didn't know Trevor Pratt at all, Vicky was thinking. She said, "He walked into my office a few months ago and said he needed help filing documents with the government to transport Arapaho artifacts into the country and arrange a cash payment to a dealer in Berlin. He said he was a collector, owned a ranch south of Lander. A couple of weeks ago, he invited me to the ranch to see his collection. Beautiful artifacts. Sioux, Crow, Kiowa, Cheyenne. The kind of things you see in museums. He said they came from collectors around the world. I asked him why he needed me because it was obvious he had filed necessary documents in the past, and he told me the process was always smoother with a lawyer involved. Trust him, he said. He knew what he was talking about. How well do you know him?"

John O'Malley gave her a slow smile. "Showed up here, said he'd heard the

54

museum was going to mount an exhibit on Buffalo Bill's Wild West and offered to donate Arapaho artifacts for the show. I introduced him to Eldon." He turned partway and looked up at the banner snapping in the wind overhead. "It would have been a special exhibit."

Vicky started for her Jeep. The sun glinted in the little clouds of dust the SUV had stirred around Circle Drive. The low roar of the SUV's engine drifted back from Seventeen-Mile Road. She opened the door, sank inside, and turned the ignition. She watched John O'Malley disappear inside the museum as she drove into the tunnel of cottonwoods that led to Seventeen-Mile Road. It hit her then. "My God," she said out loud. "Trevor knows who the thieves are. He's going after the artifacts."

4

Father John finished saying the early morning Mass, hung his vestments in the sacristy, and made his way down the aisle of the church, a chapel, really, built by the Arapahos themselves. Arapaho symbols painted on the walls — lines for the roads of life, a cluster of tipis for the people, a cross for the morning sun and for Christ. The early sun itself flared in the red, white, blue, and yellow stained glass windows, colors of the Arapaho. He scanned the pews for left-behind rosaries, scarves, and wallets. Not more than twenty parishioners this morning, and most of them elderly, on their knees, arms supported on the pew ahead, rosary beads moving through wrinkled, worn fingers. Most had gone to St. Francis school in the old gray stone building. "Come and teach our children," the leading men had pleaded with the Jesuits in Omaha. That was in 1884, the Arapahos on the

Wind River Reservation only six years. The Jesuits had come. Always at the edge of his consciousness was the sense that he was part of a long line of Jesuit priests at St. Francis. They stared out at him from the framed portraits in the corridor of the administration building, wide-eyed and all seeing behind wire-rimmed glasses, following him through the days. He never wanted to let them down.

The morning was warm with a hint of autumn coolness. The sky the color of blue iris, as clear as an inverted glass bowl; little gusts of wind ruffled the cottonwoods and the wild grasses. He cut diagonally across the grass field on the path that had been stamped out by past Jesuits, took the steps in front of the residence two at a time, and let himself into the entry hall. Aromas of coffee and hot oil floated toward him. Walks-On, the golden retriever he had found in the ditch along Seventeen-Mile Road, scrambled down the hall from the kitchen. He had taken the dog to the vet and brought him home when no one had inquired about him. Home to the mission, missing a hind leg, which had never seemed to bother him in life. That was six or seven years ago, Father John guessed. He couldn't imagine a time at St. Francis without Walks-On. He tossed his cowboy hat on the bench, scratched the soft fur behind the dog's ears, and followed him back into the kitchen.

Bishop Harry was partway through breakfast, pushing thick pieces of pancake around a plate full of syrup. Sunlight filtered through the window and glistened on the bald spot of the old man's head. A stack of pancakes looked as if it might tumble off the plate in the middle of the table. They took turns saying the early Mass, but even on mornings when he could have slept in, the bishop was up early, ready to work, as if he were the assistant pastor when, officially, he was at the mission to recuperate from two heart attacks and bypass surgeries. Except the bishop, who had spent thirty years looking after the welfare of thousands of Catholics in Patna, India, didn't take to the notion of recuperating. "I'm not ready to be put out in any pasture," he had said when Father John urged him to take it easy. "Plenty of time to take it easy when I'm dead."

So they had reached an unspoken agreement. Bishop Harry took half of the morning Masses, filled in wherever Father John needed an extra hand, and zeroed in on the social welfare committee and the education committee. "Can't get anywhere if people

58

are hungry and scared," he'd said once. "Can't get anywhere without education." He'd spent his time in India championing both causes.

"Pancakes, Elena? What's the occasion?" Usually breakfast was oatmeal, toast, jam, and two mugs of coffee. The same every day, a ritual he'd become accustomed to. He opened a cabinet, sprinkled food into the dog's dish, and set it on the floor before he took the chair across from the bishop.

The housekeeper flipped another couple of pancakes on the grill, then glanced around, gray, curly hair framing the serene, wrinkled face of a half-Arapaho and half-Cheyenne grandmother, a woman who had passed through the first three stages of life and was now in the last. She had to be in her seventies. She had been at St. Francis so long that even she didn't know the exact number of years. Cooking and cleaning and looking after generations of priests. Seeing that they ate right and showed up for meals on time. He tried, but he had never been good at marching to orders.

"I figured you needed a little pick-me-up." Elena stepped over to the coffeepot next to the sink, filled a mug, and set it down in front of him. Walks-On let out a gulping noise and settled onto his rug in the corner.

The bowl had been licked clean.

Father John slid a couple of pancakes off the stack and onto his plate, spread on the butter, and poured on a quarter cup of syrup. This was a treat. "Somebody's birthday?" he said.

"I'm pretending it's mine," Bishop Harry said. He had blue eyes that twinkled when he looked up. "And this is the best present I ever received."

Elena had moved close to the table, wringing both hands in her apron. "Just seems to me, with the artifacts missing and everybody crying about it, saying how terrible to lose them after all we already lost, going on about it not being fair and when was it going to stop. Seems to me we need to think about what we have, the good things, like pancakes."

"Here, here." Bishop Harry held his coffee mug aloft a moment, then took a long drink.

"Thank you, Elena," Father John said. It didn't surprise him that people on the rez were upset and angry over the artifacts. No loss stood by itself. Every loss added to the accumulation, as Vicky had said. He realized that pancakes were Elena's attempt to accept this new loss. She didn't believe the artifacts would ever be found.

"Eldon should've kept his mouth shut," Elena said. She turned to the sink, plunged both hands into the water, and scrubbed at a bowl as if she wanted it to disappear. "Every time you turned on the TV, there was Eldon talking about the artifacts. How great they were, how rare and valuable. No wonder crooks came and got them." She glanced over her shoulder. "Don't tell me how the fed's gonna investigate and find the thief. What does he care?"

"It's a major theft," Father John said. "I think Gianelli's taking it very seriously."

"Indian stuff stolen, that's all it is," she said, working hard on the bowl.

Father John exchanged a glance with the bishop. Understanding flickered in the old man's eyes. The assumption, unspoken but as detectible as a bad odor, that as long as nobody got hurt, and only Indian stuff was stolen, then what happened was Indian business. Let the Indians take care of it themselves. He finished his coffee, thanked Elena for a gourmet breakfast, and started down the hallway.

"I'll be in the office in a little while," Bishop Harry called after him. He could hear the kitchen chair scrape and the coffeepot clink as the old man got up to top off his mug.

It was close to noon when Father John heard the engine cut off in front of the administration building and the car door slam. Past the corner of the window, he could see the white roof of Gianelli's SUV. Footsteps scraping the front steps, the front door opening and shutting. There was a whoosh of air. Then Gianelli crossed the office and dropped a CD on Father John's desk. "Bet you don't have that," he said.

Father John picked up the plastic envelope. Puccini's *La Fanciulla del West*. It was the only Puccini opera he didn't have on a CD. He had never expected to find another opera buff on the reservation, but Ted Gianelli loved opera as much as he did and, Father John had to admit, probably knew more about it. Tough as nails. He'd no doubt faced down three hundred pounds of solid flesh without flinching, but Gianelli had a soft spot when it came to opera. Most of the time, Father John had an opera playing in the office, and he had seen tears come to the fed's eyes during a particularly beautiful aria.

Gianelli poured himself a cup of coffee over at the little metal table behind the door and took a side chair. "Any guess why Puccini decided to compose an opera about the American West?"

Father John got to his feet and inserted the CD into the player on the shelf behind his desk. "Hello, Minnie!" burst into the air. "He went to see Buffalo Bill's Wild West?" he said.

"Exactly!" Gianelli pounded the palm of one hand against his thigh. "Got all caught up in the cowboys and Indians, went home and wrote about it."

Father John sat down at his desk and tipied his hands, letting the opera wash over him. Elena's words punctuated the music. "Level with me," he said. "How important is this case?"

"To the bureau? To me personally? Tell your Arapaho friends it's damn important." Gianelli sipped at his coffee a moment. "What we don't know is whose jurisdiction it's going to fall in. Depends upon where the artifacts were stolen. If they were stolen and moved across state lines, it's federal. If they made it to Riverton, it's local. You might want to bring Eldon in."

From outdoors came the sound of footsteps on gravel, the hard thump of boots on the steps, as if on cue. "I suspect he's already here," Father John said as the director came through the door.

"I saw you drive up." Eldon pushed another side chair close to the desk with his boot. He was blinking rapidly, face flushed, as if he had sprinted from the museum. "What about the artifacts? Have you found them?"

"We know they reached New York," Gianelli said. "X-rays by Customs and inspections by the U.S. Fish and Wildlife confirm that twelve artifacts were inside the cartons unloaded from the airplane's cargo hold. Fish and Wildlife inspectors actually opened the cartons and made certain that the eagle-feathered headdress matched the description in the documents on the outside of the carton." He cleared his throat. "Documents Vicky prepared."

"That's all you know?" The color in Eldon's face had drained to a dull gray. "The artifacts arrived in the U.S.? What happened then?"

"A couple hours in a warehouse at JFK, transfer in Denver and sixteen hours in Riverton," Gianelli said. "Plenty of time for someone to break into the cartons. We have to assume the thieves had a well-planned operation that went off just as they hoped. Agents have been interviewing warehouse workers and clerks at JFK and Denver who had contact with the cartons. It's possible somebody may have noticed the cartons had been tampered with. If so, we can narrow down the time frame." He worked at the coffee another moment, then turned to Eldon. "Something I don't understand. The cartons were off-loaded in Riverton, Monday at 4:34 p.m. They were scheduled to be trucked directly to the museum, and I was under the impression you were eager to have them delivered. But the trucking company had instructions to store them in a warehouse at the airport overnight. Who gave the instructions?"

Eldon sat very still, elbows braced on the armrests, fingertips touching as if he were holding an invisible globe. He started to say something, then cleared his throat and started again. "Trevor thought Bernard Tallman should open the cartons since the artifacts belonged to his grandfather. Trevor wanted him to have the honor of placing the items in the exhibit. It was a matter of respect. We decided to have a little ceremony in the morning. You know, Bernard lifting his grandfather's things out of the cartons, blessing their return. That kind of thing. Trevor asked me to call the trucking company and arrange for the artifacts to be kept in the warehouse. It was a good idea. I didn't want them delivered here until we could secure them behind the locked, Plexiglas doors." He gave a half-committed shrug. "I guess they should have been brought here. I could have guarded them all night with my rifle."

Gianelli slipped the notepad past his leather vest into the pocket of his white shirt. He'd keep them posted, he said, setting the coffee mug on the table as he headed into the corridor. Eldon waited a moment, staring at the window, sunk in thought. Then he got to his feet. Slouchshouldered, head down, a man of regrets and defeat, Father John thought, he flipped one hand in a wave and disappeared into the corridor. The sounds of boots scuffing the gravel and an engine turning over melted through the thick walls, then dissolved into silence.

Father John turned on his laptop and watched it whir into life, the blue screen peopling itself with small, colorful icons. He tried to focus on something that had bothered him from the day Trevor Pratt had walked into his office and offered to give the museum a collection of Arapaho regalia from the Wild West Show. He typed in a search for "Indian regalia," "Buffalo Bill's Wild West." Lists of Web sites materialized.

Dozens of pages. It would take him all day to scan through them. He typed in another search for "Chief Black Heart," "Wild West" and watched other sites come up. Three pages. A more manageable number. He read down the sites on the first page, then moved to the next and clicked on the second site. The familiar photo of Chief Black Heart came up, the same photo as in the exhibition hall. The chief in his bone breastplate and eagle-feathered headdress, feathers draped in back. In another photo, the chief galloped across an arena leading dozens of Indian riders, the hooves of his black horse suspended over the ground. The caption read: "The crowd cheers at the spectacle of Chief Black Heart leading Arapaho warriors into the Berlin arena, July 23, 1890."

On the next site was the headline: "Arapaho chief's regalia recovered after 120 years." The article he brought up, dated six months ago, was from what looked like a magazine for collectors. *The regalia worn by Arapaho chief Black Heart in the 1889–1890 European tour of Buffalo Bill's Wild West was found last month during the demolition of several nineteenth-century buildings in Berlin adjacent to the arena where the performances had taken place. The regalia had been missing since 1890. Chief Black Heart was known as one of the most flamboyant of the Show Indians. He wore spectacular regalia that his ancestors had worn during many battles in the West. When reporters in the United States asked to see his regalia, the chief was quoted as saying that his adopted son would bring the regalia when he returned home. It appears the regalia had been hidden in a concrete vault deep in the basement of a condemned building. "We were lucky we hadn't set the explosive to bring the building down before we stumbled on the stuff," said Heinrich Hoelscher, contractor. He turned the regalia over to Jens Heuter, dealer in American Indian artifacts. Heuter said the artifacts could be positively identified from old photos as belonging to Chief Black Heart.*

So this was the article Trevor Pratt had run across, he thought. This was where everything had begun.

5

Berlin
July 23, 1890

Sonny Yellow Robe dodged through the crowds in the Arapaho village. People straining to get a better view of women seated outside the tipis beading moccasins, bracelets, pendants, and anything else the whites might want to buy. Every few steps someone reached out and plucked the sleeve of his blue shirt. Touch an Indian for good luck, he thought. Strange customs, these Germans had. It was like a holiday, a festival, the entire city spilling down the streets and into the village on the grassy space outside the arena. The afternoon's Wild West wouldn't start for an hour, but the crowds had come early. A long line snaked from the ticket wagon.

This morning the train had pulled into a siding alongside a row of run-down stone buildings from another time. Beyond the buildings Sonny had watched the grass-filled space stretch toward the metal poles and bleachers and canvas walls of the arena. The prairie wagons and stagecoaches, wagons loaded with buffalo and other wagons swaying under the weight of canvas tipis, tent poles, cartons of food, and more supplies than Sonny had ever seen on the plains had rolled off the train and paraded through the streets of Berlin, winding back to the arena. Thousands had lined the streets, cheering and shouting. At the head of the parade was Buffalo Bill himself, long dark hair flowing across the shoulders of his fringed jacket. He rode tall and proud in the saddle, waving his white hat to the crowds on one side, then the other. Behind him rode the Show Indians, cowboys, and shooters. Sonny had felt a chill of anticipation and excitement running through him.

By noon the Indians had set up their tipis. Arapahos here, Cheyenne nearby, Sioux over there. Tents for the cowboys and the stars, like Annie Oakley, Frank Butler, Little Johnnie Baker, and the other performers were pitched beyond the Indian villages. The large tent of Buffalo Bill with the buffalo head mounted over the flap stood between the camps of the performers and the Indians. Sonny had heard rumors of the

70

tanned hides of mountain lions, bears, deer, and wolves spread over the grassy floor and the chairs with elk-horn armrests fit for a king.

His own tipi stood at the edge of the Arapaho village, not far from Buffalo Bill's tent. BB, everyone called him. Everything in place, and everything done with precision, following BB's orders. The Wild West was used to moving, settling in, packing up, and moving on. Like the Old Time, Sonny thought, before the people were herded onto patches of their own lands that the government reserved for them. Reservations, they were called. Everything about the Wild West reminded him of stories of the Old Time. Warriors hunting buffalo, protecting the villages, attacking wagon trains and settlements that moved onto Indian lands. But the settlements and the soldiers had outnumbered the people. All the white people in the world had come to the plains, some of the old men said. The warriors had been forced to ride great distances to find enough buffalo to feed their families. They returned to the villages dusty and weary, slumped over their ponies, the future closing around them.

Sonny dodged past a group of children who pointed and smiled, stretching small white hands toward his brown hands. The buzz of voices, punctuated by shouts of laughter and exclamations of surprise, filled the air. Through the crowds moving like a white cloud along the grassy path between the rows of tipis, he could see Black Heart's tipi. The flap was closed. Flaps on other tipis had been thrown open so the visitors could see inside. Beds of baled hay covered with buffalo robes, sling-back chairs made from wood and bone and decorated with glass beads, big, black cooking pots hanging on tripods over the fires laid in pits.

Black Heart was usually out and about before the performances, chatting with the visitors. The leader of the Arapahos. Wherever the exhibition went, visitors wanted to see the chief. Pawing at his red, white, and blue flag shirt, leaning in close, smiles frozen, waiting for the photographer to jam a glass plate into a box camera mounted on a tripod and duck under a black cloth. Black Heart had the patience of the plains. Still and watchful as a deer.

The chief appeared on posters plastered on fences, walls, and lampposts across Berlin. But this morning, when the parade had wound toward the arena, the posters were nowhere to be seen. News had flashed through the village that the posters had been stripped away, and Buffalo Bill had called the cast together. Arapahos, Sioux, and Cheyennes, dozens of cowboys, stagehands, wranglers, cooks. BB mounted a wood stage, white jacket opened over a black shirt, the sun glinting in the silver strands of his dark hair. His voice rang as clear as one of the bells that had tolled in a church as the parade passed. "You all know our interpreter, Herman Marks," BB said. "He's talked to the officials here. Seems they didn't like our posters splashed everywhere. Said they wanted Berlin clean and uncluttered. Turns out the metal, cone-shaped structures we passed are the place for posters and such."

Sonny had stifled a laugh at the image of Germans lifting their noses and shaking their weighty heads at the sight of Wild West posters decorating walls and fences.

"We hope folks that saw the parade will come to the performance this afternoon." Worry had worked through BB's voice. He always sent men ahead to put up the posters days before the show came to town. "They are sure to tell their friends. I expect a full arena for the evening's performance."

Nothing to worry about, Sonny thought now, judging by the crowds pouring through the Indian village, making their way toward the arena entrance. Every city the same. Paris, Lyon, Marseille, Barcelona, Florence, Milan, Naples, Rome, Dresden, Bologna, dozens of strange cities and thousands and thousands of people crowding the arenas, the air strung with excitement. Everything had been bigger and grander than he could have imagined that day at the agency in Oklahoma when Black Heart told him that Colonel William F. Cody, Buffalo Bill himself, was coming to hire Indians for the next Wild West Show in Europe. Black Heart had gone to England with the show three years before. He never stopped talking about the people and things he had seen.

Sonny had been nervous, legs wobbly, sweat cold on his forehead. Riding on a boat across the never-ending waters! It was beyond his mind. Still he had joined the other warriors who crowded in front of the agency building waiting for Buffalo Bill to step onto the porch. Black Heart and the other older men respected Buffalo Bill. Scout, buffalo hunter, warrior who had fought Sonny's people but had kept the warrior's code: fight fairly, fight to win. And there he was. Calm and unflappable as he was today. He didn't speak. Just stood there and looked about at the faces in front of him, as if he were reading the terrain, sensing the location of the buffalo herd. It was as if he could sense the Indians he wanted in the Wild West, and he had chosen Black Heart and dozens of other Arapahos. He had chosen him, simply waved his hand where Sonny stood.

From twenty feet away, Sonny heard the angry voices in Black Heart's tipi. He broke into a run, threw back the flap, and ducked inside. The angry voices stopped. Black Heart stood directly across from the flap, a dark figure against the light glowing through the canvas walls and pouring down from the top where the tipi poles were tied together. The chief was a big man, wide in the shoulders, well filled out in the arms and legs. Features sculptured out of granite: the high, rounded cheekbones that cast deep shadows on his cheeks, long nose, and wide mouth. His eyes were wide set, his gaze fixed and steady on the man in front of him.

Herman Marks swung about. "Nobody wants you here," he said. He was a child-sized man, small and delicate looking, with brown hair that stood up like grass around his head, and gray eyes that had a fixed, dead look in them. A small brown goatee pushed up against his lower lip. "This is between me and Black Heart."

Sonny didn't say anything. The chief's

eagle-feathered headdress, bone-pipe breast-plate, beaded cuffs and leggings lay on the cot along the wall of the tipi. Next to the cot was the black leather satchel where Black Heart kept his regalia in between performances. Sonny moved past the white man and planted himself behind the chief. He would die for Black Heart. Plant his own staff in the ground and tie himself down to divert the enemy so that Black Heart could escape. The chief and One-Moon, his wife, had become his parents. Adopted him in the Arapaho Way — the way a man and his wife took in the young who needed help — after Sonny had walked away from the Carlisle School in Pennsylvania. Just set off walking toward the sunset every day, sleeping in the forests and the ditch banks, snaring rabbits and catching fish with his hands. Walking. Walking. Walking. He had walked to Oklahoma and made his way to the agency. Feet bloody stumps wrapped in bark. His boots had peeled away long before. Black Heart had taken him to his own tipi and told him that his parents had died while he was at the Indian school. Orphaned, skin hanging off his bones, nothing in his stomach for so long that he got sick when he tried to eat from a bowl of meat and vegetables. "You will be our son now," Black Heart had said. One-Moon had rubbed his feet with grease she made from plants she gathered along the streams. She held the bowl of dark broth for him to drink until he was strong enough to take the bowl into his own hands. Their son, he learned later, had left the agency to go after a stray calf the year before. A white settler had killed him.

"We're done talking," Black Heart said. "Go stay with your white brothers."

"You are a bigger fool than I took you for." The white man leaned sideways and spit a wad of yellow phlegm onto the grass floor. "The kind of money I'm talking about, you can be a free man. No more living on a miserable reservation. Live where you want."

"I want to live on the prairie," Black Heart said.

"You saw Paris. They loved you Indians there. You'd be a celebrity. Get invited to fancy parties, everybody wanting to be friends with a real Indian. Barcelona? You like Barcelona? Okay, there was bad sickness there, made some Indians sick."

"The typhoid killed four Indians."

Marks shrugged. "Never happen again. Rome? Pope loved you Indians in Rome. You could make the rounds, city to city, stay until you get bored. Never have to dress up and prance around an arena pretending to be the kind of Indian you used to be. Now's your chance to be somebody."

"Go buy some other Indian's stuff," Black Heart said.

"Relics," Marks said. "What my business associates want are relics. Authentic pieces from the plains. Got history all over them. You got the oldest relics here. You think collectors want the cheap headdresses and breastplates BB made up for some Indians?"

Sonny kept his face quiet, but inside he felt the barb, as if the white man had hurled a shaft at him. He wore new regalia BB had hired Arapaho women to make. His father's regalia as well as his grandfather's had disappeared by the time he returned from Carlisle, vanished into the dust where his family was buried.

"Talk to your old man, here," Marks said, and Sonny realized he was directing the command to him. "This is the best offer he's ever going to get. I'll bet you wouldn't mind spending time in Paris and Rome with them beautiful damsels throwing themselves at Indians. Lots of beef and wine. What do you call it? Fire water? Make you feel warm inside. No need to freeze to death in some tipi out on the prairie."

"Get out before I throw you out." Black Heart took a step toward the white man, and Marks stood his ground a moment before he hauled himself around and stomped out.

Black Heart walked over and lifted the feathered headdress. "My father wore this when he fought Custer at Little Big Horn." His voice was as calm as a memory. "Rode away from the battlefield with the other Arapahos that went with Crazy Horse, bursting with pride. Indians defeated the biggest white man of all. He knew it wouldn't be the end. All the Indians knew they had won the battle but the war wouldn't stop until the people were killed or run onto reservations." He held out the headdress and ran his gaze across the eagle feathers, still straight and forceful looking, the red felt of the band covered in red, blue, yellow, and black beads. "At Little Big Horn, the warriors stood up for what was ours. What happened back then is part of Grandfather's headdress. It can never be sold. It must stay with our people. It is a sign of who we are and what we have done."

Sonny went to the opened flap and looked out. Marks had moved a good thirty feet away. He stood talking to two white men, probably business associates. The crowd flowed like water around them. Marks turned partway back, lifted a fist, and punched the air in the direction of Black Heart's tipi, his face a hard mask.

"He won't give up," Sonny said, stepping back inside. "He'll try to take what he can't buy. He might come back tonight after the show and steal everything you have." He tilted his head toward the satchel. "We can move the regalia to my tipi tonight," he said. "Even Marks won't be fool enough to rob a tipi near BB's."

Sonny realized that the noise of the crowd outside, the whish of movement and undercurrent of voices had died back. The performance would start soon. "We must get ready," he said.

6

Mid-day quiet lay over the rez. The sun a diffused yellow ball high overhead, the sky the glassy blue of a mountain lake. The wind moved across the wild brush like an army of spirits, and the heat shimmered on Seventeen-Mile Road. Father John kept the Toyota pickup a short distance behind the empty school bus that crawled ahead. When the bus lumbered into a right turn toward Ethete, he stepped on the accelerator. The pickup jumped forward, like a racehorse given slack. He had left Bishop Harry manning the phone, which had rung all day. People wanting to know about the artifacts. How could they be gone? Who could have done this? Always the faint hope ringing in their voices that whoever stole the artifacts would bring them back. He had wanted to reassure the callers. Anything was possible. He didn't say he doubted the thieves would have a change of heart. "Quello che tacete" rose out of the CD player on the passenger seat.

He swung left onto Blue Sky Highway and after a few miles took a right onto a narrow dirt road that meandered like a cow path toward the brown-shouldered foothills of the Wind River range. The white house with the sloping gray roof stood up ahead in a clump of cottonwoods. He made another right across the cattle guard and bounced along the hard, dry ridges that crisscrossed the driveway. In the corral next to the house, a tall, skinny Indian in blue jeans and light blue Western shirt was brushing an Appaloosa. The Indian looked up from under the rim of a tan cowboy hat, brush balanced over the horse's spotted rump. Then he swung over the fence and landed on the other side. Puffs of dust shot up from his boots. He waved toward an empty space next to the fence, as if this were a busy parking lot. Except for a black truck parked in back, almost hidden by the house, there were no other vehicles around.

Father John switched off the CD player and got out of the pickup. The wind blew tumbleweeds against the corral. Mickey Tallman, Bernard's grandson, extended a ropy, muscular arm. Ten years ago, Mickey had come out for the Eagles baseball team that Father John had started that first summer at St. Francis. That would make him about twenty-four now, and the last Father John heard, Mickey had been in Afghanistan; a warrior, like his ancestors.

"Hey, Father," he said. His grip was strong and confident. "Long time no see. Grandfather's been waiting all day for good news." He turned toward the house and motioned Father John alongside. "He's been taking the theft pretty hard. He was really looking forward to Black Heart's things coming home where they belong." He stopped and gave a moment's stare across the corral. "Seemed like something was finally coming around the way it oughtta be."

Mickey opened the screened door and ushered Father John into a small living room. Shadows floated down the walls and across the sofa and worn overstuffed chairs that sagged under the imprints of countless bodies. Across the room the old man struggled to get out of a recliner.

"Don't get up, Grandfather." Father John went over and placed a hand on Bernard's knobby shoulder. Then he pulled up a footstool and perched on the edge. "How are you today?" It was never polite to launch into the reason for the visit without the usual preliminaries.

83

Feeling pretty good, the old man said, now that Mickey was home safe from Afghanistan. Gonna be better soon as Black Heart's regalia was found.

Father John told him about Gianelli's visit, how the artifacts had arrived in New York, how they had spent several hours in warehouses before the cartons arrived in Riverton. "It's possible the artifacts were stolen en route," he said.

Mickey had pulled a chair from the kitchen and straddled it backward. He wrapped his arms across the top and gave a loud snort. "How long were the cartons at the Riverton airport?"

"About sixteen hours."

Mickey shifted sideways to face his grandfather. "That's when the stuff was stolen, you ask me. That was more than Cam Merryman needed. He could've pulled off the theft in ten minutes. Ripped open the cartons, took the artifacts, taped the cartons back up so nobody'd notice. He's been waiting for this. The big score."

Bernard Tallman lifted a hand and pushed at the air, as if he could push away Mickey's words, drive them back to wherever they had come from. "None of this" — he hesitated, then spit out the word — "speculation, is gonna do good or bring back Black

84

Heart's things. Trevor said lots of people could want the artifacts. Collectors with big money to spend on real Indian stuff from Buffalo Bill's show. Just 'cause you think —"

"Know, Grandfather." Mickey was on his feet, circling the kitchen chair, slapping his palms together. "What I know is Cam Merryman hates us. He's been waiting to get even for what happened back then."

"What happened?" Father John said.

Mickey shot him a look of incredulity, as if it weren't possible for anyone not to know the obvious. "Sonny Yellow Robe was Cam's great-great-uncle. Black Heart did everything for Sonny, made him his own son, seen that Buffalo Bill chose him for the show. Black Heart trusted him. Might've given him all the regalia, you ask me. Wouldn't have surprised me none if Black Heart gave it to him instead of his own daughter." He glanced over at the old man. "Sorry, Grandfather. Your mother might not have gotten the stuff." He shrugged. "The way things were back then, girls weren't important." He shrugged and turned back to Father John. "You ask me, Sonny got greedy. Didn't want to wait until Black Heart died to get the stuff. So he took it — feathered headdress, vest, moccasins — all of it. Sold it in Germany. Oh, I've read how the Show Indians got all excited about the things they could buy in Germany. Warm wool coats, leather bags, fine shoes and suits. Lots of ways to spend money."

The old man was shaking his head. "I've told you what my mother told me. Black Heart came home, but not Sonny. He disappeared. It was real hard on Black Heart."

"Disappeared!" Mickey gave a hard, forced laugh. "People over there loved Show Indians, treated them like celebrities, big Indian heroes. I mean, not long before, some of those warriors had defeated the greatest Army the U.S. put together, led by none other than General George Armstrong Custer. Left him and his men lying in their own blood on the hillsides over the Little Big Horn River. Some Arapahos were there fighting with the Sioux. Black Heart's father was there in his headdress and vest and moccasins. That made his stuff even more valuable, 'cause it had been in the battle. Oh, I can almost understand." Mickey folded his arms across his chest, walked over to the window and leaned forward, staring past the filmy white curtains. The sky had turned hazy, the sun a blurred white ball. "Arapaho with no reason to come home. An older sister, but she had her own family

86

here on the Wind River. Nobody cared about Sonny."

"Black Heart cared," Bernard said. "It's bad enough Sonny went missing, never showed up at the dock the day they was supposed to board the ship. Black Heart's things was gone, too. We had the chance to get them back, and now they're missing again. Breaks my heart, same as it broke Black Heart's."

Mickey lifted his left hand as if he were weighing an invisible ball. "Black Heart here," he said. He lifted the right hand. "Over here all the money Sonny needed for the rest of his life, living it up in Berlin or Paris or wherever he landed. Wouldn't surprise me none if he married some French girl, started a family. Descendants probably still there. Bottom line is, Black Heart came home, and Sonny Yellow Robe didn't. Made his sister mad. Her own brother didn't care enough about the people and the Arapaho Way to come home. Made them ashamed, too, is what I think. Funny thing, nobody expected Black Heart's stuff to show up in a basement after all this time. Cam Merryman heard about it. Everybody heard about the artifacts. How they were gonna come back to the people where they belong. Cam seen his way —"

"Enough!" Bernard Tallman slammed down the leg rest on the recliner and straightened himself against the back. "Black Heart never blamed Sonny. He loved him like a true son. Don't accuse Cam 'cause he happens to come down from Sonny's sister."

Mickey took a moment. His voice was quiet when he said, "They're no good, those Merrymans. You know that's the truth, grandfather. Fruit don't fall far from the tree. Cam's just like his great-uncle. Seen the chance to make a big score and grabbed it. He already spent time in prison for hijacking auto parts and selling them. How's that different from hijacking a truckload of artifacts? Besides, he hates our family. This was his chance to get revenge."

"You're the one he's got a beef with," Bernard said.

"So I blew the whistle on his hijacking business. So what? The sheriff was looking to pin it on me. Didn't leave me much choice."

Father John got to his feet. "You're saying Cam Merryman has a score to settle with you. But Trevor Pratt bought the artifacts for the museum. How does that settle any score?"

" 'Cause of Grandfather." Mickey nodded

toward the old man in the recliner. "Meant a lot to him to get Black Heart's things back, so it meant a lot to me. Man, he could settle the score and make more money than he ever dreamed of."

Father John left the old man leaning back in the recliner, legs forward, gray holes in the boots pointed upward. The whole experience seemed to have worn him down like the soles of his boots. The loss of the artifacts was a heavy burden. There had been a flicker of hope in Bernard's eyes that maybe Father John had good news. The hope had faded, leaving behind a sadness at the idea of one of the people stealing the artifacts. He had patted the old man's shoulder and assured him he would let him know the minute he had any news. Mickey had led him outdoors, climbed over the fence and gone back to brushing the Appaloosa, without saying anything.

He had said too much, Father John thought, and yet none of it mattered. Gianelli wasn't likely to spend time investigating Cam Merryman based on Mickey's suspicions. And yet, Mickey might be on to something. Even in the Old Time, the most accurate assessment of a warrior's character came from other warriors. Men who grew up together, rode side by side to hunt the buffalo and fight the soldiers and other enemies. Each warrior knew who was brave and honest and who would turn his pony and run. When was it, three years ago that Cam Merryman had served time in Rawlins? And Vicky had defended him.

He stopped at a stop sign, then turned right and drove for Lander. Twenty minutes later, he was on a tree-lined street of bungalows, kids throwing a ball in a front yard, a young woman pushing a stroller down the sidewalk. He felt her head swivel in the direction of the Toyota as he passed, and realized his windows were open. Puccini blared from the CD player. On the corner ahead was the redbrick bungalow with the small sign in front that he knew said, "Vicky Holden, Attorney at Law." Just as he pulled into the curb across the street, the front door opened. He knew the man heading down the steps: black hair, bronze skin against the white shirt sleeves rolled to his elbows, the stride and confidence of a warrior. He sucked in his breath. Adam Lone Eagle was back.

7

Vicky felt the pull of air as the front door opened. The sound of a thud broke the office quiet. She kept her eyes on the black text that filled the computer screen, ignoring the tremor in the floor boards. Adam. Forgot to tell her something, make some point crystal clear so she wouldn't misunderstand. He had spent thirty minutes in the office trying to talk her into going into practice with him again. When that failed — this wasn't the time; she had insurance forms to complete for a client — he had made himself at home, hitching a thigh over the corner of Annie's desk, chatting and joking, Annie bestowing an upward, adoring gaze. Then he had disappeared behind the beveled glass doors that closed off the office from the reception room, boots clacking down the hall between the conference room and Roger's office.

Eyes still glued on the screen, Vicky tried

to ignore the blurred hum of voices. Adam asking about the conference room. Roger confirming that they hardly ever used it. No reason Adam couldn't take it over for his private office. Annie giggling when Adam reappeared, saying how great it would be to have the old firm back. Everything in place. Adam striding about, in control, and Annie and Roger falling into step.

Vicky could feel the knot tightening in her stomach. Why had he come back?

She tapped the print key and swung toward the desk. Through the beveled glass, the tall, lanky figure in the tan cowboy hat and blue plaid shirt and blue jeans looked as blurred and distorted as the image in a fun house mirror. She felt the tension running away. She jumped up and flung open the doors. The printer had set up a swooshing noise. "Any news?" she said.

John O'Malley turned toward her, leaving Annie smiling at whatever he had just said. No doubt he had been teasing her, wanting to know why her boss kept her chained to the desk on such a beautiful day. He had been smiling, too, but a shadow moved in his blue eyes. He shook his head. "Something else I'd like to talk to you about."

Vicky walked over to the printer on the table next to Annie's desk, scooped up the white sheets it had spilled out and straightened them into a neat pile on the table. She glanced at her watch: 3:34 p.m., and still no sign of Trevor, who had agreed to stop by and sign the papers. Annie had been trying to reach him all afternoon. There was still time to get them signed and into the mail today. "I have to drive out to Trevor's ranch," she said, holding up the forms. "Why not come along? We can talk on the way."

Vicky drove her Jeep, even though John O'Malley had offered to take the old red Toyota parked across the street. Every time she saw it, she marveled that it got him anywhere. Somehow it kept going. A rumor she had heard not long ago: one of the mission's wealthy benefactors had offered to buy the pastor a new pickup. He had turned down the offer. Of course, he would turn it down. She couldn't imagine him driving around in a fancy new pickup. Instead the donation had gone into the mission's scholarship program for kids who needed help with college expenses.

"I see Adam's back," he said. They were driving east on Main Street, sun glistening in the windows of the shops and restaurants, red and gold flowers spilling out of the baskets that lined the sidewalks.

Vicky felt a little jolt of surprise. Adam. For a few moments, she had forgotten to remember him. She glanced sideways and caught the eyes of the red-haired man beside her, hat pushed back on his head. His eyes always startled her, as clear and blue as the sky. She guessed she was five or six years old before she saw anyone with eyes that color. All eyes were brown, she had thought, and some so brown they seemed black. All complexions were dark, all hair black, but that was when she had assumed that Wind River Reservation was the entire world.

"Adam wants to practice together again," she said.

"Is that what you want?"

The way he asked the question made her flinch, the words swollen with what was implied and left unsaid. Practice together, *be* together, a couple again, she and Adam. "I'm not sure," she managed. She wanted to roll down the window and shout. She wanted to swear, utter a string of words that she never used. Instead she gripped the steering wheel and stared at the highway unrolling like a conveyor belt ahead, a scattering of pines and brush rushing past the windows. Why was she so comfortable with this man, everything so easy and natural, while everything with Adam was so complicated and strained? Unnatural, as if she were someone else when she was with him.

John O'Malley didn't say anything, but she knew what he was thinking. Do what is right for you, he had told her — how many times? She had lost track. Be happy. Be happy. She stopped herself from laughing out loud. She wasn't sure what was right for her. She wasn't sure how to be happy.

"I'm sure we'll work things out." She threw him another sideways glance, and in the blue eyes, she could see that he was reading her thoughts.

"If you want to talk . . ."

"No, I really don't, John," she said. How ironic, she was thinking. What could they talk about? How it was impossible for them? A priest, for godssake. How they would never know if there could be anything between them? How Adam had gotten stuck somewhere in the middle of an impossible situation? Not his fault. For the briefest moment, she felt sorry for Adam, still trying to make something out of such a thin and fragile possibility. She drew in a long breath and concentrated on the road. A semi lumbered ahead. She pulled close to the rear bumper and waited for two pickups to pass before swinging out into the passing lane. Then she settled back, aware of the cool air blowing out of the vents and across her arms and neck, the tires humming on the asphalt.

The silence lapped around them for a few minutes before John said, "I just came from Bernard's house. His grandson, Mickey, thinks Cam Merryman is responsible for the missing artifacts."

"Cam?" Vicky shook her head. "He made a mistake a few years back, and he paid for it. As far as I know, he's kept his nose clean ever since he got out of Rawlins. I can't imagine him getting involved in anything that would send him back to prison." She took a moment, aware of the quiet breathing beside her. "Arapahos don't do well in prison." Out of the corner of her eye, she saw John O'Malley nod. "Might as well drop us in a black hole. We're plains people. We're used to the prairie and the sky all around. Coop us up, and we fold our wings and die a little. No, I don't think Cam would get involved. Besides . . ." She tapped out a rhythm on the edge of the steering wheel. "We don't know for certain that the artifacts made it to Riverton. All we know is that the cartons arrived. The artifacts could have been stolen anywhere along the way.

Trevor said there's a huge international market for items from the Wild West."

"There's no evidence against Cam," John said, and she could sense the logical part of him asserting itself. "Just Mickey's belief that Cam Merryman would steal the artifacts to hurt Bernard. Mickey says Cam would do anything to take revenge on Black Heart's descendants for what happened to his family after Black Heart came back from the Wild West. I doubt Gianelli will spend much time following up."

Vicky took a moment before she said, "There's always been bad blood between the two families. Everybody on the rez has heard the story. Black Heart came home, but all of his beautiful regalia were missing. Worth a lot of money even in 1890. When Sonny Yellow Robe didn't return, people assumed Sonny had stolen the regalia and sold it to support himself in Europe, probably in fine style. Trouble is, Black Heart himself never believed it. He tried to tell people that Sonny would never have taken the regalia. Strange, when I think about it. Black Heart and Sonny were both southern Arapahos from Oklahoma. But when Black Heart and his wife moved onto the rez to be close to their daughter, people accepted him. He was a great man. Sonny? No one here knew him, except for his sister. He was considered the outsider. People blamed him. The worst kind of thief, one who stole from the man who had treated him like his own son. It was a black mark on the Yellow Robe family. I heard that Sonny's sister never got over the way people avoided her and her children, shunning them, always letting them know they weren't welcome here. Where were they to go? She was a widow, and not only had her brother disappeared, he was reviled. That sense of injustice can stay with a family through the generations. Maybe Cam blames Black Heart for not speaking up enough for Sonny, changing people's minds. But that doesn't mean Cam stole the artifacts."

Vicky slowed for the right turn onto a narrow dirt road that lifted itself across the dusty, sun-burned earth and scraggly sagebrush toward the Wind River range. The foothills rose ahead, rounded like buffalo humps and as brown as the plains against the blue sky. Trevor's ranch spread over a bluff that butted up against the base of the foothills. She was about to say that the collection of artifacts in the ranch house rivaled anything she had seen in a museum when a cloud of dust, like a tornado, spun around the curve ahead. It took a half second to realize that the dust was in the vortex of a vehicle speeding down the middle of the road. She jammed on the brakes and gripped the wheel hard as the Jeep rocked back and forth, rear wheels skidding. Borrow ditches ran on both sides of the road. There was no place to go. She managed to swerve to the right, out of the path of the dark sedan. Two men in the front, focused on the windshield. She could feel the Jeep begin to dig in and steady itself as the tornado slammed past, engine roaring, dust spraying over her windshield. She was still gripping the wheel, nails digging into her palms, when the Jeep came to a stop, nosed into the ditch.

"My God." In the rearview mirror, the tornado spun down the road she had just been driving. She pulled on the door handle and got out. Her legs felt like Jell-O. She had to lean against the door to keep her balance. Little clouds of dust hung over the road as the sedan swung around the curve and out of sight.

"Are you okay?" Vicky was aware of John's arm around her shoulders. She wasn't sure when he had gotten out of the Jeep; he had simply materialized beside her, as if he had always been there.

"They didn't slow down or try to get

over." She could hear herself blurting out the words, as if she were a hurt child about to burst into tears. She swallowed back the urge to start crying and gave into the anger that moved through her like boiling water. "They could have killed us." She turned in John's arm and looked up. It was inconceivable that in the last few minutes, he could have been dead. Even more inconceivable, she thought, than that she herself might have been dead.

"Where's the ranch?" he said, nodding toward the road that stretched into the foothills, gray clouds of dust hanging in the air like ghosts.

"Up ahead. The road dead-ends at his gate."

"We'd better get up there," he said.

8

Lazy Z Ranch was carved into the overhead post. Through the gate, Father John could see the log cabin ranch house, two stories high and a porch across the front with wooden chairs lined up behind the log railing. He could sense the anxiety in Vicky; it poured off her like perfume. It matched his own anxiety. The ranch house had a vacant look, half-mast blinds in the windows, flag whipping in the wind from a pole at one corner of the porch, as if it had been forgotten. Fifty yards beyond the house were the out buildings: barn, storage sheds, what looked like a garage that probably stored a truck or tractor. Three horses grazed in the fenced pasture that ran alongside the dirt road to the barn. A black SUV stood between the barn and the pasture, which made him think that Trevor Pratt was on the ranch. There was no sign of the cowboys who worked for him.

It had taken a good twenty minutes to ease the Jeep along the borrow ditch, tires spinning and balking, churning up even more dust. Father John had walked along the ditch and collected branches and twigs, which he jammed in front of the tires, and Vicky had guided the Jeep at an angle until it stood level on the road.

"Trevor knows who took the artifacts," she had said as they drove toward the ranch. Bent over the wheel, talking mostly to herself, he had thought, worry seeping through her voice.

"He should have told me." She clenched the wheel, not taking her eyes off the road, as if another speeding vehicle might appear out of nowhere. "The way he acted at the mission. He was anxious to get out of there and talk to someone. God, I hope nothing has happened."

The plains had raced past outside the window. The sky hazy through the rolling dust. They had been going about sixty, he guessed, when the sedan had come at them. In the speed and dust, he'd made out the head and shoulders of a man crouched over the wheel, with a hard, angry intent. Another man in the passenger seat. What had propelled two men — white men, he realized — to flee the ranch at a hundred miles an hour, or whatever they had been doing.

Vicky drove for the front porch and slammed on the brake. Before he could get around to her side, she was out of the Jeep and heading for the wooden steps, gripping the brown envelope in one hand, bag swinging from her shoulder. He followed her and waited as she pounded the brass knocker against the wood door. From inside, nothing but a muffled echo. He moved closer, listening for the sound of footsteps or chairs pushing back, any disturbance that suggested someone was there.

Father John lifted the knocker and slammed it down even harder. The door gave a little sigh. Still no sound inside, and after a couple of seconds, Vicky grabbed the knob. The door pushed open. "Trevor?" she called, leaning into the opening. "It's Vicky and Father John. Are you there?"

An air of vacancy drifted from the house. Vicky called again, then pushed the door back. Father John stepped inside close behind her. They stood in an entry with a woven Indian rug spread over the pine floors. Beyond the entry were a pair of rooms that flowed across the front, divided by a staircase that rose to a balcony that overlooked both rooms. On the far side of the balcony were a series of closed doors, like dorm doors. At one time, this was a working bunkhouse, he thought, with rooms for the cowboys. Hardly a home. It didn't look much like a home now. Vicky was right. The house was like a museum, the front rooms filled with Indian artifacts on the walls, arranged on tables and stuffed inside glass-fronted cabinets. Even the furniture looked antique, displaced from another time. It took a moment to take it all in: displayed on the walls like paintings were dresses, shirts, and leggings, sewn out of the tanned, white skins of deer, embroidered in blue, red, orange, green, and yellow beads, with geometric images painted around the beads. Ceremonial clothing, he knew, worn only in the sacred ceremonies. Alongside the clothing were eagle-feathered head-dresses — he counted five — that had been worn by the leading men who had earned each feather with acts of bravery, courage. Each feather had a story. There were vests that drooped with beads and chest plates made from layers of yellowed bones.

On the tables were coup sticks, painted and wrapped in red cloth, trailing eagle feathers, used by warriors to approach the enemy. Not to kill him, but to touch him with the tip of the stick — to count coup —

and prove his own courage. There were lances decorated with eagle feathers that hung off the edge of the tables, and smaller head ornaments, feathered and beaded. The cabinets were filled with beaded armlets, bracelets, medicine bags, rattles. In one corner, a large painted stick used to play games stood next to a painted shield.

"He's not home." Vicky swung about and almost hurled herself back onto the porch, as if she had to get out of there. The house was like a cemetery, Father John thought, filled with all that used to be and now was lost.

"Maybe the barn," he said, walking out after her, pulling the door shut behind them. He couldn't shake the image of the speeding sedan. Neither could Vicky, judging by the mixture of resoluteness and dread in the way she stood looking out over the ranch.

They headed down the steps and along the side of the house. Gusts of wind swept down the dirt road and smashed Vicky's slacks against her legs. Except for the sound of the wind and the scuff of their footsteps, a deep quiet suffused everything. The horses stood motionless at the fences, as if waiting for something that might never occur.

Through the opened door to a shed next

to the barn, Father John could see a small tractor in the center and tools aligned against the walls. No sign of Trevor. The barn looked unused, the wide door pulled shut. Most likely, Trevor had closed the door himself after he saddled one of the horses, then had ridden out into a pasture where he ran a herd of cattle. Or maybe he had taken an old truck to check on the fences. Nothing unusual about the ranch, Father John thought, except the quiet and emptiness. And yet the uneasy feeling had fastened itself onto him like a chain. The speeding car kept rolling through his head. "Wait here," he said, touching Vicky's arm. He could feel the tension moving through her.

"I'm going in with you," she said, plunging ahead.

He hurried past, grabbed the metal handle on the right and slid half the door across the other half. A long shaft of sunlight shot across the concrete barn floor and illuminated the stalls on either side. Blankets and tack filled the shelves and hung from the hooks on the front walls. "Trevor!" he called. His voice bounced over the concrete and around the stalls. Bales of hay were stacked in a loft overhead.

"Trevor?" He started down the middle of

the barn, checking the stalls as he went. Clumps of hay and water stains on the floor, a shovel upright in a corner. Then something different, out of place. A large wooden club had been tossed into a disturbance of hay and dust near the rear stall. He hurried toward the stall, moving ahead of Vicky. "Trevor," he said again, his voice coming back to him, tight and dry.

He saw Trevor the instant he reached the stall, slouched in the back corner, head sideways, eyes fixed on the floor, arms akimbo, like a drunk who had slumped down and couldn't get up. A dark stain spread across the front of his light-colored shirt. In an instant, Father John was down on one knee beside him about to check the man's carotid artery when he saw the dark splatters across the plank wall behind Trevor's right shoulder. He pressed his fingers along Trevor's neck. The skin was warm; there was no pulse.

Vicky folded onto her knees beside him. "Oh, my God," she said.

Father John didn't say anything, aware of the sound of her breathing beside him.

"The car we saw. It must have just happened." She threw a glance over one shoulder, as if the men speeding past might materialize in the barn. Then she drew a cell out of her bag and started punching the keys. "Come on," she said, under her breath.

Father John looked back to the dead man beside them. Trevor Pratt, benefactor to the mission, benefactor to the Arapahos. *The artifacts belong with the people*, Father John remembered Trevor saying the day he had driven onto the mission grounds, stomped up the concrete steps of the administration building and dropped into one of the chairs Father John kept for visitors. *I found them for sale on the internet and jumped on the opportunity. They wouldn't be available for long. Too many dealers and collectors eager to get their hands on Indian regalia from the Wild West. I knew right away I had to buy the stuff. Called the dealer in Berlin, got him out of bed. Two in the morning over there. Softened him up as soon as I told him what I wanted. We made a deal right then. All I knew was that the regalia belonged to Chief Black Heart, leader of the Arapahos in the Wild West. Frankly, I would've paid a lot more if I'd known then what I learned later. How Black Heart's father wore the regalia in old battles like the Battle of the Little Big Horn.* Trevor had laughed, and Father John remembered how the laughter had sounded like a cough rumbling out of his chest. *That German didn't know the whole story or he would have held out for more. The artifacts belong at the museum where Arapaho people, schoolkids, you know what I mean? can come and look at them as many times as they want.*

Vicky's voice, shaky, not like her voice at all, cut into the memory: "A man has been killed," she was saying into the cell. "The Lazy Z Ranch at the end of a ten-mile dirt road off Highway 287."

Father John made the sign of the cross over Trevor's forehead. "May God take you to himself," he whispered.

"Yes, that's it," Vicky said. "The junction just south of Willow Creek Road."

"May God have mercy on your soul. May he look upon the good in your life and forgive any sins you may have committed."

Vicky leaned in close and stared down at Trevor, the cell phone gripped in one hand. Poking out of her bag was the brown envelope that contained papers for Trevor to sign. A gust of wind swished across the concrete floor. "I'm so sorry, Trevor," Vicky said finally, her voice choked now. Father John saw the moisture gathering in her eyes. "So sorry." She pushed herself to her feet and headed back through the barn.

Three white pickups with green stripes and "Fremont County Sheriff" splashed across

109

the sides stood in front of the barn. Officers in tan uniforms moved in and out in a slow, methodical way, as if the murder of Trevor Pratt was part of the day's schedule. It had taken twenty minutes for the pickups to roll onto the ranch. Father John had stayed in the barn a few moments, praying silently over the still body of Trevor Pratt. Then he had found Vicky sitting on a log beside the fence and dropped down beside her. Together they had watched the dust clouds gathering far out on the road, coming closer. "How do you stand it?" she had asked, her eyes on the clouds. "Praying over dead bodies. So many senseless deaths."

There was no answer, and in the sad smile she had given him when she turned toward him, he knew she understood. At one time, he had needed props to hold him up. Jim Beam, gin, whatever he could get his hands on. Rubbing alcohol once, desperate for a drink. And that was before he had ever prayed over someone whose life had been taken. Teaching American history classes in a Jesuit prep school in Boston, a future with a doctorate and a position in some Jesuit university — that had been his path, until the alcohol had sent him veering in another direction. After rehab, an Indian mission in the middle of Wyoming with Father Peter

Roach, the only Jesuit who had agreed to give him a chance. There were times here when he had longed for the props. The senseless deaths, the sad history. But Father Peter's voice had stayed in his head: "I believe in you, son. You can make it."

He had made it almost ten years, and yet he could taste the thirst coming on him now, feel the dread knotting in his stomach. Would it never leave him?

"When was the last time you saw the victim?" The sheriff's investigator had walked over. Tall and wiry with light, short-cropped hair and a plug of tobacco in one cheek. He introduced himself as Detective Colsky.

Father John got to his feet. "Yesterday at the mission," he said. He and Vicky had already told the investigator and his partner, Detective Janson, a big, jowl-faced man with a pillowlike paunch above the belt of his Levi's, what they knew about Trevor Pratt. How he had materialized out of nowhere, offered to donate valuable Arapaho artifacts to the museum, and hired Vicky to handle the details. How the artifacts were stolen before they could be delivered to the museum. When Trevor hadn't shown up at Vicky's office today, they had driven out to the ranch to have him sign the insurance forms.

As he talked, Father John had read the irritated look Colsky threw his partner: Murder in Fremont county fell in the sheriff's jurisdiction, but missing Indian artifacts might be in the fed's. Gianelli would have to be brought in.

"I had the feeling . . ." Vicky hesitated, lifting herself off the log, her eyes fixed now at some point in the pasture, ". . . that Trevor knew who had taken the artifacts. He knew where they were."

Colsky considered this a moment, squaring his shoulders, drawing himself taller by an inch or two. "He give you any names?"

Vicky shook her head.

"Not much to go on." Colsky shrugged. "We'll check out the house. Might come up with something. I'm going to need both of you to come into the office tomorrow and give your statements."

Vicky started down the driveway, and Father John fell in beside her. If Vicky was right about Trevor, and she was usually right, he was thinking, then the thieves could still be in the area. Which left the possibility that the artifacts were here as well.

9

The quiet of dusk had settled over the mission grounds when Father John pulled up in front of the residence. The transition time, when the day's activities had ended and the evening's hadn't yet begun. The old trucks and sedans that appeared on Circle Drive throughout the day had disappeared. Social committee and Ladies Sodality and adult education classes ended. Kids picked up from after-school day care in Eagle Hall. Everyone gone home.

He let himself through the front door, expecting Walks-On to bound out of the kitchen, snuggle against him and lick at his hands. There was no sign of the dog. The mission quiet had invaded the house, Father John thought as he headed down the hallway. Elena would have left by now, but his dinner would be warming in the oven. The sharp smell of barbeque filled the kitchen. The dog's bed spread across the far corner.

Food bowl empty; water bowl half-full. He walked past the table and looked out the window. Walks-On wasn't in the yard.

No sign of Bishop Harry either, no footsteps overhead or muffled undercurrents of TV noise. Sometimes, after spending the day answering phones and counseling parishioners in the back office of the administration building, the old man liked to walk down by the Little Wind River. And Walks-On had a sixth sense for when the bishop was headed for a walk. He would bark and howl from the yard or house until the bishop came and got him.

Father John retraced his steps through the house and took the path through the wide swath of wild grass in the center of Circle Drive. He crossed the drive and walked down the graveled road that divided the administration building from the church. Past Eagle Hall, past the guest house. He had just turned into the narrow path that led through the cottonwoods and pines to the river when he saw the bishop coming toward him. Walks-On loped ahead, bounding up and down. From close by came the sound of the river lapping the rocks. A thick odor of damp pine suffused the air. He reached down, patted the dog's head and scratched behind his ears. "Good run, buddy?" he said. The dog's coat was cool and wet.

"Sorry you couldn't join us." The bishop's boots slapped at the hard dirt. A deep pink flush ran across the old man's face, but he looked invigorated, even younger than he had seemed this morning, slumped at the table, sipping coffee. Father John had ignored the provincial's instructions to insist upon the old man resting. Resting was likely to have killed him, he thought now. He enjoyed the old man. Wandering down the hall to his office and chatting, listening to stories about India, reaffirming his own intention to be the kind of priest that Bishop Harry was.

"I heard the news." Moisture in the old man's eyes had started to fog his glasses. "Terrible. Terrible." He paused for a moment, removed his glasses and wiped at them with a handkerchief he had extracted from his jacket pocket. "The phone started ringing late this afternoon. Seems one of the deputies at the ranch texted his brother about the murder, and the brother is married to an Arapaho." The bishop shrugged. He had been at the mission long enough to accept that the moccasin telegraph was as efficient as the internet. "Folks started putting things together. Trevor Pratt, Indian artifacts dealer, murdered. Likely he was the anonymous donor who had donated the missing artifacts to the museum. What about the artifacts? Had they been found yet? The callers sounded very disappointed when I told them that, to my knowledge, the artifacts had not been recovered. I assume that is the truth."

Father John told him it was. They might never be recovered, he was thinking, even if they were still in the area. It was as if they had disappeared into a sinkhole that plunged into the depths of the earth. If Vicky was right, any idea about who had stolen them could be gone with Trevor Pratt. He couldn't shake the image of the man who took up a lot of space, big shoulders and voice, confidence spilling off him, crumbled in the back of a horse stall.

Walks-On had already run down the road toward the center of the mission. The bishop started after him. "I understand you and Vicky found the body," the bishop said as Father John fell into step beside him.

Father John started to explain that Vicky had taken insurance forms out to the ranch and he had gone along, wanting to talk to her about the accusations Mickey Tallman had made against Cam Merryman. The words lodged in his throat. He didn't want to get into the rest of it, how he could have called Vicky, how he didn't have to go to her office at all, how he had wanted to spend the time with her.

"I'm sorry." Bishop Harry turned toward him. In the old man's eyes, Father John could see he had filled in the blanks himself.

"Does it ever get any easier?"

"Encountering death?" the bishop said. Father John knew the old man had deliberately taken a different turn. "Asking God to have mercy on the poor soul? In my experience, the sadness and senselessness of a violent death never leave you. Sometimes in the middle of the night, I think about the little boy who found his way to the mission in Patna. Skinny and beaten, shaking so hard he could hardly stand. We tried to protect him, but his father sent the police who took him away. He died a few days later. I think of the girls, so many girls we tried to protect. Also hauled away and we learned later of the terrible things that happened. One was burned to death by her mother-in-law. Such a pretty girl she was, with large, trusting brown eyes." He hesitated. "You must pray, John, that it doesn't get easier because that would mean you had lost part of your own humanity. It would mean you had learned to protect yourself by pushing the horror into a separate compartment in your mind, forgetting about the victims. Better to remember than to forget. Pray for their souls always. Pray for the brokenness in the world."

They walked past the guest house. They both knew he had been asking about Vicky, Father John realized. But how to deal with the victims, the motionless, blood-crusted bodies, the senseless deaths — that was another question to which he longed for answers. Ahead, two pickups stood in front of Eagle Hall. Father John could hear the commotion inside as chairs and tables were set up. The faint odor of coffee drifted outdoors. "I can take the AA meeting tonight," the bishop said. "You go on to the house and get your supper."

"It's okay," Father John said. "I'd like to take the meeting tonight."

1860s Cheyenne artifacts from the wars on the plains. Handcrafted bows and arrows, Winchester rifles, tobacco pouches, war shields, war bonnets. Recently purchased from a small-town museum in eastern Colorado that closed its doors. Items have been stored in temperature-controlled environments and are in excellent condition. Contact Trevor Pratt, antiquities dealer, Lazy Z Ranch, Lander, Wyoming.

Vicky scrolled to the top and searched for a date. The streetlight outside glared across the bottom of the screen, and she got up and snapped the curtains shut. The apartment instantly seemed smaller, more intimate. She had just sat back down at the laptop on the dining room table when the crack of what sounded like a gunshot came from the street below. She felt her heart start up, then told herself it was only a truck backfiring. Cowboys leaving the bars, heading out to the ranches. God, she wasn't herself. This afternoon had unnerved her, made her jumpy and scared. She had to get herself together.

She struggled to focus on the black text filling the screen. There was no date. The advertisement might have been placed yesterday or two years ago when Trevor said he had moved to the ranch. Thirteen pages had come up when she had typed in Trevor Pratt. She moved to the next page. Most of the sites seemed to be ads that Trevor had placed, like the one for the Cheyenne artifacts. But here was something different: a short article from a trade magazine dated eight years ago:

Word is that none other than the mysterious Trevor Pratt brokered the million dollar sale of Plains Indian artifacts to a private collector in Santa Fe. Pratt is considered the authority among dealers in such artifacts. We understand that he has been accumulating the items from members of various tribes. We hear that the Sioux, Crow, and Blackfeet tribes were outraged at the sale of their patrimony. They claim to have asked Pratt for the chance to bid on the items, but he refused. Our own efforts to reach Pratt have been unsuccessful. Rumored to be a recluse on a ranch somewhere on the plains of Colorado, he did not respond to numerous phone messages. No dealer is under any compunction to offer Indian items to the tribes before putting them on the market, but it might make good business sense to allow tribes to bid. Pratt seems to have made up his mind ahead of time that the tribes could not match the million dollar bid, but the brouhaha could make it more difficult for Pratt to purchase items from tribal members in the future. On the other hand, the episode might only bring more attention to the mysterious Mr. Pratt, who always seems to get top dollar for Plains Indian antiquities.

Vicky read the article again. Nothing that gave her a glimpse into Pratt, aside from the fact he was an astute businessman, focused on the bottom line. A faint whiff of admiration ran through the piece. And yet, Trevor Pratt had donated a million dollar collection to the Arapaho Museum. She wondered why.

She moved onto the next Web site, and here was something new. *Recent purchases of rare Plains Indian regalia for sale. Telephone auction to be held on August 23. Sign up below to take part. Pratt and Hyde Indian Antiquities.*

Below the announcement were pages of photos of white deerskin shirts and dresses, headdresses, gloves, vests, leggings, pants, all beaded and painted; tools of all kinds, carved from stone — hatchets, hammers, chisels; pipes decorated with strings of beads and feathers, hoops and shields, parfleches of various sizes that the people had used to carry their belongings, exquisitely beaded medicine bags. The sign-up sheet to join the auction filled the last page, along with a paragraph of ground rules. Items would be auctioned off individually. Pratt and Hyde reserved the right to begin each auction at a baseline price. If the price was not matched, the item would be with-drawn.

Vicky went back to the search page and typed in *Pratt and Hyde*. Another page of Web sites scrolled into view. She clicked on the first site, and skimmed through an article from a trade magazine: *Julia Hyde of Hyde's Fine Collectibles in Kansas City has joined Trevor Pratt Collectibles. Pratt was unavailable for comment but Hyde returned our call and confirmed the new partnership. She has closed her store in Kansas City. The new business will be based in Colorado, she said, and will operate on the internet.*

Pratt had never mentioned a partner, Vicky was thinking. She typed in "Julia Hyde" and the name of the store in Kansas City. Only two sites materialized, and she clicked on the first. A blond woman, smil-ing, in her thirties, with the small, toned figure of an athlete, arms crossed over the jacket of her dark suit, posing in front of a brick store with "Fine Collectibles" written in white across the plate glass window. A half inch of text ran below the photo: *Look-ing for the unusual gift? The perfect piece that says your home is as unique as you are? The piece from the past that cannot be duplicated? Come and see me at Fine Collectibles. I am an interior designer and I know how to incor-*

porate beautiful antiques into your modern home. My decorating services are free with every purchase. I will help you turn your home into a show home.

Vicky scrolled through several pages of photographs: all types of antiques, tables and chairs, chests, bookcases, desks with curved, rococo legs and what looked like fine wood-inlaid surfaces. Then came the accessories: lamps, vases, bowls, pitchers, candlesticks, place settings of china, silver knives, forks and spoons, heavy-looking silver coffee and tea services on large trays, the kind of household items she had seen in movies.

She moved onto the next site. *Dear Customers and Friends. Life is filled with changes. Don't we all know that to be true? Changes are usually a mixture of sadness and expectation. I am sad to announce the closure of Fine Collectibles and will miss being able to help all of you furnish your home with one-of-a-kind pieces that have their own history. But I look forward to expanding my knowledge of antiques by joining Trevor Pratt in a new adventure, Pratt and Hyde Indian Antiquities. We will be based in Colorado and will specialize in unusual, hard-to-find items from the rich culture of the Plains Indians. We will be on the internet and will always be available to you by e-mail or telephone. Look for the details on our Web site which will be up shortly."*

Vicky went to the next site: Another photo of the blond Julia Hyde, older, with squint lines at her eyes and a sunbaked look about her. The text was brief. *My dear customers and friends. After four years, Pratt and Hyde has been dissolved.*

A buzzing noise zigzagged through the quiet. Vicky pulled away from the laptop, walked over and pushed the button on the intercom. "Who is it?" she said. She knew the answer even before Adam's voice filled up the space around her

"May I come up?"

She pushed another button, listened to the beeping sound followed by the noise of the elevator creaking into action, then cracked open the door and went back to the laptop. *Pratt will continue to operate the Plains Indian antiquities business, while I return to my first passion: Victorian Americana. My store is now in Dubois, Wyoming, a small, beautiful town that still has wooden sidewalks.*

She could hear the elevator clanking upward, the swoosh of the doors opening and the familiar footfalls coming down the hallway. A part of her was glad that Adam was here, that she wouldn't be alone.

Woman Alone. The Arapaho grandmothers had given her the name. There were times when the truth of it had stung like a whip.

She made herself read on: *A perfect place for a Victorian antique shop on Main Street. If you are out in Wyoming, be sure to put Dubois on your itinerary. Stop in and see the exceptional items I have collected.*

She was aware that Adam had come through the door and shut it behind him. Still she kept her eyes on the screen. A woman named Julia Hyde had been in business with Trevor Pratt. The mysterious Mr. Pratt, the magazine piece had said, but Julia Hyde knew who he was, and she was in Dubois.

10

"You okay?" Adam said.

Vicky got to her feet and went over to the counter that divided the kitchen from the dining area. Adam leaned against the door, one hand wrapped around the knob, as if he half expected her to ask him to leave. He might have stepped out of a poster advertising a movie about the modern Native American, blue-checkered shirt, blue jeans, and belt with silver buffalo-head buckle, black hair brushed back from a wide, intelligent forehead, jaw set in confidence and eyes that seemed to take in everything about her, even the things she wanted to keep from him.

She ignored his question. "You heard the news?"

"I'd have to be deaf not to have heard. It's all over the radio and TV. Heard it on the moccasin telegraph first. Word is that Trevor Pratt donated the artifacts from the

Buffalo Bill show. Is that true?" When she didn't say anything, he nodded, as if he had the answer. He pushed himself off the door and stepped around the counter into the alcove that served as a kitchen. "Any hot coffee?"

Vicky nodded toward the half-empty coffeepot next to the stove. She had brewed the coffee when she got home from Trevor's ranch. The thought of food made her stomach churn, but she had sipped at a mug of coffee while she searched the internet for an explanation of why Trevor Pratt might have known the thieves. Trevor was so alive in everything she had read. The mysterious Trevor Pratt. Collector and dealer of Plains Indians artifacts, authority on dates and history and value. She slammed the palm of her hand onto the table. "It's stupid and senseless," she said. "Trevor knew how valuable the artifacts were. He should have known that the people who stole them were capable of anything. He shouldn't have put himself in danger."

"You're saying Trevor knew who took the artifacts?" Adam poured the last of the coffee into a mug and turned toward her.

"He was furious yesterday when the artifacts were missing. He tore out of the museum. I followed him and tried to talk to

him. He brushed me off and drove away."
She could feel the anger blossoming in her
cheeks. Stupid, stupid. "He was going to
solve the crime all by himself, a one-man
posse out to bring the bad guys in for hanging. He was like Buffalo Bill presenting the
Wild West, telling the whole story of the
West as he saw it. Well, Buffalo Bill's dead
now."

She slumped back into the chair and
Adam walked over and plopped down on
the chair next to her. "I'm sorry, Vicky," he
said. "I'm sorry you had to find his body. I
heard you weren't alone. I'm glad for that."

"The thing is, I keep thinking there's
something I should have done."

"You were his lawyer, not his keeper. You
couldn't follow him around, try to talk him
out of going after the thieves himself."

"There must have been a way," she said.
"I didn't know him well enough to know
how to help him."

Adam got up and leaned toward her. "I
got a phone call after I left your office
today," he said. "It made me realize the kind
of law you practice."

"What are you talking about?" She
glanced away, her thoughts still on Trevor
Pratt.

"Personal law. Everything is personal to

you. Clients don't just walk in off the street or pick your name out of the phone book. They're your personal responsibility. You have to help them, advise them, protect them, and if a client ends up murdered, it's because you failed somehow. You didn't know him well enough . . ."

"Please," Vicky said, lifting the palm of her hand. "You didn't see Trevor with a hole the size of a baseball in his chest."

"All I'm saying is that I finally understand the way you practice law. We have different ways. My approach isn't personal. I'll do my best for my clients, but I won't own them. I don't care about their other problems. I don't want to know where they go or who they talk to. I give them good advice. If they don't take it, I don't worry about it. Two different approaches, that's all. I'm not saying one is better than the other, only that I'm finally beginning to understand." He paused. "And appreciate your approach. The woman who called me today . . ." Another pause, and in that instant, Vicky understood the call hadn't come from a random woman looking for a lawyer. "An old friend," he hurried on, throwing up both hands as if to demonstrate there was nothing to hide. Vicky wondered where this was going. Why was he telling her this? Adam didn't talk about his former lovers, still they hovered in the background, forgotten, he assured her. But the woman on the telephone hadn't been forgotten.

She tried to concentrate on what Adam said next: how he and Mary Many Horses went back a long time, how she was someone he had once cared about.

"I haven't heard from her in years, but she's living on the reservation now. Moved here to be close to in-laws after her husband died. Anyway, she called the office, said she needed to speak with me and Annie gave her my mobile number. She's having trouble with her son. Good kid. Graduated from high school, enrolled in classes at Central Wyoming College, got a part-time job. He's been depressed for a month or so, but seemed to be coming out of it. Then last night, he tried to kill himself. Botched up job. She came home from work and found him lying on his bedroom floor. He'd swallowed some pills. Riverton Memorial has him on suicide watch. She asked me to talk to him."

Adam walked around and perched again on the stool. "When I knew Petey, he was five years old, missing the dad that left him. For a while I tried to fill that empty place, but when things didn't work out between

Mary and me, I moved on. Now Petey's in trouble. I don't know if talking to him will do any good. I don't know if he'll confide in me, and I don't even know if he needs a lawyer. But Mary's worried he's mixed up in drugs. What I'm saying is, it's personal. I intend to do whatever I can to help them, and I realized I was thinking like you. Some poor guy from the rez comes looking for a lawyer and you're ready to move mountains to help him. So I get it, Vicky. It doesn't mean I want to practice personal law twenty-four-seven. It's not my expertise. But it does mean I'll be a better partner."

Vicky set her elbows on the counter and dropped her face into her hands. Adam Lone Eagle was persistent. He never gave up. She had seen oil executives wince when he walked into a conference room with Arapaho tribal officials because the executives knew they would not be walking out of that room until Adam Lone Eagle had gotten the agreement he wanted.

"Please, not now," she said. Still in front of her was the image of Trevor Pratt slumped in the stall, the black hole gaping in his chest. And hovering about the image was the attractive blond woman named Julia Hyde who had been Trevor's business partner and might also know the identity of the thieves who had stolen the artifacts and most likely murdered Trevor. If the thieves made the same connection, Julia Hyde could be in danger.

"Okay. Okay." Adam lifted the mug and took a long drink of coffee. "But we have to talk about it," he said. "Whether we're going to put the firm back together and whether there's a chance for us."

Vicky dropped her hands and turned her head to the man beside her. A year ago he had walked out of her life. He had agreed to represent the Crow Tribe and needed to be in Montana, close at hand for the endless negotiations with coal companies and federal regulatory agencies. The firm would go on, he had said; one of the partners would be elsewhere. A simple matter for Holden and Lone Eagle, Attorneys at Law, and complicated at the same time. He would call regularly, drive back to Lander. They would still be together. Except the silence between calls grew longer and the trips fewer, until Vicky had called and told him she intended to dissolve the firm and move back into the one-woman-law-firm-size bungalow where she had once practiced alone. She had taken Annie and Roger Hurst with her. Ironically, the number of small cases — adoptions, wills, insurance claims, DUIs, and assaults — had grown enough to keep both her and Roger busy. Everything was settled now, running as smoothly as a thoroughbred horse.

"Why did you come back?" she said. "Why didn't you stay in Hardin? Or go to Lame Tree and help the Cheyennes protect their resources? Or move to L.A. and practice natural resource law from a fifty-story building in Century City? Why here?"

"I've told you," he said.

"This isn't a good time."

"When is a good time? When wouldn't you be involved in some case that hadn't taken you over, occupied all of you? Your thoughts and feelings. Look at you! It's past ten o'clock and you're still working!" He tossed his head toward the laptop on the table. "Searching for some random piece of information to figure out who killed your client. It's not your job, Vicky. Let the sheriff's detectives figure it out. Listen, what I'm saying is . . ." He leaned in close, his face inches from hers, his breath heavy with coffee. "I'm making an effort to understand the kind of lawyer you are. If there's a future for us, I need you to see my point of view. I need more of you, and as I see it, the law has all of you."

Adam stood up and slammed his fist down

hard, setting the mug dancing on the table. "Whoever said the law is a jealous mistress got it right. In your case, the law is a jealous lover."

"You'd better go," Vicky said.

"Go?" He took a moment before he swept his palm down the edge of the table, as if he could wipe away the crumbs and detritus of the past. "Okay. I get it. You're upset about today, and I don't blame you. But I need to know what kind of a relationship we might have. Just business? I'm not interested. Business and personal, yes."

Vicky studied the edge that he had just swiped clear. A blank page, she thought. She could write anything she wished, only she wasn't sure what she wanted to write. She only had to look up at him, she knew, and he would stay the night. They would be back together, figuring out how to go forward. And she would be back in a half-hearted relationship. Adam was right about that; she had never been able to bring all of herself into their relationship. He had blamed it on the law, but she knew that he knew the truth. There was a part of her that wished John O'Malley were not a priest, that things were different, that he might someday leave the priesthood. Always a part of her hanging on to the thinnest thread of hope. Stupid.

She could feel the heat of Adam's gaze burning into her. Out of the corner of her eye, she watched him swing around and head for the door. Small tremors ran through the floor when the door slammed shut.

11

Berlin
July 23, 1890

The dinner gong had sounded five minutes ago, and groups of Indians were making their way toward the big tent at the far side of the camp. Sonny Yellow Robe held back, not taking his eyes off the interpreter on the other side of the grassy road. The interpreter stood at the opened flap of Chief Black Heart's tipi, arguing again with the chief over the regalia. Sonny knew they were arguing. He had observed the conversation for the past twenty minutes. He could guess how it had gone. Marks had offered a ridiculously low price for a headdress worn by Black Heart's father in battles on the plains, even the battle against Custer. The chief just shook his head, saying nothing. Marks had cajoled and explained. He was offering more money than Black Heart had ever seen. He was angry. Arms flying side-

136

ways, head lowered like a charging bull. Probably calling Black Heart all kinds of names: fool, dumb Indian, too stupid to help himself. An Arapaho family hurried past, blocking the view for an instant. Then Sonny saw Marks stomp out a little circle in front of the tipi. Black Heart kept shaking his head. It made no difference what Marks promised or threatened, the chief would not sell what belonged to his ancestors. The argument was over, Sonny realized, but with Marks, the argument was never really over.

Marks broke away and, head still down, set out for the dining tent. Sonny followed, hugging the long, jagged shadows of the tipis, pulling back when Marks looked around. He had kept an eye on Marks for the last two hours, ever since the afternoon performance had ended and the Indians rode back into the camp. They had run the ponies into the corral where the younger Indians — training to be warriors, he thought, like the Old Time — had fed and brushed them and gotten them ready for the evening show. Marks had worked his way through the crowd spilling out of the arena and into the Indian camp. He had stopped at several tipis before he reached Black Heart's. Sonny had watched as Indians handed over beaded vests or leggings, sometimes a bow and quiver of arrows or a hatchet, and Marks placed a roll of bills in outstretched brown hands.

The feeling of shame, so strong Sonny could smell it, had welled up around him. He'd had to stop himself from running over, grabbing the relics out of the interpreter's hands, throwing the filthy wad of bills onto the dirt. The Indians needed the money, he knew. Jobs were hard to find on the reservations. They came and went. Even if an Indian landed a job driving a wagon of hay for a week, he didn't know how he would feed his family when the job ended. The wads of bills, along with the pay the Show Indians earned — well, it was a lot of money.

There had been other visitors this afternoon: three stout, serious-looking white men in topcoats and hats, walking through camp, stopping to talk to Show Indians still in their regalia, visiting with women selling beaded necklaces and bracelets and earrings outside the tipis. Always jotting something down in notepads. Sonny had avoided them, his mind focused on protecting Chief Black Heart's regalia.

An Indian family hurried toward the dining tent, kids running back and forth, hollering and laughing. Horses neighed in the corral, and a couple of dogs had started barking. Pieces of memory surged inside him. He was back in his village in Oklahoma, one of the kids racing about, playing games. One day the government men from the agency had come with the wagon and taken him away. His father had been off hunting, and he had always known in a silent space deep inside that his father would have killed the government men, had he been there. He could still see his mother running behind the wagon, calling "Yellow Robe! Yellow Robe!" It was necessary to knock the Indian out of the child, the government men told him. They put him on the train packed with other Indian kids. For five days and nights they traveled across the plains and rivers and forests to the Carlisle School in Pennsylvania, a place he had never heard of. By the time he had walked away, all of his family was dead, except for a sister who had gone north to the Wind River Reservation.

Beyond the tipis, past the block-stone buildings, he could see the train parked on the siding, red, white, and blue banners with giant words, "Buffalo Bill's Wild West," sagging across the passenger and freight cars. He had ridden another train across rivers and hills, boarded a ship called the *Persian Monarch* and sailed across waters more immense than he could have dreamed. He had heard that one of the Arapahos at Wind River, Chief Yellow Calf, had refused to go with Buffalo Bill. How could they ever find their tracks on the water when it was time to come home?

At Le Havre, Black Heart had taken him by the arm and led him onto the Wild West train, knowing Sonny might bolt, run off and try to walk back home. Since then he had ridden the train across Europe, through France and south into Spain, east into Italy and north to Germany, giving two and sometimes three performances almost every day.

Sonny ducked inside the dining tent. Panic hit him like a star falling from the sky. Marks was nowhere about. The man was sneaky, capable of running back for Black Heart's regalia. Black Heart had removed the regalia in his tipi after the performance and packed it inside the black satchel. Sonny had carried the satchel to his own tipi, bent around the treasure, hurrying through the field of brush and trees between the camp and the old stone buildings. He had stored the bag under a buffalo robe that Black Heart had given him when he returned from Carlisle. Marks would go to Black Heart's tipi first. When the bag wasn't

140

there, he would go to the tipi of Black Heart's adopted son, but at least Sonny would have more time to stop him. Marks could find the regalia in the flap of a robin's wings. He would smell it.

Finally Sonny spotted Marks seated at the end of one of the four long tables that extended from the head table. Not the interpreter's usual place, but a good place from which to disappear, Sonny thought. He would not allow the white man out of his sight again. He walked sideways down the length of the next table and took his seat next to Black Heart. The afternoon heat had gathered inside the tent, and the air was heavy with odors of grilled meat, hot oil, and fresh coffee. "I don't trust Marks," he said.

"If anything happens to my ancestor's things," the chief said, "we'll know who took them."

"Marks says he has buyers waiting." He nodded toward the tent opening, the Indian camp and the arena. "They could be out there now. He's been buying relics this afternoon."

A long moment passed before Black Heart said, "Two Eyes, the Ogallala, told me he didn't want to sell his headdress, but now he's thinking about it. The white man pays

141

a lot of money. He said he can make another headdress when he gets home." Black Heart shook his head. He looked tight with worry, lips drawn across his teeth, cheeks sunken. "It took years for Two Eyes' ancestors to earn those feathers. They did brave things, faced many dangers. What brave deeds are left to us warriors now? What danger do we face? Growing hay? Looking for a job? The old man won't live long enough to get himself another headdress." He gave a small bark of laughter that sounded as if he were stifling a sob.

Sonny started to say he would talk to Two Eyes, but another thought crashed through. If Two Eyes sold his headdress, Marks might be satisfied and leave Black Heart alone. He and Black Heart could stop worrying, stop moving the relics from one tipi to another, stop watching the white man every minute. He pushed the thought away. The relics were part of Black Heart, of his history, of who he was. Two Eyes' headdress was part of him. He would talk to the old man.

"Ladies and Gentlemen." The voice rang like the sound of a familiar melody, low and solid with authority, working through the buzz of conversations around the tables. Buffalo Bill stood tall and square-shouldered at the center table, gazing out over the dining tent. He wore a white suit that shone against the late afternoon daylight filtering through the canvas tent. His hair and trimmed goatee flowed long and dark over his shoulders. Colonel William F. Cody, famous everywhere. Army scout and Indian fighter and buffalo hunter in the old days.

Sonny noticed that the strangers he'd seen in camp earlier were seated on either side, heavyset men in dark topcoats and ties, perspiration glistening on their foreheads, hair slicked back and wet looking. "It is my honor to formally introduce our esteemed guests. The United States Consul General to Berlin on my right." Buffalo Bill nodded toward the flushed-looking man who made an effort to rise halfway out of his chair and give a little nod. "On his right is the Legation Secretary." A smaller man leaned back against his chair as if he wanted to disappear. "And here" — Buffalo Bill turned to the left — "The United States Consul to Hamburg." The consul glanced over at his comrade before getting to his feet and bowing.

"I have invited these eminent gentlemen to visit our exhibition this evening. I hope many of you have had the chance to speak with them, and I trust you have given their questions honest answers. They are here to determine the kind of treatment Show Indians and their families receive while performing in our educational exhibitions. I purposely chose not to tell you they would be with us because I did not want to make you think you should answer with anything but the truth. Despite the nasty rumors that have appeared in the *New York Herald* about your treatment, you have stood up and told the truth. These gentlemen have heard the facts from Show Indians themselves. Your pay represents a fair share of profits. The food you receive is good food. Meat, bread, canned milk, vegetables — your meals are the same as mine. These gentlemen have told me that you are the best-looking and apparently the best-fed Indians they have ever seen."

A shout of laughter burst over the tables, and Buffalo Bill waited a moment before he went on. "Are you held here under any constraints? No. You may return to your homes whenever you choose, and the Wild West will pay for your trip. I thank you for providing the facts to these worthy gentlemen. They have assured me they will contact the *New York Herald* and demand that the truth be printed. I remind you, if you ever encounter mistreatment, report it to me immediately. I will not allow my people to be mistreated. Enjoy your dinner." He nodded toward the plates heaped with beef, potatoes, and carrots that had been boiling most of the day in large pots in the nearby cooking tent.

Sonny cut into the meat on his plate and took a bite. So the important-looking men were investigators, here to see for themselves if the rumors started by that crazy Indian, White Horse, had any truth. White Horse had walked away from the Wild West and taken money from the newspaper man to tell lies that could cause the commissioner of Indian affairs to ban Indians from going with Buffalo Bill. Sonny had heard the thin thread of worry in BB's voice.

Marks was gone! In the few seconds that Sonny had kept his eyes on BB, Marks had disappeared. Sonny dropped his knife, pushed back his chair and jumped to his feet. He didn't remember covering the length of the tent or running outside, but now he was running down the grassy road, past the tipis with bales of hay that served as chairs, all of it blurring into the arena on the right and the field and old buildings and train on the left. He could hear the noise inside Black Heart's tipi, as if a wild animal had gotten inside and was rooting through

Black Heart's belongings.

Sonny threw back the flap. He stood in the opening, the graying daylight shooting past him over the white walls. "Get out," he said.

Marks had been leaning over a trunk, pulling out shirts, trousers, undershirts. On the floor was a tan cowboy hat, the brim stained with Black Heart's sweat. How many times had he seen Black Heart riding across the prairie, the hat bobbing against the blue sky? Next to the hat was a box of inlaid wood that, Sonny knew, Black Heart treasured. A white man had given him the box after Black Heart found the man's stallion wandering the plains. He could have kept the stallion, improved his own horse stock, but Black Heart had searched for the owner and taken the horse home.

"Don't seem like it's any of your business," Marks said. "What's gonna happen if the chief takes his stuff home? They'll get lost, trampled in the dust. Some relative will sell them for pennies to buy a bottle of gin. These relics stay here with collectors, they're gonna get the best of care, be preserved for future generations, you might say."

"You heard Yellow Robe." Sonny realized Black Heart had come up behind him. He

146

moved past him into the tipi, wide shoulders and back blocking the shaft of daylight. "Get out of my home."

"I'm raising my price, Chief," Marks said. "We both know there's nothing like your relics. None of them other Indians got head-dresses and regalia that were in the Custer fight. So I'm gonna give you more money than you can count. Hell, you can do the grand tour and send money home for the folks if you want. Isn't that what you want?"

"Buffalo Bill would like to know what you're up to," Sonny said.

"What?" Marks pivoted about, eyes wide, mouth flapping like a hooked fish.

"You'll be fired, Interpreter. Sent on your way like you deserve. Get out of here and forget about Black Heart's regalia."

"You talk to BB and I swear . . ."

Sonny closed in on the white man. "You think you can scare me?" He felt the heat in his face; he was spitting out the words. "I killed a man like you with a hatchet once," he said. Another white man. He could still see the white face and blue eyes coming at him in the creek bed where he'd been hiding on the long walk home. The white man wanted his boots. "Take them off," he'd ordered. Then he had clenched his fist and hit Sonny hard, knocked him into the brush

147

and rocks and jumped on top of him. Sonny had managed to get the hatchet out of the man's belt and slam it into his head. He had set off running into the woods, away from the creek bed, the man's blood hot and then cool on his face and hands.

"Get out," he said again, waving toward the opened flap. He had killed once, he was thinking. He didn't want to kill again.

12

"You heard about Trevor?" Father John stood in the doorway to the director's office. Eldon White Elk was bent toward the computer screen. A cigarette burned in a saucer next to his fist that looked as if it might have just been driven into the desktop. Sandra Dorris occupied a chair by the window, flipping through a catalogue of some sort, black hair flowing like a veil around her face. A pile of catalogues lay scattered at her feet.

"Heard last night." Eldon glanced up. Sandra pushed herself off the chair. "I'll go to my office and finish this," she said, bending down to scoop up the catalogues. Father John stepped into the small office as the girl hurried past, dipping her head and giving him a shy smile as she went.

"We're researching the cost of artifacts like those that are lost," Eldon said. "Haven't found anything yet with the same kind of history. But we'd like to replace them with other regalia from the Wild West, if we can. We'll need a generous benefactor. What a tragedy, Trevor getting murdered. He might have identified the thieves."

"What makes you so sure?" Father John dropped into one of the side chairs against the wall. He had spent the last hour and a half at the sheriff's office in Lander giving a formal statement. Just as he was leaving, Vicky had come in, looking drawn and tense. He wondered if she had been up all night, and decided she probably had. Wide awake, unable to settle into sleep, walking the floor and going over and over in her mind the horrible scene in the barn. He had asked how she was doing, and she had assured him she was okay. Not great, she said, but okay. All she wanted was for the men who killed Trevor to be brought to justice. She had thrown a challenging look at the sheriff's investigator when she said this.

"You saw the way Trevor ran out of here after we opened the cartons." Eldon swiveled sideways, picked up the cigarette, fitted it in his fingers, and took a long drag. "Been in the collecting business for years, knows everything about Plains Indian art. You can bet he had a good idea of who was likely to come after the artifacts."

"I meant, what makes you so sure the artifacts are lost?" The morning light flooded through the window and danced across the framed certificates and college degrees on the wall behind Eldon. A thin twist of smoke rose from the saucer; the office smelled of smoke.

"A million miles away by now." Eldon drew on the cigarette and blew the smoke out of the side of his mouth. "I've posted photos on the internet that Trevor gave us. 'Be on the lookout for stolen artifacts from Buffalo Bill's Wild West.' Every collector and buyer in the business has most likely seen the photos. Nada. Nothing. Those artifacts dropped into a big empty void. The buyer has seen the postings, you can bet on it. He knows they're hot. So they're gonna disappear into a special room in his mansion. Probably great art hanging all over the place. Wows his guests. But only a few special guests get to see the special room. 'My really valuable art is in here.' " He had switched into the deep, confidential voice of a radio announcer. "Guests feel special, like the room. Maybe they'll see the postings and realize the SOB had bought stolen goods, but are they going to report what they've seen? Not on your life. It would be the last time any collector invited them into his special room."

Father John didn't say anything.

"It's my job to know these things," Eldon said. "Collecting, preserving, and exhibiting valuable artifacts, pieces of the past, if you will, is what I do. I have to be on top of all the ways the crooks would like to stop me."

Out of the corner of his eye, Father John caught sight of the white SUV curving onto Circle Drive. He watched it pull up in front of the administration building and rock to a stop. Gianelli, white shirt, tan vest, blue jeans, jumped out and headed up the steps. Father John got to his feet. "The fed just drove up," he said.

Eldon snuffed the cigarette in a saucer and stood up. Father John was aware of the director's boots clacking down the corridor in rhythm with his own.

"Suppose you tell me exactly what happened yesterday at the ranch," Gianelli said. He had settled into one of the old chairs Father John kept in his office for visitors, pen poised over a notepad the size of his palm. "Sheriff faxed me the statements you and Vicky gave this morning. We're cooperating here on the assumption that Trevor's murder and the theft are related. I've gone over the statements, but I'd like to hear it from you."

Father John started with the two men in the dark sedan, racing away from the ranch in a cloud of dust. "Ran us into the ditch," he said.

"Two men?" Eldon sat forward in the chair across from the fed. "There you go. The thieves and murderers."

"Either you or Vicky get a view of their faces?"

Father John shook his head. "Not really. I think they were white," he said. Then he told the fed about going to the ranch, not finding anyone around, and looking in the barn. "Trevor was in the back stall." The image planted itself again in his mind's eye. He looked away, taking a moment. *Pray that it never gets easier.*

Gianelli scribbled something in the notepad, flipped the page and continued writing. Finally he looked up. "No sign that the cartons were tampered with either in New York or Denver. They were loaded onto the Denver flight and transferred immediately to the flight to Riverton. Arrived here 4:34 p.m. Signed into the warehouse at 5:13 p.m. Stars Shipping picked them up Tuesday morning and delivered them to the museum thirty minutes later." He flipped the notepad closed. "During the night, someone managed to open the cartons, remove the artifacts and reseal the cartons. I've put out a be-on-the-lookout for a dark sedan with a driver and passenger to every law enforcement agency in the area. If those guys are still around, a patrolman or deputy could spot them."

"Confirms my theory." Eldon shifted sideways, crossed one leg over the other and bounced a black cowboy boot into the middle of the office.

"What's that?" Gianelli said.

"Who had the most incentive?" Eldon said. "Who knew how to sell them, how to locate buyers?" He paused for a second and rubbed a fist against his mouth, a desperate look about him as if he longed for a cigarette. "I don't like to blame anybody, but all the signs point the same way. Trevor set this whole thing up himself. He had connections. My guess is he already had a buyer lined up when he made the deal to purchase the artifacts. Brought in a couple of thugs he knew to take the artifacts from the warehouse. Who knows what happened between him and those guys?" He shrugged. "Falling out of thieves, is my guess. Maybe they didn't like the size of their cut for doing the dangerous part. Probably put the squeeze on him. Got into an argument and

Trevor ended up dead." He stared into the middle of the room. "Now they don't have to cut him in."

"You're assuming they know the buyer."

"I'm thinking they were supposed to make the delivery as soon as Trevor gave the all clear. It wouldn't do for him to have any contact with the artifacts or to try to deliver them to Colorado or Nevada or California himself. Too many chances for things to go wrong."

"I'm not following you," Father John said. He couldn't shake the impression of the man who had walked into his office as if it were a corporate boardroom and announced that he intended to make a donation to the mission. "Trevor could have sold the artifacts legally," Father John said. He had asked Trevor why he wanted to donate them to the museum and Trevor had hesitated before he said, *I've sold a lot of Indian artifacts in my time. Sold them out of the tribes. Let's just say I'd like to see the artifacts go where they belong.*

"You're forgetting something, John," Eldon said. "The million-dollar insurance policy. Trevor could sell the artifacts on the black market and still walk away with insurance money. The perfect scam."

The director stood up and went over to

the window. He stared outside for a couple of seconds before he turned back. Lips drawn into a thin line against his teeth; eyes darting about the office, as if he were searching for something solid to hold onto. Father John had seen the same look on the faces of parishioners during counseling, just at the moment they finally faced themselves and whatever they had done — cheated on their wives, stolen from an employer, neglected their children. "I can't stop thinking . . ." Eldon seemed to struggle with the words bunching in his throat. "I could have prevented this."

The office went quiet. From the back office came the clack of computer keys — the bishop writing this Sunday's homily. Gianelli sat motionless, not taking his eyes from Eldon White Elk. An experienced interrogator, the fed, Father John was thinking. Like a counselor, knowing when to speak and when to listen.

Eldon folded himself back into the chair, clasped his hands between his knees and leaned forward. "I never should've listened to Trevor. Never should have called the shipping company and told them to keep the cartons in a warehouse at the airport." For a moment, Father John thought the man might burst into tears.

Gianelli took a moment before he stood up and started for the door. He turned back. "Riverton police are checking the warehouse security cameras. If it looks like that's where the artifacts were stolen, they'll have jurisdiction. Right now, we're all working together. Call me if anything comes to mind," he said. Then he disappeared into the corridor. The door wheezed open and slammed shut.

Eldon was shaking his head. Finally he stood up and began backing toward the door. "He'll never find those men," he said. "They're gone, like the artifacts."

Father John listened to the director's footsteps on the old wooden floor in the corridor. Again the opening and shutting door. Maybe the idea of Trevor Pratt arranging for the artifacts to be stolen made logical sense, he was thinking. But it was like the piece of a puzzle that didn't fit anywhere, a lost piece mixed up in the wrong box. He couldn't shake his own sense of the man. Looking for redemption for whatever he had done in the past, the Indian artifacts that he had helped to take away from the tribes. A man who had wanted to atone for the past.

13

The house looked deserted, small with faded gray paint and blinds half-pulled in the front windows. The Toyota pickup bumped across the borrow ditch and nosed over the bare dirt yard. So much land and sky and emptiness surrounding each house, Father John thought, that the houses themselves seemed empty. Even with laundry flapping on lines outside, breaking the quiet. But there was no laundry outside the gray house. Behind the house, the barn doors were open. He parked a few feet away and walked into the cool shadows inside the barn. Daylight splayed on the dirt floor, the tack hanging on the walls, the horse stalls facing each other. The faint, hollow rhythm of metal on metal mixed with the whistling noise of the wind. A dun-colored horse stood silent in a stall on the right. Seated on a stool, shoeing the horse's left hoof, was a man in a yellow checkered shirt and dark cowboy hat.

"Cam?" Father John said.

The man in the cowboy hat gave the horseshoe another tap before he dropped the hoof and stood up. "Heard that old pickup of yours," he said, tossing his head in the direction of the road. He was probably in his mid-twenties, slim, muscular build, black eyes slitted against the afternoon brightness, and the rough, crooked face of a man who had been in too many bar fights.

"Got a minute?" Father John said.

"You here about the missing relics?"

Father John nodded.

"Mickey Tallman said I know anything, he's a liar. Been holding a grudge since we was kids. Man can't stop living in the past. You want to talk? Sure we can talk." Cam set the hammer on top of the stall's half wall, shouldered past Father John and went outside. "One condition," he said, starting across the yard toward the gray house. Father John fell in beside him. Boots made a soft thud on the hard, dusty earth.

"What's that?"

"You gotta give me a hand, Father, talk sense into Mickey Tallman, tell him to stop lying. I gotta share the blame with my great-uncle for what happened more than a

159

hundred years ago? It's crazy. Now Mickey's put the word on the moccasin telegraph that I must've stole the artifacts before they got to the museum." He ignored the two steps, hopped up onto the wooden stoop at the back door and flung it open. "I'm clean now," he said, stepping inside. Father John followed him into a closet-sized kitchen that felt hot and damp with the smells of coffee. A green Formica-topped table had been pushed against the wall below the window. Dishes, pots and pans, and an assortment of cereal boxes and cans of soup were stacked on the counter next to a white plastic coffee brewer with a half-full glass container.

"No more doping," Cam said. He nudged a chair away from the table with his boot and motioned for Father John to sit down. "No more drinking and hanging out with lowlifes and fighting. Left all that behind. Got me a nice wife now. Donna Wolf. You know her? Folks used to live on the rez."

Father John nodded. He remembered a little girl with a quick smile and long black braids squirming between her parents at Mass Sunday mornings. The Wolfs had moved to Oklahoma to take care of elderly relatives. Evidently Donna had come back. She couldn't be more than eighteen, he was thinking.

"We're gonna have a kid," Cam said. "I got me a fine spread here, raising a little hay out in the field, and I been picking up jobs at a garage in Riverton. Donna works at the diner." He plopped down across from Father John. "Made some bad mistakes, I'm not denying it. But I paid my debt to society, did three years in Rawlins, and I ain't never going back."

"Why do you think Mickey blames you for the missing artifacts?" Father John said. With Mickey's accusations on the moccasin telegraph, he was thinking, Gianelli might decide to have a talk with Cam after all.

"I hate him, and Mickey knows it." Cam jumped to his feet and turned toward the counter. "Fixed up some coffee a while ago. Want some?" He was already filling two mugs that he had dragged from behind a cereal box. He handed one to Father John, took his chair, and sipped from the other one. Through the archway, Father John could see the dim light filtering past the blinds in the living room. The coffee was barely warm and strong, laced with coffee grounds. "Damn near ruined my life," Cam said. "I got reason to hate him, the dirty snitch. Him and me were hijacking stuff together, but he turned snitch, got himself a

161

deal and walked off. He was the one got me involved. Easy way to make some bucks, he told me. Wasn't for Mickey Tallman, I never would've gone to Rawlins. So now he's saying I want revenge, so I stole his ancestor's belongings."

Cam took a drink of coffee, then set the mug down. "We go back a long ways, Mickey's people and mine, all the way to the Buffalo Bill days. My ancestor, Sonny Yellow Robe, got himself adopted by Mickey's ancestor, Chief Black Heart. I remember the stories my grandfather told about Sonny. How he escaped from the Carlisle School. Walked all the way from Pennsylvania to Oklahoma." He shook his head. "Can't blame him. I would've done the same if they'd locked me up in that place. Indian kids got beaten for speaking their own language. Had to speak English all the time, 'cause they was trying to turn them into white kids. Grandfather said Sonny used to go out into the fields and sit behind a tree and talk to himself in Arapaho, he was so scared he'd forget how to speak to his own family if he ever got home. When he did get back, all his family was dead, except for Lulu, his sister. She had moved here, 'cause her husband was a northern man, Emmett Merryman. I come from them."

"When did the bad blood start?" Father John took a sip of the coffee.

"Early on, from what I heard," Cam said. "Chief Black Heart got back from the Wild West, but Sonny never came home. Seems when they got ready to board the ship, Sonny was nowhere around. Grandfather said the Show Indians could come and go as they liked. All Buffalo Bill expected was that they showed up for the performances. He wasn't their keeper, you know what I mean? He treated them with respect. So if Sonny didn't want to go home, that was okay with him."

He took a moment, regarding the coffee as if he had just noticed the grounds floating around. "Trouble started when Black Heart's regalia never arrived. So his people started saying that Sonny must've stolen it. Black Heart never said that, my grandfather told me. Fact is, Black Heart tried to stop the stories. He said Sonny wouldn't do such a thing. He claimed something happened to Sonny, and somebody else took the regalia. But a lot of people on the rez still think Sonny Yellow Robe was a no-good lowlife that stole from the chief that adopted him."

Father John took another sip of coffee.

"What did your grandfather think happened?"

Cam shook his head. "He didn't want to believe what the Tallman clan said. What could he do? Sonny never showed up, and neither did the regalia. There was other stories, he said, about Indians that sold their valuable stuff. Sooner or later, most of them came home, but some didn't. Maybe Sonny was one of them, only he sold Black Heart's stuff." He pushed the chair back and got to his feet. "Hold on a minute," he said before he disappeared into the dimness of the living room.

There was the sound of drawers opening and shutting and papers rustling. Cam was back, clutching a small brown envelope. He spilled the contents onto the table: three yellowed postcards. "One thing Sonny learned at Carlisle was how to read and write," he said, dropping back onto his chair.

Father John picked up the nearest postcard. The paper felt like fabric, flimsy and worn, the black writing faded almost to dark red. The postmark at the top said, "Paris, May 20, 1889." A brief message, a few sentences scribbled in a painstaking, schoolboy hand: *Dear Sister, We arrived in Paris with no troubles. Indians that said we would fall off the edge of the waters was real sur-*

prised. Everybody here loves Indians. Try to touch us, checking if we're real. Your loving brother, Yellow Robe. On the back was a black-and-white photo of the Eiffel Tower.

He looked at the second card. A photo of the *Monumento a Colón* in Barcelona, the postmark dated January 17, 1890, and another brief message. *Dear Sister, We are on tour now and have been in Spain for three weeks. Some Indians got sick in Barcelona. Four Ogallala died, and they're buried far from the ancestors. I am fine. Will write more later. Your loving brother, Yellow Robe.*

The last postcard came from Berlin, mailed on July 23, 1890. *Dear Sister, We have been to many cities in Italy. The pope himself blessed the Wild West Show Indians. We are in Germany now. I'm almost used to riding the train. Everybody here wants our regalia for keepsakes. They pay a lot of money for headdresses. Herman Marks, the interpreter, buys things from Indians and sells them to Germans. I won't sell anything. Will write later. Your loving brother, Yellow Robe.*

"Three postcards, that was all grandfather got from his mother," Cam said. He swept the postcards back inside the envelope. "He said she was real sad her brother never came back. She always missed him. She never believed what Black Heart's people said."

"If he wouldn't sell his own things," Father John said, "it's hard to imagine he would have sold Black Heart's."

"Tell that to Mickey," Cam said.

Father John got to his feet, thanked the man for the coffee, and started for the door. He turned back. "The fed might stop by to ask you a few questions."

A look of bafflement crossed Cam's face, followed by the shock of understanding. He straightened his shoulders and thrust his head back. The muscles in his jaw twitched. "You saying he believes Mickey's lies?"

"Look, Cam," Father John said. He didn't want Cam to be surprised when Gianelli's white SUV drove up. He had counseled a lot of ex-convicts. They believed they carried a bull's-eye on their foreheads, that the police and the sheriff and the fed would always look at them first, ask a lot of questions about whatever crime they were investigating. If was as if they could never wipe the slate clean, get away from the past. A couple of men he'd counseled had panicked when a police car drove into the yard, fled out the back door, taken off running. They had spent time in jail for evading police officers. "Agent Gianelli's talking to anybody on the rez who might have a connection to the artifacts. You can explain that Mickey

166

Tallman blames you for what your ancestor might have done."

"I'm not talking to the fed or any other cop." The anger in him seemed to have hardened into something more implacable. For the briefest moment, Father John wondered if Mickey Tallman was right, if Cam Merryman was capable of taking revenge on the man who had sent him to prison.

"Can you account for your whereabouts Monday night?" he said.

"Right here, where I belong, minding my own business The fed can go chase his tail around."

"Donna can vouch for you?"

He took a moment, swiped his tongue over his lips. "Donna was at the diner 'til midnight."

Father John closed his eyes and pinched the small part of his nose. Plenty of time to take the artifacts before midnight, he was thinking. And yet, all Gianelli would get from Mickey Tallman was a theory of a man looking for revenge. Unless . . . He looked at the man sitting statuelike. "Anything else between you and Mickey?" he said.

Cam took his time, drawing an invisible square on the table with his mug. "He thought Donna was gonna marry him.

Drove him crazy when she left him and started up with me. He thinks he can lay the theft on me, I'll go back to prison, and Donna will come running back to him. I'm never gonna let that happen."

14

The tribal offices sprawled over a flat patch of earth south of Ethete Road. Father John wheeled between clumps of sagebrush and gold-tipped wild grass into the dirt parking lot. He stopped at the end of a row of pickups and road-weary sedans that faced the one-story, gray frame building. The double glass doors parted, and an Arapaho, tall and stocky looking, black cowboy hat pushed high on his head, headed toward a pickup, clutching papers in one hand. Father John got out and followed the imprints of the man's boots. A wild-goose chase, he was thinking. A hunch. The afternoon was hot, the sun beating down and the wind whipping the heat. He could feel the heat burning through his shirt.

The temperature dropped ten degrees inside the building. The whir of a motor blowing cool air through the vents mingled with the low buzz of voices behind closed doors that ran down the corridor and the muffled clack of footsteps on hard vinyl floor. On the right were the offices of the tribal council, called the business council because, along with the Shoshone business council, the members conducted the Wind River Reservation's business with the outside world. Oil and gas leases; timber and water rights.

"Hey, Father!" Betty Youngman clasped her hands on the counter and leaned forward. Last spring she had graduated from the University of Wyoming, pretty girl, exuding college idealism, with wide-set intelligent eyes and black hair that hung about her shoulders and shone in the overhead light. "What brings you to the center of the world?"

"Buzz Moon in?"

"Officially tied up with important matters," she said. "Always in for you." She motioned him after her down the corridor to a door with a plaque that read: "Cultural Resources." She rapped once before pushing the door open halfway. "You got company, Buzz," she said. The girl gave Father John a smile and turned around.

The door sprung back and a large man in his fifties with the fit look of a man half his age and long, gray-streaked black hair pulled into a ponytail loomed in the opening. "Good to see you, Father," he said.

"Got a minute?" Father John stepped inside the small office with books and file folders piled on shelves that made a U around three walls and crowded the narrow window overlooking the back parking lot. The books had an unsettled look, as if they might break free and topple over a desk nearly buried under piles of papers. "Excuse the mess." Buzz busied himself clearing stacks of papers and books from a straight-back chair. He motioned Father John toward the chair and, wedging himself between the desk and a wall of shelves, dropped into a chair. "Hot for this time of year," he said, wiping at his forehead. He might have been standing in the sun, dripping sweat.

Father John balanced his cowboy hat on one knee. The polite preliminaries came first. Talk about the weather, the latest news on the rez. Fifteen kids heading off to college this fall, and wasn't that great? He was accustomed to the Arapaho Way — live in dignity with respect for others. He liked the slower motion, the willingness to take a little time, acknowledge the other person's humanity before launching into business.

Finally Buzz said, "I been feeling like somebody sucker punched me in the gut

171

ever since I heard about the missing artifacts." He pushed back, lifting the chair off
the front legs and crossed his arms over his
chest. The top of his head brushed the
books balanced on a shelf. "Important part
of our heritage, gone like so many other
things." He dropped the chair and frowned
at a stack of papers. "It doesn't matter how
much money the artifacts are worth. They
represented something. They showed how
Arapahos were part of what happened on
the plains. We fought for our lands. Protected our villages. Lost our people at the
Sand Creek Massacre. Joined the Sioux,
listened to Sitting Bull and rode with Crazy
Horse against Custer. We even went with
Buffalo Bill and reenacted the Old Time
across Europe. Helped educate millions of
people about who Indians really were.
Those artifacts would have reminded us to
be proud of our past. Young people could
have taken a lot from them."

He let his gaze run across the cluttered
desktop, drumming his fingers on the edge.
"Gone now," he said, as if he were talking
to himself, struggling to find acceptance for
the reality. "I know how these things go.
Burial sites dug up, artifacts taken. Indian
stuff stolen out of museums and shops.
Petroglyphs cut out of stone. There's big

money for antique Indian regalia, tools, weapons, you name it. The kind of money that doesn't care how the items were obtained." He locked eyes with Father John. "Rich people that got everything else, so they want what belongs to us."

Buzz shook his head, as if what he had said was hard to imagine. "Arapaho regalia from the Wild West is pretty rare," he said. "Fact is, not many Arapahos went with the show. Most of the Show Indians were Sioux and Pawnee. But Buffalo Bill took Chief Black Heart and about a hundred other Arapahos for the 1890 show. Black Heart's regalia had history. Somebody put a lot of money on the table for that regalia." He shook his head. "Ugly business. I hear the anonymous benefactor was murdered yesterday."

Father John nodded. "Trevor Pratt. He was a dealer and collector. He might have confronted the thieves. The fed traced the artifacts to the Riverton area, which makes me think the thieves might still be in the area."

Buzz considered this a moment. "A long shot," he said. "Unless they're waiting for a buyer to show up, but I doubt it. Usually the thieves get out of the area and make the exchange in another state. Even if the

173

exchange took place here, my guess is it happened right away, and the buyer left with the artifacts."

"What's the chance the thieves are local?" Father John said. Arapahos like Cam Merryman or Mickey Tallman, stealing their own heritage. He didn't want to believe it, but he had heard too many confessions, counseled too many parishioners to think that Arapahos and Shoshones were any different from everyone else.

"They're out there." Buzz tilted his head toward the window. A pickup lurched past, belching a cloud of black smoke. "Indians willing to sell their own heritage. It's been quiet the last two, three years. Nobody digging where he shouldn't be or hunting artifacts in sacred places."

"Anybody you suspect might have stolen artifacts in the past?"

"One or two families the cops keep an eye on, but like I said, things have been quiet lately. If you're fishing for a local tie to the stolen artifacts . . ." He pulled in his lower lip and looked at Father John out of narrowed eyes. "Could be somebody on the rez saw an opportunity. Certainly was enough publicity. Everybody knew Arapaho artifacts from Buffalo Bill's Wild West would be at the museum for the exhibit opening.

Wouldn't have been difficult to watch for them at the airport. Small airport." He gave a little shrug. "Only a few planes coming in every day. Somebody working there could have passed along the information when the artifacts arrived."

Father John didn't say anything. Something was missing, the minor premise in the logical syllogism. "You're saying somebody saw the opportunity and jumped into the business of stolen artifacts? Where would a beginner find a buyer?"

"The internet," Buzz said. He switched his eyes toward the computer screen at the corner of the desk. "I've been checking the obvious sites. Nothing suspicious, but there are a lot of sites." He clasped his hands and rounded his shoulders forward. "Maybe the thieves didn't have to go looking for a buyer. Maybe the buyer or his representative found the thieves."

Father John worked the folds in his cowboy hat a moment. "You're saying somebody showed up on the rez and found an Arapaho or Shoshone to steal artifacts?"

"You think greed stops at the rez border?" Buzz waved a thumb at the window as if he were hitching a ride. "It's happened in the past. Outsiders show up, find somebody to help them steal petroglyphs or dig up grave

175

sites. Outsiders need local help. We hear of outsiders working the powwows, trying to talk people into selling their regalia. They ingratiate themselves, dangle a lot of money in front of people's noses." He shook his head. "Some of them sell. Perfectly legal to sell their own possessions, even if the items are ancient. Treasures that should stay with the people. We try to discourage folks from selling. If they need money, and most of them do, the tribe tries to find a way to buy the pieces. Sometimes we're successful, and sometimes we're not. The pieces are already sold and gone from the rez before we hear about it. We have managed to save a few items. They're in the museum."

Father John nodded. The collection was growing. Families donated artifacts that belonged to their ancestors. Other Arapahos brought in items they wanted to sell, and sometimes Eldon found a benefactor willing to purchase them and donate them to the museum. Like Trevor Pratt, except that Trevor had found the museum.

He put on his cowboy hat and started to his feet. He felt as if a heavy load had been strapped to his shoulders, the same feeling that came over him after hearing confessions all afternoon. Buzz had confirmed what he had hoped couldn't be true: somebody on the rez could be involved. Somebody Trevor had suspected and confronted. He could see Cam sitting at his kitchen table, talking about his new life. Wife, kid on the way, little ranch, part-time job. You think greed stops at the borders? Buzz had said.

He realized Buzz was still talking about outsiders approaching Indians. "Had some show up at the powwow in Arapahoe two weeks ago," he said. "Nobody ever saw them before. Walked around, visiting with Indians, complimenting them on their regalia, saying they could get them good money. Making nuisances of themselves, you ask me." He stood up and set his knuckles on a stack of papers. "Couple white men. Dark blue car. Colorado license plates. Far as we know, nobody took them up on any offers, so they drove off."

"Who did they talk to?"

Buzz was studying him again. "You think they had something to do with the theft?"

"The fed's looking for two guys in a dark sedan," he said.

"Wilma RunningFast," Buzz said. "Tried to talk her out of her great-grandmother's deerskin dress. Made her mad. They didn't understand what no means. She had to get her grandson to shoo them away. Guess they went off and bothered somebody else." He wedged himself around the desk again and opened the door. A shaft of cool air shot into the small office. "Wilma's not gonna want to talk to the fed, not with her grandson on probation for that bar fight he got into last spring. Maybe she'll talk to you."

"Maybe she will," Father John said.

Father John turned on the ignition and rolled down the windows. The hot breeze swept through the cab. He hit the button on the CD player and listened to "Oh, se sapeste" a moment, his thoughts on Wilma RunningFast. He had met Wilma on his second day at St. Francis Mission. Still unpacking his books and opera tapes — it might have been yesterday, the memory was so vivid. He could see himself back then, trying to settle into a new office, adjust to a new job on an Indian reservation, where he had never imagined he might find himself, unsteady on his feet and trying to ignore the thirst that clung to him like a bad odor, anxious not to disappoint Father Peter the way he had disappointed just about everybody else in his life. The provincial, the other Jesuits at the prep school where he had taught American history, his own family. Everybody.

And there was Wilma. Short and almost as wide as the doorway, gray-haired, a grandmother in a pink dress with a red and blue shawl thrown over her shoulders and feet swelling out of black slippers. Everything you might ever want to know about patience and acceptance and forbearance written all over her. "Welcome to our place," she had said.

She had plopped down on a side chair and, after a few minutes of niceties, told him she wanted him to be happy at St. Francis.

"Any advice?' he'd said.

That's when she told him to get to know the people. "Lots of outsiders come to the rez," she'd said. "They already got their ideas of Indians. Even priests. They know all about us 'cause they seen old westerns. They read the newspapers about troubles some Indians get themselves into. So they think they got us all figured out. You'd be surprised how they go along, month after month, year after year, with all those ideas in their heads and they never shake them out so other ideas might come in."

He had tried to remember Wilma's advice for almost ten years now, and it had paid off. They were his family, the Arapahos. They had become part of him, and he felt part of them. This was home.

The gear was stiff and cranky as he shifted into low. Still the old Toyota kept going, and there was a lesson in that, he thought. He guided the pickup out onto Ethete Road, turned left at the intersection and drove toward Arapahoe where Wilma RunningFast lived.

15

Father John parked close to the wooden stoop, let a couple of minutes pass, then got out and stood by the pickup. He had left the CD player on, and the sounds of Puccini floated around him. A hollow sound came from inside the small white house that duplicated itself up and down the dirt road. Squeals and shouts of children drifted on the wind from the school a short distance away. The community of Arapahoe spread over the flat, brush-smeared prairie west of the mission. At night, from the kitchen window at the residence, Father John could see the lights that broke through the layers of darkness on the rez.

The front door flung open and Wilma RunningFast stood with hands dug into her broad hips. She gave him a wide smile and motioned him inside.

"I been thinking you might show up," she said.

"You must be reading my mind." He stepped into a narrow living room about as big as the corridor outside his office, stuffed with a sofa and chairs that hugged the walls. The air was warm and filled with odors of simmering meat and something spicy.

"Let's go out back where there's some shade," she said, leading the way across the living room and into an alcove that served as the kitchen. She wore a yellow print dress that hung loosely around her stout frame. The wide neckline revealed a patch of brown skin below the back of her neck. She glanced over her shoulder. "Just made a pitcher of herbal tea? Want some?"

He said that sounded good and waited while she plunked ice into two glasses and poured the tea. She picked up the glasses and, pushing the screened door open with one hip, stepped outside. He followed, took the glass of tea she offered, and sat down in a webbed folding chair. A rectangle of shade cast by the house stretched into the dirt yard.

"Minute I got the news on the telegraph," Wilma said, settling into the chair across from him and foregoing the polite preliminaries, "I told myself, Father John's gonna be stopping by. He's gonna want those artifacts back. I figured sooner or later you'd

182

hear about the white guys at the powwow. Looks like I figured right."

"What about the fed? Has he been here?"

"I got nothing to say to him." Wilma shook her head and snapped her eyes shut, as if that were the end of it. Then she said, "I can't have him nosing around. Robert's been staying with me — you know, my grandson."

He nodded. A small brown boy with black hair and big eyes dodging away from Wilma and running off with other kids at the powwows. But that was almost ten years ago. Robert had gotten into trouble last spring and was on probation.

"Robert gets the shakes just thinking about going to prison." Wilma was saying. "The fed shows up, he'll take off. I know that boy. Needs time to readjust, get his life back together. He's got himself a good job. This is a safe place for him, but no cops, no fed. You understand, Father?"

He told her he understood, then took a sip of the herbal tea. The sharp, spicy taste pricked at his throat; it smelled of sage and lavender. Wilma would tell him about the white men in her own time, if she decided to tell him at all.

After a few seconds, she said, "Never seen those guys before. Like they dropped out of the sky. Just showed up after I moved my chair into a shady spot at the powwow. Said they greatly admired the white deerskin dress my grandniece, Bonny, wore in the young woman's traditional dance. They asked her about the dress. Went right up to her after she came out of the arena and said they wanted to buy that dress. Well, she told them it belonged to her ancestor and wasn't for sale. She came and found me and told me to look out for a couple of white guys. The dress come down from my great-great grandmother. She made it herself, tanned the hide, sewed it up with sinew and sewed on the trade beads. She was one of Chief Black Coal's wives, so she had to look good, make him proud whenever other chiefs came to the village. That dress has been in the family a hundred years or more. It's part of us. Every time I take the box off the shelf, unwrap the tissue paper and take out the dress, I get a shiver up and down my spine.

"You told them how important the dress was?" The more history attached to an item, the more valuable it was, Father John was thinking. If the white men had stolen the artifacts, they might set their sights next on a dress handmade by a wife of one of the last Arapaho chiefs. He took another drink of the tea aware of the uneasy feeling clamping onto him. An old habit, the sense of danger. Perfected on the streets of Boston when he was a kid, walking home from baseball practice in the long shadows of Commonwealth Avenue, wondering if the sounds behind him were footfalls or just the wind rustling the branches, all his senses on alert. Not a bad habit. It had probably saved his life more than once.

"Of course I told them. I said my great-great grandmother's dress was never leaving our family. It was gonna stay right where it belonged."

"Did they offer a lot of money?"

"Two hundred and fifty dollars," she said.

Father John tried not to choke on the tea he had just swallowed. "Not very much for a beautiful and authentic artifact with a history," he said.

"I laughed in their faces." Wilma said. "I wanted to tell them they was stupid if they thought I was stupid enough to believe that's all it's worth! I told them I wasn't interested at any price. Turned sideways in my chair, quit looking at them. I was looking for Bonny, 'cause I was getting nervous about her walking around the powwow grounds in the dress. I was hoping she'd gone out to the parking lot and changed clothes in the trailer. She wasn't gonna be in any more dances. Thinking about her out in the trailer alone made me even more nervous."

"What did you do?"

"Turned back to those white guys. They was still standing there, like they was sure I'd change my mind. They don't put off easy, I'll say that for them. I started talking, you know, keeping them there so they wouldn't see Bonny come out of the trailer and figure that's where the dress was."

"You thought they might just take it?"

"Steal it," she said. "They wanted it bad, I could tell. I got a real funny feeling about those two. I said, 'What else you looking to buy?' The big guy with a lot of gray hair and scars all over his face, like a tornado run over him, said they wanted Indian stuff that had been on the plains and could tell stories. The way they talked! Like they wanted stuff that was alive and had memories of what it was like in the Old Time. Anyway they said they had people waiting to buy artifacts like that."

Father John set the empty glass down in the dirt and leaned forward. "Did they say where they were from?"

Wilma shook her head and kept her eyes on the ground, like a schoolgirl who hadn't completed an assignment. "I tried to get it out of them," she said after a long moment, "but they didn't want to say. I asked them if they had a store somewhere. 'Not exactly,' the big guy said. What's that mean — 'not exactly'? You either got a store or you don't."

"What was the other guy like?" Father John said.

"Younger, maybe thirty or so, looked Mexican. Light-skinned. The older guy could've been his father, except he didn't act like anybody's father. The young guy had a scary look, brown hair plastered to his head, and whiskers. Red nose, I remember, like he was a drinker."

An older gray-haired man, a younger man with brown hair and the beginnings of a beard. A drinker. They could have been in the dark sedan speeding away from Trevor Pratt's ranch. He couldn't be sure. Even if he were to face the two men in a lineup, he could never identify them as the men in the sedan — a dark object hurtling by, his own attention on the Jeep gyrating over the road and veering toward the borrow ditch.

"Gianelli's looking for them," Father John said.

"Looking for who?" The man at the corner of the house was about six feet, in his twenties with a high, sloped forehead and black hair slicked back from a sculptured face with high, prominent cheekbones and a jaw that jutted forward. He kept his hands in the pockets of his blue jeans as he started over. "Mind if I join you? Find out what's going on?"

"You remember my grandson Robert?" Wilma said.

"How're you doing?" Father John wouldn't have recognized Robert Running-Fast if he had run into him somewhere on the rez. Another slightly familiar face, and he would have had the vague feeling that he ought to know the young man, remember him from somewhere.

"Go get yourself some iced tea," Wilma said as Robert skidded a webbed chair across the dirt.

He hesitated a moment, looking from the chair to the back door. "Hold on," he said finally. "Don't want to miss the gossip." A gust of wind plastered his denim shirt against his back as he headed toward the house. The mixture of dust clouds and tumbleweeds swirled around.

The screened door banged shut and Wilma leaned so far forward that Father John put out his hand, afraid she might tumble from the chair. He had set his cowboy hat on his knee, and he had to grip the brim with his other hand to keep it from blowing away. "After Robert walked over, those white guys took off. But I seen them talking to other people." She was whispering, the words barely audible in the wind. Father John scooted his chair forward.

"Anybody you know?" he said.

Wilma sat very still, holding her breath. "Sometimes the younger generation all look the same. If you don't keep up with them, know what I mean?"

He knew, he told her.

"They was just wandering around, stopping people. Oh, I kept my eye on 'em, 'cause I didn't want them heading out to the trailer. I swear, if they'd gone in that direction . . ." She let the thought trail off, but he got the idea. The old woman would have gone after them and challenged them with a rock or stick or whatever she could pick up. She would have screamed her head off.

"I think they talked to that young Merryman," she said. "Never liked him even when he was a kid. Used to come around here and get Robert to go riding with him. Them two kids rode their ponies all over the rez, up in the mountains, out on the plains. They'd be gone all day. Then he sort of disappeared. You ask me, he should've stayed disappeared. Instead, he shows up some years ago and tried to get Robert in a lot of trouble. Robert told him to get lost. Heard Merryman went to prison.

"No sense in reliving old history." Robert's voice boomed from inside the house. Father John wondered whether the young man had overheard his grandmother or was just issuing a peremptory remark.

Wilma leaned back in her chair and shook her head. She was breathing hard now, her chest moving up and down with agitation. There wouldn't be anything else, Father John thought, but he had something: Cam Merryman had spoken to the two white men at the powwow two weeks ago.

Robert slammed out the door and dropped onto the webbed chair, a blue plastic glass in one hand. Ice cubes tinkled as he sipped at the tea. Wilma didn't take her eyes off him. After a moment, he wiped the back of his hand across his lips and said, "This about the artifacts, right?"

16

Father John waited. Finally Robert said, "Fed's already come around asking a lot of questions."

"Why didn't you say so?" Wilma seemed to choke on the words. For a minute, the tension between the woman and her grandson snapped like electricity.

"What difference does it make? I get myself the first decent job ever, and they won't leave me alone. Come around first time anything goes wrong. I'll be real lucky if the airport don't fire me."

"Airport?" Father John said.

"Baggage handler." The young man nodded. "Loading and unloading baggage and cargo."

"Were you working Monday when the artifacts arrived?"

"You might say I was the last one to handle the cartons. That's why the fed come to see me and the other handler on duty.

We off-loaded the cartons. Hell, we didn't know at first what was inside. Just three cartons to us."

"How did you figure out they contained the artifacts?"

"They were shipped from Germany. Wasn't no secret the artifacts were arriving. You had to be dead not to hear the news."

"What did you do with them?"

"You sound like the fed," Robert said.

"He wants the artifacts back," Wilma said, a touch of scolding in her tone.

"Me and another guy off-loaded them and set them on the tarmac. A truck was supposed to come pick them up. Pretty soon the boss paged me and told me, soon's the truck arrived, to help load the cartons, then ride over to the warehouse and help unload them." Robert's voice was flat, like an atonal aria, Father John thought. He could have been talking about cartons that contained nothing but air. "Delivery truck was gonna pick 'em up in the morning." He went on. "We stacked them inside the warehouse with other cartons and baggage waiting for pickup. Some of 'em probably waiting for a plane the next day to Billings or someplace. That's all I know."

"Were the cartons lightweight?"

Robert took another drink of tea,

scrunched up his forehead and studied the rim of the blue glass a moment. "Heavy enough," he said. "Not like empty cartons."

"How long were they on the tarmac?"

Robert shook his head. "What, you and the fed go to the same school? Nobody bothered them on the tarmac. You can see the area from the airport. Anybody try to open the cartons and take out the artifacts would've been spotted by — oh, I'd say a dozen people." He held up a hand. "Next questions? I already know 'em. Yes, there's an old guy that's worked at the warehouse forever. Alan Newsome's his name. Leaves at six o'clock. Last of the planes has come in for the day by then. It's not DIA, you know. Only get a few planes a day."

"I assume Newsome locks up?"

Robert nodded. "There's a keypad on the door and an alarm inside. I know 'cause it went off once while I was working night shift. You should've seen the guys scurrying around trying to shut it off. Anyway, there's security comes around all night. You ask me, nobody grabbed that stuff out of the warehouse. They got it somewhere else."

"You told Gianelli this?" Father John hoped that was the case, but it if weren't, he was going to have to convince Robert to do so.

"Yeah. Told him about the white guys I seen bothering Grandmother, too. Soon's I went over, they took off. He wanted to know if I could identify them. What's he think? I'm blind?" He shrugged. "All the time I'm talking, the fed kept watching me. Had that look on his face like, You got something to do with this? I was one of the last guys that handled those cartons before they got delivered to the mission. So that puts me right up there on the fed's bad list."

"What about the other handler?"

"He ain't Indian." Robert drained the tea in his glass, puffed his cheeks and blew out a stream of sugary smelling breath. "Fed comes around again, I'm outta here."

"No, Robert." Wilma turned sideways and clamped a hand over her grandson's arm. "You'll look guilty, and you didn't do anything."

"Your grandmother's right," Father John said. "Look, if you think the fed is harassing you —" He paused. Gianelli had always played fair, he thought. But the fed was determined. "Call Vicky Holden. She'll help you." He got to his feet and set a hand on the young man's shoulder. "Stop by the mission anytime you want to talk."

Father John waited, but Robert didn't say anything. Finally he thanked Wilma and started around the house toward the front. Behind him, he heard the old woman huffing out of her chair. Footsteps hurried after him. He stopped and waited for her to catch up. "I understand why you're worried," he said.

"This isn't just about the stolen artifacts." She was out of breath, her chest blowing like a bellows. Little beads of perspiration popped on her forehead. "Those white guys killed that rich white rancher, ain't that right?"

"It's possible," he said.

"So if the fed thinks Robert had something to do with stealing the artifacts, he's gonna think Robert's up to his neck in murder." She turned halfway around toward the backyard, and Father John followed her gaze, half expecting to see Robert coming toward them. There was nothing but the breeze scudding over their footprints.

Wilma gave a little shudder. "I could go talk to the fed, tell him what happened at the powwow."

"I think that's a good idea," Father John said. "Another thing, Wilma. There's a vault in the basement of the museum, if you'd like to store your grandmother's dress for safekeeping."

The old woman gave him a quick nod. He

watched as she pulled herself around and
headed for the backyard. The sounds of
Puccini spilled around him. He got inside
the pickup, started the ignition and backed
into a U-turn. The wind blew some of the
heat through the opened windows. Out of
the corner of his eye, he saw Wilma hurrying back, yellow dress blowing against thick
legs that worked like pistons. He stepped on
the brake.

"There was somebody else," she said as
she came up to his window. "I saw those
white guys talking to that new guy on the
rez. You know, the Arapaho that works at
the museum. Eldon . . ."

"Eldon White Elk?" he said.

"That's the one."

The two white men could be anywhere,
Father John was thinking as he guided the
pickup between the ruts in the dirt road.
Hiding out in an abandoned barn or falling-
down house or motel, lost in the great open
spaces, biding their time until . . . what?
They could steal another artifact? Anything
was possible, he guessed, but it wasn't logical. Why would two men who stuck out like
patches of snow on the summer prairie hang
around and risk being arrested, if they had
possession of the artifacts? He grasped at

the shadowy thought forming at the edge of his mind. They didn't have the artifacts. They were still looking for them. That would explain why they had gone to Pratt's ranch. They thought he knew where the artifacts were. But why would they have thought that, unless Pratt was also involved?

A truck ground past on Seventeen-Mile Road ahead, and his hands burned against the steering wheel. He put the visor down to block out the red ball of fire moving across the sky. He had never gotten the feeling that Trevor Pratt wasn't the man he claimed to be. A collector and dealer in Indian artifacts who believed that Arapaho artifacts from Buffalo Bill's Wild West belonged with the Arapahos. But he had been wrong about people. The smiling, congenial, glad-handing and back-slapping people — easy to spot as phonies. Trying too hard, covering up something. It was the others, the Trevor Pratts, who had stumped him, he realized. The honest, well-intentioned. Whole. Later he had discovered the brokenness and realized their camouflage was even better, more practiced and smoother, than that of the glad-handers. They were better actors.

He slammed on the brake at the stop sign. Seventeen-Mile Road was clear, but he didn't move. His thoughts kept twisting around the fact that Trevor Pratt might not have been what he seemed. Finally he turned right and drove toward the large blue sign, like a billboard, that said St. Francis Mission. He saw the red and blue lights flashing through the cottonwoods the minute he turned into the mission grounds. In front of the museum ahead, beyond the field of wild grasses, were two sedans — Wind River police cars, lights gyrating on the roofs. He pressed down on the gas pedal and sped around Circle Drive. He pulled in next to the police cars. The pickup was still rolling forward as he jumped out and ran for the museum. He took the concrete steps two at a time. The big wooden door swung open just as he grabbed the handle. He could hear a sobbing noise from somewhere deep inside.

"Here you are." Bishop Harry held the door as Father John walked into the entry. "I've been calling your mobile," he said. Father John remembered turning off the phone before he went to see Cam Merryman. A phone jangling into a conversation was always impolite.

"What's going on?" The sobbing came in loud, jagged bursts.

"Museum's been broken into," Bishop

Harry said. "Office ransacked. Blood on the floor. There was some kind of altercation."

"Where's Eldon?"

"The director seems to be missing," Bishop Harry said.

17

"Be right with you." The white-skinned, blond woman waved from the back of the store as Vicky let herself inside. The bell attached to the front door was still jingling.

Vicky glanced around the shop. Every available space crammed with Victorian furniture and artifacts: velvet loveseats, gilded armchairs, Oriental rugs, brass lamps with fringed shades, china sets painted in intricate pink and rose designs, porcelain dolls in elaborate silk dresses. Despite the slight breeze blowing through the opened door in back, the shop had the stuffy feeling of small, closed-in spaces. There was an undercurrent of muted sounds: people streaming past the plate glass windows, footsteps clacking on the wooden sidewalks and voices trailing away; traffic humming on Dubois' main street.

The woman in back was occupied with two men who wrestled a credenza across the floor. Through the rear door, Vicky could see a truck with "Reliable Movers" emblazoned on the side. The woman looked older, thinner, and more drawn than the Julie Hyde in the photo on the internet. But there were still similarities. The light, curly-thick hair, the long face and deep, shadowed eyes.

The woman waited until the men had finished loading the credenza, then she shut the door and rounded the counter of Victorian jewelry. She wore a flowery white blouse and a long blue skirt that swirled about her ankles. Strands of white pearls flowed over her chest toward the white belt, encrusted with glass baubles. "Vicky Holden?" she said. "I'm Julia."

Vicky nodded. "Thanks for seeing me."

"No problem." The woman tilted her head toward the plate glass windows. "If one of those tourists gets a yen for Victoriana and drops in, I'll have to stop . . ."

Vicky put up a hand and said she understood.

"Just me here. That's always what it comes down to in the end, isn't it? Should have learned a long time ago. Rely on yourself, Julia, 'cause you're all you've got." She waved a hand in the air. "Whatever." She swung around and began clearing the seats

201

of two red velvet chairs. A doll in a flowing dress was squeezed between two other dolls on top of a chiffonier; a pile of gilded-edged books was set on the floor. "This is about Trevor, I assume. We'd better sit down," she said, claiming one of the chairs.

Vicky took the other. The seat was stiff and scratchy with horsehair threatening to break through the velvet surface. "I'm sorry about Trevor," she said.

"So am I." Julia kept her face as expressionless as the surface of a rock, a habit, Vicky knew, that required years of training. She had seen that lack of expression on the faces of her own people, honed by more than a century of having to accept what could not be changed. "How did you hear about me? Oh, the internet," Julia said. "I keep forgetting about that monstrous intrusion into our lives. How can I help you?" She crossed her legs and in the space between them began dangling a white satin slipper with a thick, curved heel, the kind of slipper white women must have worn in the 1890s, Vicky thought.

"I represented Trevor —"

"So you said on the phone."

"I've had the feeling he might have known who took the artifacts. I was hoping . . ."

"Authentic Arapaho regalia worn at per-

202

formances of the Wild West with the famous Buffalo Bill himself! Oh, I read all about the artifacts coming to the museum at St. Francis Mission. I knew immediately that Trevor had to be the donor. I must say, it was very surprising."

"That he intended to donate the artifacts to the museum?"

"No, no, no." The satin foot did a little jingle. "Just like him to donate the artifacts. Trevor was on the road to redemption, or so he thought. What surprised me was the amount of publicity. I couldn't turn on the radio without hearing some local yokel going on about the valuable artifacts found in a basement in Berlin, hidden for a hundred and twenty years, and how a local benefactor had purchased them for the museum. On and on and on. Same with the *Gazette*. Every week recapitulating the story. Artifacts coming. Artifacts coming. The thieves had ample time to make plans." Julia uncrossed her legs and leaned forward. "All a smart crook had to do was keep an eye out or pay somebody at the airport to make a phone call when the cartons arrived."

"Is that what you think happened?"

"Doesn't take a genius to figure it out."

"I don't think Trevor was happy about the publicity."

Julia gave a sharp explosion of laughter. "No kidding," she said, sitting back and crossing her arms over the frilly white blouse. "He was very private. Worked quietly on deals, never breathed a word until artifacts were delivered. Last time I saw him was a few days before the publicity started. He didn't say anything about the artifacts, but I knew him well enough to tell something was up. You had to get inside Trevor by reading between the lines. I became an expert."

"You were partners for four years."

"He was my husband." She shrugged and fixed her gaze on some point in the middle of the store. "Four years of misdirection in my life. My love and expertise, if I have to say so, is Victoriana. I ran a perfectly lovely little shop in a regentrified neighborhood in Kansas City. Hardly getting rich, but making a few bucks off the young professionals buying up old Victorian houses nearby. One day the doorbell jangled and I looked up from my desk and saw Trevor Pratt. It was like the earth shifted beneath my feet. Sounds stupid, but that's the way it was. I took one look and knew that was my future. Turned out to be a short future. He said he was in the neighborhood, and he could never pass an antique shop. Especially one specializing in the Victorian period. He bought and sold Indian artifacts, he said, and often shops such as mine carried some. After all, artifacts came from the same period, 1830s to the turn of the century. Did I have any? Well, yes, as a matter of fact, I had a collection of arrowheads in a framed case. Some farmer out on the Blue River had been picking them out of his field for fifty years. A lot of Indian battles on the Blue River, Trevor told me. I had a stone hatchet decorated with leather thongs and beaded ribbons that I'd gotten in an estate sale. He loved it. I could tell by the bland expression plastered on his face, as if he had seen thousands of hatchets and this wasn't special. People do that with the things they like the most. They want you to think they're gonna walk away if you don't meet their price. But I knew he couldn't walk away. He bought the arrowheads and the hatchet. You probably don't want to hear all this."

"Please go on," Vicky said.

Julia gave another shrug. "Trevor went back to his ranch in Colorado and called me every day. After about a month, I went out for a visit. Short version, I never went back to Kansas City. Except to sell my store and the lovely things I had accumulated." A hint of sadness and regret ran through her words. "I became a dealer in Indian artifacts, Trevor's right-hand woman. I was second best. Customers always demanded to talk to Trevor. They relied upon his word that the artifacts we were selling were authentic. He was an expert. Who did the Denver Art Museum and the Museum of Nature and Science call upon to authenticate items they were considering? Trevor Pratt."

"What about the illicit side to the trade?"

"What about it?'

"Why would Trevor know who stole the Arapaho artifacts?"

The bell clanged and a stream of warm air flowed into the store. Julia jumped to her feet. "Excuse me," she said, sweeping past Vicky toward the woman and small girl standing hand in hand inside the door. "Welcome," she said in a tone exuding confidence and good cheer. "Anything in particular you're looking for? I have a large variety of Victoriana," she said, waving her hand like a flag over the contents of the store.

"We're interested in the yellow house in the window," the woman said. The little girl clutched a cloth doll to her chest and looked up at Julia with big, hopeful eyes. "How much do you want for it?"

"Oh, the Henders house," Julia said. "Lovely, isn't it? Hand built in 1892. It's a miniature replica of a house in Ann Arbor, Michigan, which no longer stands, I'm afraid. Would you like to see the inside?" She took hold of the top of a painted divider screen and shifted it away from the window.

"Don't go to any trouble," the woman said. "I just wanted the price."

"I'm afraid the house is rather expensive, given its provenance. I purchased it directly from the great-granddaughter of Cecil Henders who built it. It's worth at least $1,500, but I could let you have it for $1,350."

"My goodness." The woman took a gulp of air and turned to the little girl. "I told you, Amy, that it was probably more than we could afford. I'm afraid we'll have to keep looking."

"I really like that house," Amy said. She craned her neck to look around the screen as her mother pulled her toward the door.

"Thanks so much for your time," the woman called out as the door shut. The bell jingled a moment before the sound was swallowed into the quiet.

"A thousand? That's my best price," Julia said, under her breath. She moved back to the red velvet chair and plopped down. "I've got to take it out of the window. Draws too many looky-loos who don't appreciate the value of antiques. I need serious connoisseurs wandering around the shop, touching the patina on the cabinets and the velvet on the cushions, and discovering the yellow house. *Quelque* surprise! Someone who says: 'I'll give you two thousand on the spot. Deal?' What were we talking about? Oh, yes. Thieves that Trevor might have known. Obviously you didn't know Trevor long enough to learn how to read between the lines. Thieves? That depends upon whether you're referring to the new Trevor or the old."

"I'm not following," Vicky said.

"Don't feel bad," Julia said. "I was married to the man for almost two years before he told me the truth. His real name was Thomas Plink. The day he walked into my shop marked his first anniversary as a free man after a year in jail for illegally trafficking in Indian artifacts. He assured me he had turned over a new leaf, become a new man. He was building a new business under a different name, of course. No one would trust a convicted thief. You should see the resume he invented for himself: Trevor Pratt, Ph.D. in cultural studies of indigenous

Americans, or some such fancy degree. From Athabasca University in Canada, because he figured nobody would bother to check with a Canadian university. Ten years as curator of First Persons artifacts at a museum in Alberta. Nobody questioned the resume because Trevor could deliver the goods. He knew what he was talking about. He was the best."

Vicky felt as if the air had been sucked out of the store. The world seemed like an untrue place, a funhouse with sofas, chairs, and furnishings from another time rising around her, taking on lives of their own, mocking her. Another Trevor Pratt? Different from the man who sat in her office and told her he needed legal help to make certain all the shipping documents and insurance forms were in order for a half-million-dollar purchase of Arapaho artifacts?

It was a moment before she could say anything. "Where did he get his expertise?"

" 'School of hard knocks,' he used to say. Little Tom Plink, growing up in East Texas, Comanche country, kicking up arrowheads and stone tools with the toes of his boots, selling them to folks passing by on their way to somewhere better. He learned how to study each artifact for its special markings. Nobody could tell you more about a stone club than Trevor. He was still in high school when he graduated into digging up Indian graves and became an expert on beaded clothing, headdresses, Indian harnesses and saddles, all the valuable things Indians like to be buried with. He had quite a business in the illicit artifacts trade when the feds caught up with him."

"How about insurance scams?" Vicky could hear the tightness in her voice.

"Once, but the feds never caught on. Made a couple thousand dollars on artifacts he had purchased legally and shipped to a buyer. The artifacts never arrived. He didn't like doing it. Too risky, he said. Too many people involved. Too many chances for a leak. Anyway, the new Trevor had left all of that behind." Julia clasped her hands in her lap. They disappeared into the folds of her skirt. "The business was strictly legitimate. He said he had to redeem himself."

"By donating artifacts back to tribes?"

"Exactly," Julia said. "One of the big issues we argued about. He blew a couple of our best deals by returning Apache and Hopi artifacts. Gave them away. The tribes got enough old stuff, I told him. They'll just sell what you give them. He wouldn't listen. He'd trafficked in enough stolen Indian artifacts that it kept him awake at night. He said he needed his sleep."

"Is that why you left?"

"That and lots of other reasons. Let's just say, Indian artifacts and Victoriana don't mix. Our divorce was amicable. We remained friends. Still are." She hesitated and blinked hard. "We were. Trevor gave me a fair settlement. I found this little shop for sale, so I moved to Dubois and started over. Two years ago, Trevor decided to buy the ranch outside Lander. Colorado was getting too crowded, he said."

"What about the people he used to work with?"

"You mean the crooks?" Julia gave a snort of laughter. "Whoever they were, they didn't come around. Except . . ." Her eyes slid sideways in thought. "One time two creeps showed up at the ranch. Trevor had gone to La Junta ten miles away. I was alone. They pounded on the door. The minute I opened it, I knew they were trouble. You don't grow up in a city like St. Louis without developing survival instincts, and my instincts went on red alert. I told them Trevor was on his way home, which wasn't true. I didn't expect him until evening. They said they'd wait, and I said I wouldn't advise it. Trevor didn't like men hanging around the ranch. I guess they knew Trevor well enough to believe me 'cause they got in a beat-up old pickup and drove off. I got out the shotgun and sat on the porch, waiting for them to come back. When Trevor got home, he told me not to worry. They wouldn't be back."

"Did he say who they were?"

"Hol Chambers and Raphael Luna. Artifacts thieves." Julia glanced away. "I remember, because I kept looking for their names in the newspaper, thinking sooner or later they were probably gonna murder somebody. Trevor said, forget them. They weren't important. They were from that other time."

Another time. Another man. What else had Trevor Pratt neglected to mention? Vicky kept her foot on the brake along Ramshorn Street, trying to stay a comfortable distance behind the car ahead. The red sedan behind her seemed to be crawling up her trunk. The windows were down. She preferred the smells of the prairie and sage and empty spaces to air conditioning, but exhaust fumes mingled with the air blowing through the Jeep. She tried to focus on Trevor Pratt. The man had hired her to shepherd the artifacts safely from Berlin to Riverton. He wasn't required to lay out his background. *Oh, by the way, I was a thief in another life.* The fact he'd been involved in an insurance scam in the past would have raised a lot of red flags, had he told her. She laughed out loud. Why would he have told her? According to his ex-wife, he had never been charged. As a matter of fact, there was no proof it had ever happened.

The line of traffic ahead finally reached the main intersection and Vicky crawled through the turn south. In a few minutes, she was at the edge of town, still following SUVs, campers, and pickups. She dragged her cell out of her bag and called Gianelli. "You have reached the Lander office of the Federal Bureau of Investigation. Please leave your name and telephone number." She waited for the beep then told the fed she had just spoken with Julia Hyde, Trevor Pratt's ex-wife. Then she gave him the names of Trevor's past associates. "Dealers in stolen artifacts," she said. "It's possible they're the men Father John and I saw racing away from Trevor's ranch."

Traffic started to speed up. She ended the call, pressed down on the gas pedal, and went back to trying to figure out Trevor Pratt. She tapped the steering wheel. You never knew about people. Trevor Pratt, expert on Indian artifacts, collector, dealer, rancher. Thief. A chameleon, changing colors. He had left that other life behind, his ex-wife said, but it had still been there, hadn't it? Still a part of him, like a bag of tricks he hauled around, ready to pull out when the chance to move artifacts on the black market and still collect a million dollars insurance money presented itself?

Too risky. Too many people involved. The words looped through Vicky's mind. Who had he turned to? A couple of scary white guys who knew how to play the game? Okay, one might be Hispanic. Raphael Luna. She struggled to follow the line of thought to its logical conclusions: something had gone wrong. Trevor could have sold the artifacts right away and held out on his accomplices. The other men had found out. Or the deal Trevor thought he had with a buyer could have fallen through, but the two men still wanted their share. Either way they had gone to Trevor's ranch and shot him.

The highway opened up ahead, and Vicky gripped the wheel and stared at the asphalt rolling toward her. Supposition, conclusions based on fantasy. Nothing admissible, nothing that could be proven or upheld in a courtroom. She had to stick with the facts. Trevor Pratt was dead and two men had been at his ranch. She had seen them driving away. But the facts led to other possibilities. The men could still be in the area. If so, the artifacts could also be here.

18

Screams rolled through the museum like cannonballs. High, piercing, and uncontrolled. Father John hurried past the bishop toward the sounds. Officers in the gray uniforms of the Wind River police materialized in the corridor between the back office and the exhibition hall. Out of the corner of his eye, he saw other officers milling about the display cases in the hall. Elena stood outside the door to the office, ringing her hands in a white apron. Inside, Gianelli and two plainclothes officers surrounded the girl sprawled on the chair next to Eldon's desk, half-sitting, half-lying. Intermittent sobs punctuated another sharp burst of screams. For an instant, he wondered if the girl really was Sandra Dorris, the competent, pretty assistant Eldon had hired last spring. She seemed like someone else, black hair hanging in strips about her face, as if she had been pulling on it, a crazed look in the tilt of her head and the way her eyes bounced over the ceiling.

The fed and the officers stepped aside as Father John sat on his haunches beside her. "Sandra, listen to me," he said, keeping his voice low and calm. He waited a moment, hoping she would drop her head and try to focus. "Sandra!" he said again. He took both her hands into his. Her fingers and palms were limp and cold, like those of a corpse, and he started massaging them to restore some warmth. "It's Father John," he said. "You don't have to be afraid."

"An ambulance is on the way, and we've notified her mother." Gianelli's voice floated past Father John's shoulder. "Whatever happened here has traumatized her."

"Look at me, Sandra," Father John said, his voice still low. It took a moment for the girl to lower her head. She scrunched her brow in an obvious attempt to focus. The screams gave way to quiet exhalations of grief. "Are you hurt?" He could see the effort in the way she shook her head.

"Somebody get her a glass of water." He kept his eyes on the girl. There was a scrambling noise behind him, followed by the scuff of footsteps in the hallway. "Tell me what happened." he said. "Take your time." The traumatized needed time, he was thinking. Words that fit the reality were hard to find. He had dealt with traumatized people before: the dazed woman sitting on the side of a road last winter, hugging her knees, watching ambulance attendants remove the lifeless body of her husband from a wrecked pickup; the man seated in his office, sobbing and reliving the sight of his son's body in the creek bed, half of his head blown away; the teenagers frozen to the cushions of a worn sofa, eyes glazed, as he told them their father had been killed out on the highway. Too many sad, inexplicable events that had broken into ordinary days.

"He's gone!" The girl let out a long wail. "They're gonna kill him."

"Eldon? What did you see?"

"You have to find him while he's still alive."

"Were you here when they took him?"

She shook her head so violently, it was like a shudder. After a moment, she pulled herself up straight and squared her shoulders. "I came back after classes to see if there was anything Eldon wanted me to do. He's been working hard on the internet to find the artifacts."

"Let's start at the beginning," Gianelli said. Father John realized the fed had slid over a chair and was seated beside him. "You said you returned to the mission. You were here earlier?"

An officer appeared and held out a glass of water. The girl yanked her hands free, took the glass, and lifted it to her lips. A little tremor seemed to run through her. Finally she said, "Came in at nine like I always do."

"Anything unusual happen?" Gianelli said. "Anyone drop in?"

Father John moved onto the chair someone had pushed toward him. The interview had passed to the fed, he realized, which was just as well. The girl gripped the glass with both hands, a lifeline someone had thrown her.

"It's been real quiet," she said. "Ever since the artifacts got stolen, there haven't been a lot of visitors. I guess people were waiting to see all the Arapaho stuff from the Wild West. Now all we got from the Wild West is Sioux and Pawnee stuff. I guess people on the rez don't care as much."

"No visitors this morning?" Gianelli said. "No one stopped in?"

"A white couple wandered around for a while. Said they came over from Nebraska. I think they were in a hurry to get to the casino. Lots of visitors go to the casino."

She dropped her eyes and seemed to ponder that fact a moment. The casino out on the highway drew people from neighboring states, and Father John knew Eldon had hoped, with the exhibit of Buffalo Bill's Wild West, to make the museum a destination stop of its own. The Arapaho artifacts would have been the big draw.

"A couple of teachers brought in a third-grade class." She gestured with her head in the direction of the elementary school beyond the mission.

Gianelli jotted something in the small pad in his hand. "Nobody suspicious? No one who made you uncomfortable?"

The girl shook her head again and bit at her lower lip. "Just me and Eldon," she said. "I brought some sandwiches and soda. About noon, he locked the front door and we went out back and ate lunch on the bench."

"Did he seem worried or distracted?"

"He's been real worried about the artifacts. Yeah, I'd say he's been distracted. We had this great exhibition planned . . ." She seemed to swallow another sob. "All that work for nothing. He's sure the artifacts are gonna show up for sale on the internet. It's like he was obsessed."

"When did you leave?"

"I had a one o'clock class, so I must've left about twenty minutes to one."

"And you got back when?"

"Three thirty, I guess." Sandra flattened her palms against her face. "It was terrible." She sounded as if she were underwater. Throwing her hands free, she rose a little way out of the chair before dropping back down. "You gotta find him!"

"Tell me what you saw when you got here." Gianelli was gentle with the girl, Father John thought, but persistent.

"Front door was locked," she said. "I thought Eldon must've left early. I never dreamed . . ." She started to cry softly; her shoulders shook. Moisture pooled at the corners of her eyes. "I used my key to get in, and I knew right away that something was wrong. I could feel it. I called for Eldon, but he didn't answer. I looked in the exhibition hall. Everything looked okay, but I knew. Then I saw that the outside door in the back hall was opened, and we never keep it opened. I saw Eldon lock it after we ate lunch. I saw drops of blood down the hall to the door. They hurt him! He was bleeding!"

The girl managed to get to her feet and grab the rim of the chair to steady herself. "You've got to find him!" she wailed, her voice edged with hysteria.

Father John stood up, set a hand on the girl's shoulder and guided her back into the chair. "They're going to do everything possible to find Eldon," he said. "Let's not lose hope."

There was the dull thud of the front door slamming shut, followed by voices and shuffling noises in the corridor. A large, blond woman in a white shirt and blue slacks rounded the corner into the office. Behind her was a ropey, thin man who might have been a bronco rider, except for the wire-framed glasses perched on his nose. He wore a similar uniform and carried a flat, black bag that resembled an overstuffed briefcase. "This the patient?" the man said.

Gianelli was on his feet, nodding toward the girl. "Sandra Dorris," he said. "She's had quite a shock."

"What's this?" Sandra let out another wail.

Father John pushed his chair back as the man extracted a blood pressure cuff from the black bag. In a second he had wrapped it around the girl's arm and was studying the small glass readout.

"I don't need this," the girl said.

The man kept his eyes on the readout. "Little high," he said. "Any physical injuries?"

"Leave me alone." The girl was attempting to stand up, but there was no room. "There's nothing wrong with me. It's Eldon that's hurt."

"Who's Eldon?" the blond woman said.

"The director," Father John said. "He's missing."

The woman nodded, as if a traumatized girl and a missing man were part of her routine. "She wasn't hurt?" she said, gesturing toward Sandra.

"You don't have to pretend I'm not here," Sandra said. "Nobody hurt me. I want to go home."

"We can take her to the hospital for observation," the woman said.

"I want to go home."

"Up to her," the man said, folding the cuff and placing it inside the bag. "Had there been any physical altercation, I would suggest we take her. If that isn't the case . . ."

"I want to go home," Sandra said again.

"Her mother should be here any moment," Father John said.

"Like I say, it's her call."

Gianelli nodded, which seemed the signal the attendants needed because they swung around and started back down the corridor. The heave of the door shutting punctuated the clacking of their boots. In another

223

second, a motor roared to life outside.

Father John realized that the fed had pulled a folded piece of paper out of his shirt pocket. "Vicky left me a message a little while ago," he said, opening the paper in front of the girl. "Do the names Hol Chambers and Raphael Luna sound familiar?" he said.

The girl ran her eyes over the sheet. "I never heard of them."

"Could be they had been trying to buy artifacts at a powwow?" he said.

The girl shook her head.

Gianelli handed the sheet to Father John. He stared at the names and shook his head.

The fed focused again on the girl. "I'll want to talk to you tomorrow. Sometimes things come to mind after the initial shock wears off."

"Where's my daughter?" The voice was as high and shrill as Sandra's. The boom of footsteps got louder, and Barbara Dorris, all flushed cheeks, mussed black hair, and swishing blue jeans, threw herself into the office. She muscled her way forward, encircled the girl with fleshy arms and drew her close. "Sandra, baby! Are you all right?"

"They killed Eldon." The girl's voice was muffled against her mother's chest.

"We don't know what happened to Mr.

White Elk," Gianelli said.

"I told her" — Barbara Dorris pulled away and tossed her gaze about from Father John to Gianelli to the two officers — "the museum was dangerous. Those people that took the Buffalo Bill stuff might come back looking for more stuff. I told her to stay away. Now look what's happened. She could've been killed, like that boss of hers."

"Barbara," Father John said, struggling to keep his voice on a reasonable footing. "It appears Eldon is missing. That's all we know."

"I want to go home," the girl said.

Her mother was already guiding her into the corridor. "Forget about going to that creepy apartment. You're coming home with me," she said. Then she shouted over one shoulder: "She's sure as hell not coming back here."

Father John waited a moment until the charge had seeped out of the atmosphere. He turned to the fed. "Why take Eldon?"

"They also took his computer and rifled the files." Gianelli ran his gaze over the paper-strewn floor, the empty surface of the desk with a shadow of dust outlining the place where the computer had stood. "They're looking for buyers, and they think the museum director might have an idea

225

where to find them."

"If that were the case, he would have told you," Father John said. Another thought began working its way into his mind, and he looked away, trying to grasp it. "Maybe he found something on the internet," he said. "Maybe he contacted someone looking for information, and it got back to the thieves. They might have decided he was getting too close."

Gianelli seemed to ponder this a moment before he said: "We know the artifacts were stolen from the warehouse at the airport. Riverton Police got the surveillance video. Three men entered through the front door, went right to the cartons stacked against a wall, slit them open, stuffed the contents into a large carton they had brought with them, resealed the original cartons, and left. Took three minutes."

"Any way to identify them?"

"They wore ski masks."

Father John walked over to the window. Except for the police cars and Gianelli's SUV in front, the grounds looked peaceful and normal, the breeze riffling the branches of the cottonwoods. He turned back. "I spoke with Buzz Moon today. He said two white guys were at the powwow a couple of weeks ago trying to buy Arapaho artifacts."

Gianelli held up a hand. "I've talked to Moon. Robert RunningFast said he saw the white men. His grandmother called on my way over here. I'll talk to her later."

It could be tomorrow before the fed interviewed Wilma, Father John was thinking, and Eldon was missing now. He said, "I understand the white guys also talked to Cam Merryman and to Eldon."

The fed's face remained immobile, but Father John caught the flicker of interest in his eyes. "Every law enforcement officer in the area is looking for the two white men that you saw racing away from Trevor Pratt's ranch. They can't hide forever."

So much emptiness, Father John thought, pockmarked with arroyos, brush shelters, abandoned barns and sheds. People could get lost on the rez.

"You ever seen a couple of white guys around the mission?"

"Nobody that looked suspicious," Father John said. Pickups and sedans drove in and out of the mission all the time: visitors to the museum or to the church where they gawked at the stained glass windows and murals created by Arapaho artists; parishioners dropping off and picking up kids for religious education classes or coming for the social committee, liturgy, sodality and altar society, and AA meetings that took place each week. He never paid much attention to the sound of vehicles out on Circle Drive.

"Whoever came here used the back door." Gianelli crooked his head for Father John to follow. They walked down the corridor to the intersection with the hallway that led to the back. The door hung open, and even from several feet away, Father John could see the gouges in the wood around the lock.

"They must have surprised Eldon in his office," he said. Uniforms were milling about outside. The rez police would scour the premises. Cast footprints and tire tracks, lift impressions of fingerprints, and take samples of blood drops that trailed down the hall, but Gianelli would handle the investigation. *We work together,* the fed had told him once. *Too much space, too many distances for law enforcement agencies not to cooperate.*

"Looks like it. There was definitely a struggle. We figure they took the back way from Rendezvous Road. We'll collect any evidence they left behind, but it's a long shot. Unless somebody saw something . . ."

"I was in my office, I'm afraid." Bishop Harry came walking out of the exhibition hall. "Pardon my eavesdropping. I was

228

admiring, not for the first time, the lovely Indian artifacts from Buffalo Bill's time. My, if only they could tell their stories. I'm afraid the museum isn't visible from my office."

"I saw a car driving away on the back road." Elena stood at the bishop's shoulder. Of course she had seen a car, Father John thought. She saw everything. She knew every vehicle that drove into the mission.

"What kind of car?" Gianelli said. "When did you see it?"

"All I know, it was a dark color. Dusty. Walks-On was sleeping on his rug. The car didn't bother him any. I seen it before. It always comes down the back road. I figured it made deliveries to the museum. I just put a cake in the oven this afternoon when I seen it. Three o'clock."

"Did you see it drive in?"

Elena shook her head and looked away. "Odd," she said. "Not many cars on the back road. I should've heard it drive in."

19

Berlin
July 23, 1890

As far as Sonny could see, there wasn't a vacant seat. Seventeen thousand tickets sold for the evening show. An undercurrent of voices and motion spilled through the air. The arena was alive, a gigantic animal shimmying with anticipation. The performers were already in place in the staging area at the entrance to the arena. Sonny found his pony, Dolly, saddled and waiting for him. The other Arapahos were already mounted. He was late. He had brought Black Heart's regalia to his tipi and waited until the chief had put it on. When the chief set out with the others for the arena, Sonny had hung behind and kept an eye on Marks.

Now Sonny could see Black Heart mounted on Settler, looking like a chief about to lead the warriors on a buffalo hunt or into battle against the enemy. Gas flares and lamps lit up the arena. Bonfires were burning. Dusk was coming on, and it would be dark before the show ended, but it would be like daylight. Another of the wonders of the Wild West, he thought, changing night into day. He wondered how many people had seen the exhibition? A million? At times, Sonny thought all the white people in Europe must have seen it, but in every city, more people streamed into the arena. He could feel the pride swelling in his chest as he walked over to Dolly. This is how it was in the Old Time, the sense of purpose and focus that had taken over the warriors and filled them with courage.

Something was wrong with Dolly. He knew the horse well; they had traveled together across Europe, and before that, he had ridden Dolly over the plains, sometimes imagining that they were free, the two of them, and life was the way it had been. The horse was skittish, nervous. She backed up, lifted her head, and neighed as he took hold of the reins. She was always ready to burst into the arena and show off, enjoying the freedom as much as he did, he thought. Balloons of dust rose as she pawed the dirt. A blur shot past the edge of Sonny's vision. He swung around as the wrangler who'd taken Dolly into the corral after this afternoon's show took off running in the direction of the camp.

Sonny patted the horse's nose. She was beautiful, brown and smooth, but he could feel her trembling. "It's okay, girl," he said. "You're okay." He wasn't sure she believed him; he didn't believe himself. Out in the arena, the brass band had started playing, and shouting and clapping rose over the arena. The show was about to begin.

He walked around, set his boot in the stirrup and swung into the saddle. Dolly reared back, and he tightened his knees against her flanks to keep from being thrown. He patted the side of her neck. It was moist with perspiration. She reared again, and the horses just ahead picked up on her nervousness and started pawing and shuddering. "Settle down, girl." Sonny used the most soothing tone he could muster.

The brass band had launched into the entrance music, and Sonny could feel the waves of excitement rolling through the air. Buffalo Bill himself, wearing his white buckskin trousers and shirt, fringed and beaded, waving his white Stetson overhead, rode into the arena. The crowd jumped up and cheered and shouted over the music as Buffalo Bill raced around. The old scout, the old buffalo hunter and Indian fighter, riding like the wind, reining with one hand, waving the Stetson in the air with the other. It occurred to Sonny that Buffalo Bill was no different from the Indians, reliving the past, trying to recapture the best of what used to be. After circling the arena, Buffalo Bill drew up in front of the section where city officials and other important people were seated. Sonny could see the three men from the consulate who had been talking to Indians in camp all day. The crowd had gone as quiet as the wind settling down.

"Ladies and gentlemen!" Buffalo Bill's voice filled the space. "Permit me to welcome you to the Wild West. Let our show begin!"

The crowd rose like an animal to its feet and cheered over the sound of the band. Buffalo Bill, still waving his hat, rode back and motioned for the grand entrance to begin. Sonny watched Black Heart ride out first, long headdress flying, beads on his shirt and vest and buckskin trousers glinting in the flickering lights. The other Arapahos thundered behind, warriors on the trail again. Behind them, he knew, would be the cowboys, the Brule and Ogallala warriors, the Cheyennes, the white frontiersmen and cowboys, the flag bearers holding aloft flags from the different tribes. And then Buffalo

Bill again riding as the head of the Army scouts.

Sonny struggled to keep Dolly headed forward, but she balked and tried to pull to the side of the other riders. In an instant, she was up on her hind legs, pawing at the air, the other horses and riders thundering past and the crowd shouting with joy. It was all he could do to stay in the saddle. He'd been thrown by horses before, but to be thrown here . . . it would be death. He would be trampled under the hooves pounding past. He managed to get Dolly down, but now she began kicking and jumping. The only fatality in the Wild West Show, he knew, had been when a rider was thrown and trampled. A good rider, too. He leaned over the horse's neck, rising a little out of the saddle, and that seemed to calm her. He guided her into the race around the arena, but they had fallen behind the Arapahos and were riding now with the Cheyennes. The horse was trying to throw him. It was all he could do to stay mounted. They rode back into the staging area and Sonny jumped off, knowing Dolly would try to throw him again. He walked over to the side. Another roar had gone up in the arena. The horse races with Indians, cowboys, and Mexicans were underway.

Sonny undid the cinch and lifted off the saddle. He removed the blanket. A clump of burrs as big as his fist had been pressed down into Dolly's back, tiny needles digging into her skin. Anger surged inside him like bile. He picked out the burrs, taking care to remove the needles. Then he shook out the saddle blanket and ran his hand over it checking for other needles. The horse races ended, and a different sound exploded in the arena, familiar shrieks of delight as Annie Oakley came out. A little woman, so small it was hard to notice her in the camp with all the people about, but she could shoot the eye out of a raven. Sonny had watched her entrance many times; she never walked. She ran and stopped and waved, and took off running again. Then stopped and waved and blew kisses. Frank Butler, her husband, looked after her. By now he would have laid out her guns on a table in the center of the arena. The first shot burst through the air. Then a concussion of shots as she brought down the clay pigeons Butler released. One pigeon, then two, three, and four at a time. The crowd shouted with delight.

The shots set Dolly off again. She started pawing and snorting, and Sonny rubbed his hand over her sore back until he could feel the trembling begin to ease. He laid the blanket over her again, lifted the saddle and let it settle into place. He took his time tightening the cinches, getting her back to normal. He knew what had happened. Marks had wanted him dead. What did he suppose? That he could get Black Heart's regalia if Sonny were out of the way? The white man would never get Black Heart's regalia. He finished saddling Dolly in time to ride out for the surprise Indian attack on a wagon train. Buffalo Bill would then ride at the head of cowboys and frontiersmen to defeat the Indians and save the train. The battle would look real, and it always felt real, Sonny thought. As if the Indians could turn back the wagon trains and change history.

Dolly performed as usual through the battle and the other acts: the attack on the Deadwood stagecoach, the attack on the frontier village. Buffalo Bill always riding in command of the cowboys, always defeating the Indians. But there was the buffalo hunt, where the Arapahos and other Indians would never be defeated. This was what they knew; this was what they had done. The buffaloes, released from the corral, tore around the arena, and Dolly bore in close, as if they were on the plains. Responding to his lead, dodging and sidestepping as if she and the massive beasts were in a dance as they drove the buffalo back toward the corral. There was no killing. So few buffaloes left now, they had to be carefully tended. "Don't know where we'd get any more if something happens to these fellows," Buffalo Bill had told the troupe.

The flares were burning down, the bonfires giving off a blue glow that kept the darkness out of the arena. The wranglers were in the staging area to take the horses back to the corral. Sonny looked for the wrangler who had run away, but he wasn't there. Buffalo Bill rode out alone and gave the final salute. The arena filled with the noise of clapping, cheering, and stamping of feet. Sonny could feel the ground tremble. He would deal with the wrangler later. Tonight he would deal with Marks.

He waited while the Indians and cowboys made their way out of the staging area toward the camp. Marks was nowhere around. Then Sonny caught up with Chief Black Heart. Crowds of people poured out of the arena, heading in different directions. Flares stuck in the ground threw shimmers of light over the paths. "I've been looking for you," the chief said. "*Pahaska* wants to see us right away."

Wants to see us? The words rang like a

bell inside Sonny's head. *Pahaska* was the name the Lakotas had given Buffalo Bill. It meant Long Hair. Maybe BB already knew about the way Marks kept pestering the Indians for their regalia. Maybe he wanted to confirm the rumors that reached him. Sonny stayed in step with the chief as they made their way with the other performers toward the camp. The crowd got smaller as Indians peeled off into the tipis. The cowboys and frontiersmen kept going toward their camp just ahead. Buffalo Bill's tent stood at the junction, and Sonny followed the chief to the closed flap. A lamp burning inside cast a yellow glow on the canvas walls.

"We have come," Black Heart said.

The flap snapped open. Buffalo Bill, still in his white buckskin shirt and trousers, beckoned them inside. The tent was double the size of the tipis, set up like a house, with a bed on a metal frame against the left wall, a desk in the back, and four chairs around a table on the right. Sonny recognized the two white men seated at the table: Major John Burke, black hair and black beard surrounding a white, moon-shaped face, rounded shoulders inside a white shirt with black suspenders. Burke talked to the newspapers, ordered the flyers and posters that went up in every city the show visited, and made sure the public knew the Wild West was coming. Next to him was a stick-thin man with a wormlike black mustache. Nate Salsbury, Buffalo Bill's partner, Sonny realized, although he had seen him in camp only once. They must have just arrived because neither man had been at dinner this evening.

Buffalo Bill pulled out two vacant chairs. "Have a seat," he said. "I'm afraid we have some bad news." He started pacing around the center of the tent, pulling at his goatee. Sonny waited until the chief had sat down before he took the other chair. He was thinking that somehow Buffalo Bill must have heard Marks had tried to kill him tonight.

Salsbury emitted a short cough that sounded as if he were clearing his throat. Then he said, "The commissioner of Indian affairs is calling for the removal of all Indians from the show."

Sonny could feel the chief tense beside him. The commissioner had given Buffalo Bill permission to put Indians in the Wild West. The government agents on the reservations also had permitted the Indians to leave. Now if the officials said Indians could no longer travel with the show, they would have to go home.

"It will be the ruin of us." Buffalo Bill

stopped pacing and faced the table. Deep creases of worry lined his forehead; the lamplight flickered in his blue eyes. "How can we tell the story of the West without Indians? Our exhibition will be a sham. Don't those knuckleheads in Washington know the good we're doing? We're bringing the heroic story of America to people everywhere. We present the true story of civilization reaching across our great continent."

"The commissioner has been duped by the outrageous lies White Horse gave to the *New York Herald*," Salsbury said. "Unfortunately he believes the Show Indians are mistreated and starved."

"White Horse is a fool," the chief said.

"The men from the consulates were here all day," Buffalo Bill said. "They spoke to the Indians. They saw the camp. They will tell the newspapers what they saw with their own eyes." He leaned toward Black Heart. "I've tried to tell John and Nate that as soon as the *Herald* prints the story . . ."

"Unfortunately we don't have any more time." Major Burke sat with his hands clenched on the table. "We must speak to the commissioner before he orders us to send the Indians home."

Buffalo Bill drove a fist into his opened

palm. "This isn't just about White Horse's lies. Folks that hate the idea of Indians being in the show have gotten to the commissioner. The so-called reformers say we're encouraging Indians to relive uncivilized ways, when they want Indians learning white ways. Well, I say they don't know what they're talking about. But the commissioner has left us no choice. We have to cancel the next season so I can go to Washington and talk some sense into folks."

"But we can't cancel right away," Salsbury said. "We'll lose all our money on preparations for the shows into October. The soonest we can cancel will be after the Stuttgart show. Then we can go into winter camp while you take the Indians to Washington and meet with the commissioner."

"We've called you here to help." Burke gave a little bow toward Chief Black Heart. "You are the leading man of the Arapahos." He turned toward Sonny. "You are his adopted son. You both speak good English. We want you to go to Washington and talk to the commissioner. We must gain time to finish this season before the colonel himself can travel to Washington."

Black Heart nodded. "We will go."

Sonny could feel the pride swelling in his chest. To have an important mission, to save

241

the other Indians in the show so they could collect their pay and go home with money for their families — they were warriors again, he and Chief Black Heart.

"When do we leave?" Black Heart said.

"Tomorrow," Burke said.

Black Heart would take his regalia, Sonny was thinking. It would be safe from the grasping hands of Herman Marks. For a moment he hesitated about telling Buffalo Bill about Marks, then decided BB would want to know. Sonny stood up and walked over to the big man. "Could I speak with you privately?" he said.

20

A two-year federal investigation into the theft and illegal sale of Indian artifacts came to a close yesterday when the ringleader was sentenced to one year in the county jail. Thomas Plink, Kiowa, Colorado, had pleaded not guilty to misdemeanor charges of theft, sales of Native American property, and conspiracy to transport stolen Native American goods across state lines. A day-long trial ended in a guilty verdict. Other alleged members of the gang, identified as Hol Chambers and Raphael Luna, remain at large. They were charged in absentia.

According to Ann Cambert, assistant district attorney, the gang specialized in robbing Native American graves in Nevada, Arizona, New Mexico, and Utah and stole items such as bonnets, spears, hatchets, spear points, bows and arrows,

and buckskin clothing. Such Native artifacts are becoming more and more rare
and bring high prices from collectors on
the illegal market. "It is difficult to bring
thieves like Plink to justice because they
operate below the radar," Ms. Cambert
said. "Most of the gravesites are in rural
areas. Months can pass before Native
American families realize their ancestors'
graves have been robbed. Collectors
protect the thieves because they supply
the items they want. We are very pleased
with the results of our investigation and
the guilty verdicts."

Ms. Cambert said that Plink is believed to
have been involved in the theft and sales
of Native artifacts since he was a boy. "He
grew up in East Texas and learned early
on that Native people bury valuable items
with the dead. Over the years, we believe
he dealt in millions of dollars worth of
stolen items."

The front door slammed. Vicky jerked her
head away from the computer screen and
squinted past the beveled glass doors to the
outer office. In the faint glare of light, she
could make out the figure of a man. Something changed in the atmosphere. She got

to her feet as the French doors swung open.

"You here alone?" The ceiling light flooded over Adam. "You should keep the front door locked."

Vicky dropped back onto her chair, her heart hammering. "Annie must have forgotten to lock up." Annie and Roger had left together, she was thinking. The only thing on their minds, each other.

"You should talk to her."

Vicky didn't say anything. This was how it had gone when Adam was her partner: take care of this or that, handle this or that. Adam issuing orders, moving on to more important things, not giving the small details a second thought.

Adam put up the palms of his hands, as if he had sensed her annoyance. "Old habit, I'm afraid. Must be a big case to keep you here so late."

"What brings you here?" Vicky said.

"I was hoping to find you." He plopped down on a side chair. "I have some news and . . . well, I have a favor to ask. Want to get a bite to eat?"

Vicky hesitated. Except for a granola bar, she hadn't eaten since breakfast. The little hunger cramps she'd ignored now seemed more intense. "Give me a minute." She turned back to the computer, clicked through a series of screens and tapped the print button. From the outer office came the noise of the printer choking into life and spitting out pages. Annie and Roger had been about to leave when Vicky returned from Dubois. She had spent the last couple of hours searching the internet for two men: Trevor Pratt and Thomas Plink. She had found more information on Trevor. On YouTube, the keynote speech Trevor had given at a conference in Santa Fe for collectors and dealers of Indian artifacts, Trevor's face almost lost in the glare of spotlights. *Collectors* magazine had listed him among the country's top ten dealers of Native American artifacts. Other than the blurred YouTube video, there were no other photos that she could locate. She wondered how he had managed to scrub photos off the internet. There were only a few articles on Thomas Plink. All related to his trial and conviction. The man had kept a low profile, buried in darkness like the artifacts he dug out of graves.

She turned off the computer, and lifted her bag out of the bottom drawer. Adam ushered her through the opened French doors and across the outer office. She adjusted the main light switch until a faint night-light worked its way through the bungalow, then dug in her bag for the keys and locked the front door on their way out.

The restaurant had that late, about-to-close feeling. Customers at only two tables finishing coffee and dessert. A hostess with red curls plastered to her head looked half-asleep at the front counter. Vicky half expected her to tell them the kitchen was closed. Instead, the hostess lifted two menus out of a box and headed into the dining room. Vicky slid across the blue plastic cushion of a booth next to the plate glass window, and Adam settled himself across the table. Outside, old-fashioned street-lamps lit the sidewalk. The occasional vehicle crawling down Main Street shot a flare of yellow light along the asphalt. She liked the quiet, the sense of winding down, that settled over Lander in the evenings.

"God, Vicky, I've missed you." Adam looked at her over the top of the menu.

"Is that the news you wanted to tell me?"

He laid the menu down. "Yeah, maybe it is. Have you thought about us?"

"About practicing together again?"

A waitress in dark slacks and a white blouse with coffee stains dribbled down the front materialized at the table. They both ordered hamburgers and coffee. After the waitress walked away, Adam shook his head

247

slowly, as if he'd reached a reluctant conclusion after a lot of thought. "You're set up in the bungalow now. There isn't room for a partner." He gave her a smile tinged with sadness and regret. She had moved her office once out of the bungalow and into a sleek brick building on Main Street with two story windows. How intimidating the building must have been to people who found their way off the rez and into her office. Still they came. She and Adam had hired Roger Hurst to relieve Vicky of the nuisance cases, as Adam had called them. Except those were the cases, helping her own people, that had made her feel like a lawyer.

"I've taken a lease on an office at the end of Main Street," Adam went on. "Small, nothing fancy. Perfectly fine for handling natural resources cases. Anyway, I'll be traveling as usual." He leaned over the table. "We can still work together, as colleagues, I mean. Run things by each other. It would be helpful."

"As long as there's no conflict."

"You mean, I'm trying to protect tribal rights to oil and gas on a rez and you're representing a rancher who might get screwed?"

Vicky smiled. "Something like that."

The waitress appeared with a tray of hamburgers and mugs of coffee. She balanced the tray on one hand like a contortionist while offloading the plates and mugs. After she turned away, Adam took his time spreading ketchup and mustard over the hamburger patty and closing the bun. He took a bite and chewed for another long moment. Finally he said, "What do you think?"

Vicky spread a little ketchup on her own hamburger and lifted it to her mouth. "About your office? I think it's fine."

"About us," Adam said.

Vicky worked at choking down a bite of hamburger. She took a drink of coffee and winced. The hot liquid burned a trail down her throat and into her chest. "I don't think there is an 'us,' " she said.

"But there was once, and there could be again." Adam ate for another minute or two before he said, "It's up to you, Vicky. Either we try to put things back together, or we forget the whole idea. I came back because I don't want to do that."

"How can I trust you?" she said. It had been the same problem with Ben Holden, all those years of wondering and suspecting and smelling other women on his clothes, until she had finally summoned the courage

249

to divorce him and strike out alone.

"That should never be a problem."

"What about the Crow Reservation? Are you telling me there wasn't another woman?"

Adam picked up a french fry and chewed it down to the end. "You and I were estranged."

She shrugged. It was true. She had to give him that.

"What about you and John O'Malley?"

"What about us?"

"Don't tell me . . ."

"Oh, for godssake." Vicky wadded up her paper napkin and threw it onto the table. "You know there has never been anything . . ."

"Things could change," Adam said. "He could leave the priesthood. It's happened before. What would you do?"

"This conversation is ridiculous."

"I'm trying to have an honest conversation. You're the one who wants to make certain we can trust each other."

Vicky plucked her napkin back into her lap and went on eating. God, Adam could cut so close to the bone, as if he knew exactly where to strike at her nerves. She didn't want to think about John O'Malley anymore. They worked together when the situation presented itself. Artifacts her client had donated to the museum had been stolen, so they were thrown together again. She was fairly certain he didn't want that any more than she did.

She watched Adam Lone Eagle finish the last of the hamburger, then push the french fries across the plate before he ate another one. He took a sip of coffee, avoiding her eyes, she felt, but knowing she was watching him. He was not perfect, but he was a good man. He cared about their people as much as she did. Every case he worked on had helped the tribes benefit from their own oil, gas, water, timber, and grazing lands. The big things, he called them, that brought jobs and money to reservations and gave people hope and helped to cut down on the DUIs and bar fights and assaults and drug cases that walked into her office. She laughed.

Adam lifted an eyebrow. "What's so funny?"

"I was thinking the way you help our people could put me out of business." She waited a beat before she said, "I wouldn't mind that."

He gave her a lingering smile. "We've got a lot going for us, Vicky. What do you say?"

She took her time trying to sort it out, all

the implications and consequences of getting back with Adam, all the changes that had come into her life. She was tired of being Woman Alone. The truth of it sat like a heavy stone inside her. The name defined her, but she knew the grandmothers had also intended for the name to give her strength. Even drawing on that strength had taken its toll.

"We can try," she said finally.

Adam gave her a smile that said he had already known the answer. "Good," he said, covering her hands with his.

"You need a favor?" Vicky said, pushing on as if she weren't aware of the warmth of his palms flowing into hers, as if the tectonic plates of her life hadn't just shifted.

"Favor?" Adam seemed to hesitate. "Oh, yes, as a matter of fact. You remember the friend I told you about on the rez? Mary?"

Vicky pulled her hands free. She felt as if she had made a turn into familiar territory. There was always a "friend" down the street, across town, in Casper or Hardin, on the rez.

"There's nothing between us, Vicky," Adam said. "I can't prove that to you. No irrefutable evidence. You have to trust me." He shrugged and, not waiting for a response, said, "I talked with her son, Petey.

You know the family?"

Vicky nodded. She had gone to high school with the boy's father. Petey must be in his mid-twenties now, a little younger than her own kids, Susan and Lucas. In her memory, he was still a little kid running around the powwow grounds, stealing cookies from the food booths.

"The hospital released the kid today, but he's still depressed," Adam said.

"I'm not sure what you think I can do."

"I tried talking to him. No response. He doesn't trust me." Adam shrugged. "Look, I knew Mary before he was born. We went to high school together on Pine Ridge. Anyway, I told her I'd ask you to talk to him. Besides, I think you'll be interested."

"Adam . . ." Vicky began. There was so much going on right now: the missing artifacts, Trevor's murder. She'd been sucked into a whirlwind.

"You should know that Petey just got fired from his job," Adam said. "Until yesterday, he worked for the security company at the airport."

21

The house floated ahead in a globe of light dropped into the darkness of the plains. Overhead, pinpricks of stars shimmered and twinkled in the black sky. Father John followed the shaft of headlights down the dirt road for a half mile, then turned right and bumped over the borrow ditch and across the hard-packed yard. The house was small and rectangular, lights flaring in the windows and streaming onto the yard. He parked close to the front stoop and waited a couple of minutes. He had called Sandra Dorris's mother an hour ago and said he would like to drop by. She had told him to come anytime.

All afternoon shock waves had rolled over the mission like thunder claps. The phone had started ringing almost immediately. How could the museum director disappear? For more than a hundred years, the mission had been a safe place, a cottonwood-brushed oasis in the turbulence that, at times, bore down over the rez. He had left the phone to Bishop Harry, who was good at handling emergencies — he'd seen his share in Patna, India — and walked down to the dirt road that ran parallel with the Little Wind River. Elena had seen a dark sedan leave the mission. Whoever had broken into the museum had come by the back road. Father John wasn't sure what he might find. Officers from the rez had already combed the area. Nothing out of place, except for the sagebrush and wild grasses knocked down in places, but that could have been caused by wild animals — coyotes, squirrels, raccoons. Even the officers might have trampled the brush.

He had spent the dinner hour in the office, thinking about Eldon, trying to recall everything the man had told him about himself when he had applied for the museum job last winter. A master's degree in museum management, class work completed for a doctorate from the University of Wyoming. He was writing his dissertation. Expected to finish it by the end of the year. Oh, the practical experience of running the Arapaho Museum would be of immense help, he'd said. He'd held other museum jobs, mostly as an assistant to department managers or curators. Never actually managed a museum before, but Father John had seen the ambition, the willingness to do whatever it took to get a job done, an eagerness to get ahead, shining in the man's eyes. He had proposed an exhibit on the Show Indians in Buffalo Bill's Wild West. Father John had taken a chance on Eldon White Elk, an Arapaho from Oklahoma. He liked the man's enthusiasm and ideas. And it seemed appropriate for an Arapaho to manage the Arapaho Museum.

Now Eldon was gone. Kidnapped, abducted, held against his will, whatever it was called now. But the man knew the museum business, and Father John kept coming back to that. He understood the importance of obtaining provenance for items the museum purchased. He knew that a shadowy world of illegal trade in Indian artifacts existed. He had been approached by two outsiders who could be responsible for Trevor's murder.

Sandra had worked beside him, three or four hours a day, five or six days a week, for several months now. It was possible the girl knew more than she realized. Father John had already called her mother when Bishop Harry stopped at his door and said he'd take the men's committee meeting this evening. He thanked the bishop. He didn't say he had forgotten about the meeting.

The front door flung open as he got out. "That you, Father?" Barbara Dorris stood in the doorway, backlit by the light inside. The noise of a TV rumbled toward him. She had already answered her own question because she was moving backward, motioning him into the living room.

"How's Sandra doing?" The instant he stepped inside, he saw the girl curled up on the sofa, legs tucked under her, chin bent into a black and white pillow shaped like a bear. She stared glassy-eyed at the TV across the room, a detective show, judging by the sirens and gunshots.

"You can see for yourself." Her mother nodded in the girl's direction. "She hasn't moved from that sofa since we got back from the mission. I don't know what to do. Maybe she's in shock or something. Maybe she should've gone to the hospital. See if you can talk to her, will you, Father?"

Father John went over and sat down at the other end of the sofa. The girl hadn't taken her eyes off the TV. "Feel like talking, Sandra?" he said.

A minute passed before a commercial for insurance blasted into the room, several decibels higher than that of the program.

257

Barbara walked over and switched off the TV. "Do you mind?" Sandra said. "I'm watching that."

"Father's come all the way out here to see how you're doing."

"I'm doing just fine." The girl turned toward Father John. Dark shadows ringed her eyes. She hiccoughed a couple of times and jammed a fist against her mouth. "You don't have to worry about me."

"I'm worried about Eldon," he said.

Sandra threaded the corner of the pillow through her fingers. "Yeah," she said. "Me, too."

"You were upset this afternoon when you realized he could be hurt."

"Blood on the floor," she said. "What was I supposed to think?"

"I know you want to help find him."

"What are you suggesting?" Barbara had sat down on a chair next to the TV. "Sandra doesn't know anything. How could she? She's wasn't even there."

Father John didn't take his eyes from the girl. Something about her was off: the way she averted her eyes and dug at the pillow with nervous fingers. The aftereffect of shock. This afternoon, she had been distraught, almost out of her mind, but now she seemed distant and cool, as if someone

258

else had found the museum office ran-sacked, blood on the floor and her boss missing.

"Look at me, Sandra." He kept his voice low and firm, the counseling voice to pull people out of the memory and into the present. The girl took her time lifting her eyes to his. "Did Eldon ever mention the two men who approached him at the pow-wow a couple of weeks ago?"

The girl shook her head.

"The men were trying to buy artifacts from Arapahos," he said. "It's possible they were involved in the theft, and they could be involved in Trevor's murder."

"Are you saying two men came to the museum and attacked Mr. White Elk?" Barbara's voice had moved up a half octave. "Why doesn't the fed arrest them?"

"Gianelli's trying to find them."

"Well, how would Sandra know anything? She works part-time at the museum. What does she know about theft and murder?"

Father John looked back at the girl seated a cushion away. "I've been thinking Eldon might have been alarmed at the idea of outsiders trawling for artifacts. He was always looking for benefactors to help purchase any Arapaho artifacts that became available. He didn't want them to leave the rez. Do you remember when I brought Trevor Pratt over to the museum?"

He waited until the girl gave a reluctant nod, as if she remembered but wished she didn't.

"Eldon was beside himself at the idea of getting Arapaho artifacts from the Wild West Show. He started planning right away to make Black Heart's things the centerpiece of the exhibition, and you helped him."

"I still don't see . . ." the girl's mother said.

"Try to remember, Sandra," Father John said. "Eldon wouldn't have liked the idea of outsiders hunting artifacts. He might even have tried to contact other Arapahos the men talked to. I'm thinking he would have explained that he would try to find the money to purchase any artifacts they wanted to sell. Maybe he kept a list of Arapahos who might be willing to sell. It could explain why the intruders took Eldon's computer. It could explain why they took Eldon. They're trying to identify possible sources."

"Sandra doesn't know anything about this," Barbara said.

"You worked with Eldon." Father John watched the girl. "You helped him with all kinds of tasks. Did you help him contact any Arapahos the outsiders had talked to?"

"I was working on the exhibition," Sandra said.

"Someone might have agreed to sell to the two men. Someone could know where to find them."

"This is upsetting my daughter," Barbara said. "I wish you would stop."

Father John pulled back until the armrest pressed against his spine. "I'm sorry," he said. "But I'm afraid Gianelli will ask the same questions."

"He already did," Barbara said. "Sandra doesn't know anything."

Father John turned toward the girl again. "I was hoping you may have recalled something that might help locate Eldon."

"You think they're gonna kill him like they did Trevor?" The girl's eyes were fever bright.

"I think he's in danger. He's hurt. He has to be found soon."

The girl dipped her head into the pillow. The lamplight shone in her black hair.

"I'm not trying to upset you," he said.

"But you have, Father." A plaintive note sounded in Barbara's voice. "See for yourself. My daughter doesn't know anything. She's an innocent victim."

Father John got to his feet. "If you think of anything," he said, looking down at the girl hugging the pillow, "even in the middle of the night, will you call me?"

The girl's mother flung herself toward the door. She yanked it open, stood to the side, and gripped the knob. "I don't mean to be impolite . . ."

"I understand." Father John put up one hand. He wished them both a good night's sleep and went out into the evening. The cool breeze brushed his face and neck. An uneasy feeling lodged inside him; something not quite right. The hysterical girl from this afternoon sitting glassy-eyed in front of the TV, immersed in a detective show — she had objected when her mother turned it off — disengaged from what happened, as if it had happened in the show.

Father John took a U-turn and headed out to the road, uneasiness sticking with him like a shadow as he plunged after the headlights that shot into the darkness. She had taken something, he decided. Something to calm her down, disengage her. Alcohol had once done that for him. God, after what the girl had been through, he couldn't blame her.

22

Father John spotted the pickup as he came around Circle Drive. He pulled into the curb in front of the residence, slid out from behind the steering wheel and slammed the door, all senses on alert. The pickup stood off to the side under an enormous, century-old cottonwood, as if the driver had tried to hide the vehicle. He could feel pinpricks of danger on the back of his neck. "Who's there?" he called.

"Cam." The man's voice came from the vicinity of the pickup, as if the pickup itself had spoken. Father John saw the tiny red flare of a burning cigarette and realized someone was leaning against the hood.

"How's it going?" Father John said.

"We need to talk." The man flicked the cigarette onto the ground. Little red flames spit into the air like dying fireworks.

"Let's go inside." Father John started up the walk. He could hear the clack-clack of the man's boots behind him.

A dim night-light cut through the darkness in the residence. Father John flipped the switch, and lights burst overhead as Cam Merryman stepped into the entry. Father John shut the door. He could hear Walks-On scrambling to his feet in the kitchen. A low, rumbling growl erupted from the dog's throat as he came down the hallway. "It's okay," Father John said, leaning over to take hold of the dog's collar. Walks-On kept his nose pointed in Cam's direction. He had only to loosen his grip on the collar, Father John knew, and the dog would be on the man. Usually Walks-On was friendly. He and the bishop had a running joke about how the dog would welcome burglars and show them around. Not tonight.

"Coffee?" Father John looked up sideways at Cam.

"I wouldn't turn it down."

"Kitchen's this way," he said, nodding toward the end of the hallway. He could feel Walks-On relaxing beneath his hand. He held onto the collar and crab walked the dog behind Cam Merryman. He waited until the man had sat down at the table, then guided Walks-On over to his dish before he let go of the collar. He shook out some dog biscuits. The spicy odor of meat-loaf filled the kitchen. Elena would have left dinner in the oven, the way she always did when he didn't show up at six o'clock, which was most of the time.

Father John lifted the coffee canister out of the cabinet and set about brewing a fresh pot. "Hungry?" he said to the man drumming his fingers on the table.

"You offering something to eat?" Cam jerked his head back in a nod.

Father John turned on the coffeepot, pulled the plate out of the oven, set it in front of the Arapaho and peeled back the foil. Hot steam rose off the large slab of meatloaf covered in tomato sauce and helpings of boiled potatoes and green beans. He got the man a fork and knife and slid the napkin holder across the table. The sound of dripping coffee mingled with the noise of the dog pushing his dish into the corner. By the time the coffee was done, Father John had found some cold meatloaf in the refrigerator and made himself a sandwich. He poured out two mugs of coffee, put them on the table, and sat down across from his visitor.

"What's on your mind?" he said.

The Indian had already finished most of the meatloaf and potatoes. Now he sipped at the coffee. "You tell me why the fed thinks I got something to do with the guy from the museum getting kidnapped."

"Gianelli came to see you?"

"Second time since the artifacts got stolen. Harassment, you ask me. First time was because Mickey Tallman's gonna see me go back to prison or die trying. Told the fed all kinds of lies about how I had reason to take off with his ancestor's stuff. Second time was tonight. I figure you must've told him something that sent him over to my place."

Father John took a bite of the sandwich. He waited a moment before he said, "Was it supposed to be a secret that you spoke with two white men at the powwow?" He followed the food with a drink of coffee. "A lot of people must have seen you."

Cam set his fork down and leaned over the plate so far that tomato sauce licked at his shirt. "I don't know who the hell they were. I never seen them before or since. I don't need the fed sniffing around thinking I steal artifacts and kill people. 'What happened to Eldon White Elk?' he says. Hell, I don't even know Eldon White Elk."

"How about Trevor Pratt?"

The Arapaho surveyed the rim of his mug. Finally he lifted his eyes. "He came around once. Wanted to know if we had any stories in the family about when Sonny Yellow Robe was in the Wild West Show. What did we think happened to Black Heart's stuff? What happened to Sonny?" He stretched his shoulders into a long shrug. "Hell, even Buffalo Bill never knew what happened to him. Only story the family had was about Buffalo Bill himself showing up on the rez and knocking on my great-grandmother's door. Said he wanted to express his sorrow about Sonny not making the trip home. Never got on the ship with Black Heart. Made Buffalo Bill real sad, 'cause he said Sonny was a good man. He said that when the Ogallala holy man, Black Elk, went with the Wild West Show, he got lost and missed the boat home. Showed up in Paris a couple years later and Buffalo Bill bought him a ticket home. It was like Buffalo Bill was hoping Sonny would show up the next time the show went to Europe."

"You tell Gianelli this?"

Cam shook his head, leaned back, and began tapping his fork against the edge of the plate. "What difference does that old stuff make? The fed wanted to know about the white guys that stopped me at the pow-wow. They come out of nowhere. Couple of outsiders. I could tell by looking at 'em they were trouble, and I don't need trouble."

"What gave you that impression?"

"The way they acted. They were white, so that put them in charge, even though one was Mexican, I think. They said they had money to buy Indian artifacts, like they was used to flashing money around Indians and getting what they wanted." He blew a stream of air out of his nostrils, then forked the last of the meatloaf and potato into his mouth. Finally he said, "I hate white guys like that."

"I don't like them much myself," Father John said. "What did they want to buy from you?" He had seen Cam Merryman dance at powwows. He didn't remember anything out of the ordinary about his regalia.

"That's the weird part." Cam took a drink of coffee and blinked at Father John over the rim. He sat the mug down, pulled a folded sheet of paper from his pocket, and smoothed it open between them. "I copied this out of a book some years back. This here's the group picture of the Arapahos who went with the Wild West Show in 1889 and 1890."

Father John leaned toward the photo. At least a hundred Arapahos standing in rows on bleachers, looking wide-eyed into the camera. Each row loomed over the one below. Cam set a finger on the tall, dark-haired bearded man in white buckskins, head high and shoulders straight, in the middle of the front row. Father John could have identified Buffalo Bill from across the room. "Colonel William F. Cody," Cam said. "Got the name Buffalo Bill 'cause he killed so many buffalos." He shrugged and moved the tip of his finger to the imposing Indian on his right. "Chief Black Heart," Cam said. The regalia the chief wore were familiar: striped shirt, beaded vest, breastplate, wrist guards, leggings, and moccasins, the headdress with dozens of eagle feathers.

"Sonny Yellow Robe," Cam said, sliding the tip of his finger across the image of the man next to Black Heart. "See how close he's standing to Black Heart? You can tell he was the chief's bodyguard. He was Black Heart's adopted son, so he protected him. That's why Black Heart never believed Sonny took his regalia. You ask me, the Tallman clan likes holding grudges. All except for Bernard, the old man. I heard him say once, 'We don't know what happened, so let it go.' Too bad he can't rein in that grandson of his. Anyway, see the vest Sonny's wearing?"

The vest was beautiful, Father John said. Not as intricate or spectacular as the vest worn by Black Heart, but impressive nonetheless. He wondered if someone had made it for him. Perhaps his sister. He had never heard that Sonny Yellow Robe was married.

"The white men wanted that vest," Cam said.

"You have the vest?" Father John heard the surprise in his voice.

Cam shook his head, then took another drink of coffee, as if he were considering the possibilities, the might-have-beens. "Sonny must've kept his stuff with him. I don't guess he had much. Nothing but a vest with a few beaded designs, a headband with a couple of feathers. No breastplate or fancy fringed shirt. No wristbands or gloves. Looks to me like he's wearing canvas trousers, not buckskin. Most of the other Indians in the front row are wearing beaded moccasins. Sonny's got on boots."

Father John squinted at the photo. What Cam said was true. Compared to the other Indians, Sonny's regalia looked thin and worn. Even the boots, scuffed and curled at the toes. If Black Heart had adopted him, it must mean the man had lost his parents, maybe his family. Nothing had come down to him from his own ancestors. It struck him that Mickey Tallman could have drawn the same conclusion. A man with almost nothing might be tempted to steal his adopted father's regalia.

He tried to concentrate on what Cam was saying: If Cam wanted something like Sonny's, he would have to make it himself. "Last year, I shot a deer and dressed it out. We had real good meat all winter. I tanned the hide and made myself a vest, did the beading myself, just like my grandmother showed me when I was a kid. Those dumb white guys thought the vest was Sonny's. They said they had buyers for Wild West regalia. Offered a hundred dollars. I laughed in their faces and walked away."

"Did you see anybody sell to them?"

"All I wanted was to put as much distance between them and me as I could. I got the feeling they might just help themselves to my vest, pull it off my back."

"You told Gianelli this?"

"I told him." Cam got to his feet. "Mind if I help myself to more coffee?" he said, refilling his mug. He swung the coffeepot toward the table. "How about you?" Without waiting for an answer, he topped off Father John's mug, set the coffeepot back and took his chair. "All he's got in his head is what Mickey Tallman told him. How I been wanting to get even for him snitching on me, how I been waiting my chance. So I stole his ancestors' stuff, just like he keeps saying

271

Sonny stole Black Heart's regalia." He cupped the mug, sipped for a long moment, then said, "You gotta talk to him, Father."

"Gianelli?"

"Mickey. You gotta tell him I never wanted his ancestor's stuff. What would I do with it? Sell it? Who'd I sell it to? Couple of guys that show up at powwows? Hell, they showed up two weeks before the stuff even arrived." Cam seemed to grasp the implications of what he'd said, because he leaned back. His forehead creased in thought. "Mickey must think I made a deal to get the regalia and sell it to them guys. I swear on my ancestor's grave, wherever Sonny's buried, I didn't do that. You gotta make him believe that, so he'll get the fed off my back."

"I can try to talk to him," Father John said. He doubted it would do much good. Grudges between families took on lives of their own, moving downward through generations until nobody remembered how or why they had started. Still families nurtured the grudges, fed and tended to them as if they were some sickly, diseased creatures they had inherited and had to keep.

Father John stood at the window in his study and watched Cam Merryman's taillights flicker and jump around Circle Drive and out into the cottonwood tunnel that led to Seventeen-Mile Road. It was a moment before the sound of the pickup faded, leaving the mission grounds plunged in quiet, streetlamps carving out circles of light in the darkness. He prayed for Cam Merryman and Mickey Tallman and all the Arapahos caught up in a tornado of evil moving across the reservation. He prayed for the soul of Trevor Pratt. Most of all, he prayed for Eldon White Elk who was somewhere out there in the vast, empty darkness.

23

"Petey got fired from his job." Mary Many Horses wrung her hands on her jeans-clad lap. White knuckles bulged like pebbles in the dusty ground. Her chest rose and fell beneath the pink and white blouse with a dipping neckline that showed her cleavage. "Everything crashed around him. He just couldn't take it. The counselor says he's . . ." She ran her eyes across the ceiling in search of the words. "Vulnerable, fragile. Even the drugs don't guarantee he won't try to kill himself again. Oh, God."

The woman pressed both hands against her eyes, as though she might block out the image. She was nearing fifty, Vicky guessed, not far from her own age, and she was quite beautiful, with a golden glow to her dark skin and straight, black hair stylishly cut. The anguished look on her face heightened the symmetry of her features. She carried a few extra pounds, but Vicky suspected that thirty-five years ago, when Adam met her, Mary Many Horses probably had the figure of a Miss Indian America contestant. The type of beauty that could stop trains, and stop Adam Lone Eagle. Vicky pulled her lips tight to keep from laughing. She had to give it to Adam. He had never been able to resist a beautiful woman.

"I understand Petey worked for a security company the night the Arapaho artifacts were stolen," Vicky said.

"First job since he got laid off from the highway department last year," Mary said. "He's been trying to save enough money to go back to college. Everything was going great. Then, wham, it's like he gets hit by a bolt of lightning. Adam's been such a good friend," she said. "A real comfort."

"I'm sure," Vicky said.

"Please don't get me wrong," Mary said. "Adam told me he was hoping to work things out with you. What Adam and I had, well, that was a long time ago. Two Lakota Indians lost in L.A. Oh, Adam had a good job with a law firm, and I was working in a hospital. Nurse's aide, basically. Friends from Pine Ridge got us together. Loris, my husband, had taken off. It was just me and Petey. Adam was real good to Petey, tried to fill that big gap that his daddy left. Didn't work out, but we've stayed friends, Adam and me."

"Tell me about Petey's job," Vicky said, trying to keep the conversation on track.

The woman lifted her eyes back to the ceiling. "First, I want you to know why we moved to the rez. Loris came from here. Maybe you knew him? Loris Many Horses?"

Vicky nodded. The Many Horses were a large family that sprawled over the reservation. She was struck by the effort Mary was making to convince her that Adam Lone Eagle played no role in her decision to move to the rez.

"Couple of years ago, I heard Loris got killed on the freeway near San Diego," Mary was saying. "Petey took it real hard. Always had a dream he was gonna get together with his father, and that wasn't gonna happen. That's when he had the first of his . . . episodes. Real bad depression, like he thinks he's to blame for everything wrong in the world. Blamed himself for his dad leaving. Even blamed himself for his dad getting killed." She waved a hand between them. "Only reason I'm telling you this is so you'll see why Petey's got himself into another depression. Anyway, I talked him into moving to the rez where he has family. I figured maybe Loris's people might take an interest in him, give him a sense of belonging. Hard to belong in L.A. when you're Indian."

"Is Petey here?"

"You will help him, like Adam said?"

"I don't know how I can." Vicky felt as if she were being sucked into quicksand. She had to make a decision to keep sinking or jump out while she still could. Any lawyer could talk to Petey Many Horses, find out why he was fired, see about the possibility of filing a wrongful termination suit, but Adam had asked her for what he'd called a favor. A favor for whom, she wondered. For Adam? Was this a way to draw her to him, bring her into a case that he cared about? Or had he just asked a favor that might help relieve the mind of a beautiful former girlfriend? She tried to blink back another thought. What if Adam hadn't trusted himself around Petey's mother?

"I'll get him." Mary jumped to her feet. Beneath the long legs of her blue jeans, she wore black high-heeled sandals that clacked across the vinyl floor as she walked down a hallway. The flowery smell of perfume trailed behind. A door opened and closed, followed by the hushed, clipped sounds of an argument. A moment passed before the door swooshed open. There was the syncopation of footsteps in the hallway.

Mary walked into the living room first; Petey a few feet behind, hanging back in a rumpled white shirt and jeans that hung low on his hips, and barefooted. He had a marine haircut that emphasized the redness around his eyes, as if he'd been crying for a long time. His nose was veined and red, his face flushed. Still he was good-looking, in his early twenties, Vicky thought, with the carved features of an Arapaho warrior in the Old Time. She held out her hand. "I'm Vicky Holden," she said. "I'm a lawyer. Adam asked me to speak with you."

"Where's Adam?" The young man threw a frantic glance around the living room, as if he could conjure Adam Lone Eagle from the sofa or chairs or among the papers stacked on a side table.

"Adam thinks Vicky here is the one to help you," his mother said.

Petey sank onto the sofa. His mother sat down beside him and tried to take his hand. He pulled away and leaned into the armrest. "You gonna get my job back?"

"Why don't you start at the beginning and tell me what happened," Vicky said.

"Nothing happened!" The words came like a shriek of pain. "Except the world's out to screw me. What's his name, Gianelli, comes here, says how come you weren't making your rounds the night the artifacts got stolen. I said, 'What're you talking about?' He says the boss told him I never clocked in for work. Hell, no, I didn't clock in. They switched my schedule so I was supposed to work on Saturday night. I got a call from the office about six o'clock saying don't come in."

Mary scooted forward on the sofa. "I'd gone out to run a couple errands in the afternoon, but I called Petey to make sure he was all right. He'd been a little under the weather, so I told him he should stay home from work and rest, but he said work would make him feel better. I was home when they called. I heard Petey say, 'What'd'ya mean, you switched me?' Then he said 'okay' and hung up. He was in his uniform ready to go to work." She turned sideways toward her son. "You ask me, that's when you started feeling bad again, before anything else happened."

Looking back at Vicky, she said, "Petey doesn't handle change very well. A big change moving here, and it's been hard. Especially after he lost the job with the highway department. Now this." She threw out both hands in a kind of supplication, as if she expected Vicky to make everything right.

"It made me mad, pulling me off the job when any day the Arapaho artifacts was gonna come in," Petey said. "I started thinking, maybe they're coming tonight. Maybe the boss wants somebody with more experience on patrol. Made me feel helpless, 'cause there's nobody cared more about keeping the artifacts safe. Next morning I hear the news on the moccasin telegraph that somebody stole the artifacts. Oh, man, it was like fireworks popping in my eyes, I was so mad. Then I seen where this was going. I'd been set up. The fed was gonna say I didn't go to work so the coast would be clear. He'd say I knew all about the theft. Maybe I was, what you call it, an accomplice?"

Mary was shaking her head hard. "I never seen him so terrified," she said. "Started on a downward spiral. Then the fed shows up here and asks a lot of questions, just like Petey figured would happen."

The room went quiet a moment before Mary said, "Tell her the rest of it."

Petey chewed on his lower lip a moment, then rubbed at his eyes. Finally he said, "The fed told me he already checked with the boss, and the boss said, far as he knew, I was supposed to work my regular shift. He swore nobody changed my schedule."

"Who called you?" Vicky said.

Petey shrugged. "Dean somebody. Said he was calling for the boss. I don't know all the guys in the office. They work in town; I'm out at the airport. I sure as hell never clocked in."

"How could he?" Mary said. "Petey was right here most the evening."

"Did you go anywhere?"

"After a while, I figured, what the hell. I don't have to work."

"I tried to tell him it was like getting a little time off that he wasn't expecting. Why not enjoy it, instead of getting upset."

"So I went out and drove around looking to see if there was a party going on."

"And was there?" Vicky said.

Petey closed his eyes and shook his head. "There's always a party, but I didn't know where to find it. So I came home."

"You see the trouble he's in?" Mary said. "The fed will make a case that Petey went out to the airport and stole the artifacts, when all he was doing was driving around the rez. The boss says Petey's lying about getting a call. Who's the fed going to believe? Some white boss at a security company or an Indian kid? That's why I called Adam. He came right over and said we needed a lawyer to look after Petey's rights, but he hadn't practiced that kind of law for a long time. He suggested you."

"That's not all of it," Petey said.

"You don't have to talk about it."

"If you want me to help you," Vicky said, "don't hold back."

Petey clenched his jaw so hard, the veins in his temples bulged. "It got to me real bad. What right did those bastards have to take stuff that belongs to Arapahos! They're gonna get away with it. That's what made me lose it. I mean, the more I thought about it, the more I wanted to go find them and get the artifacts back. I wanted to kill them."

"Petey isn't very . . ." His mother worked her lips over the word a moment before she said, "Strong."

"I'm strong enough."

"I'm afraid he gets emotional over anything that has to do with his father's people. Since we've been on the rez, he's heard a lot of old stories about the injustices and crimes. Sometimes they set him off. But I tell him, it's good to care so much," she said, patting her son's shoulder. "I been telling him, he needs to go back to college, become a lawyer like you and Adam, and use all that anger he's got pent up to make sure bad things don't happen anymore."

Vicky glanced away from the image of

herself that had materialized in front of her. Maybe she had cared too much, gotten too involved, taken everything too personally, on a one-woman mission to change the way things were. First she'd had to change herself. Stop denying that eventually Ben Holden would kill her if she didn't get out of the marriage. Admit that her children, Susan and Lucas, would be loved and cared for by her own parents, and that what she had to do would be best for them in the long term. Woman Alone. *I will go to school. I will become a lawyer. I will fight for the rights of my people. Rights? The grandmothers had mocked her. Since when do we have rights?*

"Who is the boss?" she said.

"Max Ritter."

"I'll try to talk to him," Vicky said. "Are there any other reasons he might have for firing you?"

Petey stared at her as if she had uttered an obscenity. "What? I show up on time, do my job. I like keeping things safe. Especially things that belong to the people."

"Anything else about your job you'd like to tell me?"

"What are you suggesting?" Mary said.

"There can be reprimands in a personnel file. Tardiness, slacking off on the job, not getting along with other employees. A company can start looking for a reason to fire an employee like that."

"You forgot one thing," Mary said. "Being Indian."

"I'm saying," Vicky said, turning toward Petey, "if your employment record is clean, we can make a stronger argument for reinstatement." Not every case of injustice, she was thinking, was about race.

"I'm telling you it's clean," Petey said.

Vicky had turned onto Seventeen-Mile Road, heading east, when the cell burst into the first chords of Willie Nelson's "On the Road Again." Fitting the Bluetooth into her ear, she said, "Vicky Holden."

"How did it go?" Adam sounded so close, he might have been sitting beside her. My God, she had left Mary and her son not more than ten minutes ago, and the woman had already called him.

She sucked in her breath to give herself a moment before she said, "You didn't tell me how unstable Petey is."

"Let's just say, he has a few emotional problems. But he's been working on them. The job's been a stabilizing influence in his life."

"I'm on my way to speak with his boss," she said. The blue billboard with St. Francis

Mission in large white letters passed outside the passenger window. "It's complicated. Maybe the thieves figured out a way to pull the security guard off the job, or maybe Petey just decided not to go to work."

The line went quiet for so long that Vicky thought she had driven into a dead area. Then Adam said, "He had nothing to do with the theft, if that's what you're thinking."

Vicky stopped at the sign where Seventeen-Mile Road butted into Highway 749, waited for a semi to pass, and turned north. Warehouses, drive-up liquor stores, trailer parks bunched together on both sides of the highway outside of Riverton. "We'll talk later," she said, and pushed the End key. Odd, how Adam had rejected the idea that Petey could be involved in the theft. Why? Petey wanted to save money to go back to school. Maybe he'd seen the chance to pick up a nice sum. She tried to focus on what he and Mary had said without coloring the story with possibilities and conjectures. Now she wondered if Adam wasn't trying to protect Petey from something more serious than not showing up for work.

24

Vicky waited at the front counter while the woman at the first desk tapped the keyboard, eyes on the computer screen. Other clerks occupied the desks stretching across the office toward a window that overlooked the alley in back and the redbrick wall of another office building. The air buzzed with the syncopated rhythm of clacking keys and ringing phones. Vicky had left the Jeep in the parking lot behind a sign that said, "Reserved for Security Services." She had debated about calling ahead for an appointment, and rejected the idea. Surprise had a way of throwing people off balance, catching them before they'd had the chance to create a narrative. She had decided to take a chance that the manager was in and would want to see her. She rapped her fingers on the countertop. The clerk at the front desk bent closer to the screen. Finally Vicky spotted the small metal bell at the end of the counter. She walked over and slammed her palm against the ringer. The shrill, high-pitched sound reverberated across the office, breaking through the other noise.

The clerk looked up and made a show of swiveling her chair partway round. Placing both hands on top of the desk, she pushed herself to her feet. A large woman. Sand-colored hair spiked around her head, and she had narrowed, suspicious eyes. The short sleeves of her white tee shirt cut into the flesh of her arms. "What can I do for you?" she said, plodding toward the counter, as if she were walking in mud.

"I'd like to speak with Max Ritter," Vicky said. "Is he in?"

"You got an appointment?"

Vicky slipped the small leather folder out of her bag, extracted a business card, and slid it across the counter. "I represent Petey Many Horses," she said. Behind the clerk, the young man seated at the second desk — Arapaho, Vicky thought, in his twenties, black hair cut short, sleeves of his blue shirt rolled up over ropey, brown arms — looked over. Vicky could feel the intensity of his gaze on her. "Mr. Ritter will want to speak with me," she said.

The young man jumped up, walked to the end of the counter, and bent down. He began rummaging in whatever was stored below.

"Max is real busy," the clerk said. "You want an appointment?" She nodded toward the computer, as if she could walk back to the desk, tap some more keys, and settle everything right away.

"Tell him I'd like to speak to him about Petey's wrongful termination." When the woman didn't move, Vicky added, "I'll wait."

The woman seemed to consider this with some distaste, annoyance flickering in her eyes. After a long moment, she propelled herself around and disappeared past the door that bisected the left wall.

Vicky glanced sideways at the young man thumping files onto the counter and making an effort to look interested in the contents. She should probably know him. Chances were she had seen him at powwows or rodeos. The rez was like a small town, everybody knew everybody, or thought they did because they saw the same faces day after day. He was about Lucas's age. They could have gone to school together. She moved along the counter. "Vicky Holden," she said. The young man jerked his head up and stared at her with the startled look of a deer caught in the headlights. "Are you from the rez?"

"Yeah," he said.

"You must know Petey Many Horses."

He was shaking his head. "Seen the name is all. He worked out at the airport. Never come around the office that I know."

"You worked here long?"

"Best get back to your desk, Jason." The woman appeared at the counter and shot a glare of disapproval toward the young man who started backing away, colliding with the edge of the first desk, finally whipping around and heading toward his own desk.

"Mr. Ritter's too busy to see visitors," the woman said. "I suggest we set up an appointment for another day."

Vicky noticed she had left the side door open. Max Ritter was most likely on the other side. "I suggest you explain to Mr. Ritter that my next stop will be the *Gazette*. I intend to make it clear that my client received a call from this office ordering him not to come to work the night the artifacts were stolen. No doubt the *Gazette* will contact Ritter wanting to know why the security guard was pulled off duty hours before the robbery."

A large man with graying hair combed over the top of his bald scalp, the veined, reddened nose of a drinker, and the bellicose attitude of a bluffer strode through the opened door. In a few steps, he was at the counter. He lifted the hinged section and gestured for Vicky to walk through.

She followed him into the hallway and through an opened door into an office lined with filing cabinets. Ritter made his way around the paper-cluttered desk and dropped onto a black mesh chair. "Looks like you Indians like to play hardball," he said.

Vicky pulled a metal side chair out of a corner and sat down. "We like justice," she said.

"Don't we all? That make you special? You think justice is giving that scumbag his job back?"

"Petey was a good employee," Vicky said. "On time, did his job satisfactorily. There's nothing in his personnel file to suggest otherwise. Am I right?" God, she hoped Petey hadn't held out on her.

The man on the other side of the desk was breathing hard. A red flush had started to move up his neck into his cheeks. He seemed to be having trouble gathering his thoughts, constructing his narrative, and she pushed on: "If we have to file a suit, your records will be subpoenaed."

He clasped beefy-looking hands together

and leaned over the desk. "Many Horses did not show up for his regular shift. Valuable artifacts were taken from the warehouse he should have been checking on. We could get our butts sued over this. Other clients might decide we don't know what we're doing and go with that company in Lander. Enough said. I had the right to fire him."

"Petey received a call from this office at 6:00 p.m. instructing him not to come to work. He was told his shift had been changed and he would work next Saturday night instead."

"Bunch of bull."

"Dean called him."

"Dean? There's nobody named Dean in this company. Your client's lying to save his own ass. You ask me, he took a bribe to stay away, give the robbers a free ride. No chance later that Many Horses would be called on to testify under oath about who he saw at the warehouse. Not with him out of the way, that's how I see it."

"Does the office keep a log of phone calls?"

"Of course we keep a log. No call went from this office to Petey Many Horses."

"Isn't it possible someone could have made the call and not logged it in?"

"Impossible. Anybody do that, I'd fire

'em. We keep meticulous records. It's part of our business."

"The readout on Petey's cell said the call came from this office."

Ritter lifted his head and sucked in another long breath. "That's what he says."

"I intend to get his phone records. They will show the time the call came in and the origin. I trust you will consider reinstating him after you've seen the records."

"You consider backing off after you find out your client is lying?"

"We have a deal?" Vicky said.

"You gotta get the proof first." Ritter shook his massive head.

"Oh, I will," she said.

Vicky drove south on 749, the white-hot sun blasting the passenger window and lighting the leather seat, the stunted brush along the side of the highway flying past. She had no idea what the phone records might show. They could show anything, and she could have just made a fool of herself. The Indian lawyer jumping off a cliff for her lying client. All she had was Adam's word that Petey and his mother were telling the truth, and Adam seemed to know. It kept coming down to that — he *knew* Mary and Petey Many Horses. He knew them from before; he knew them now. What she couldn't be sure about was how well he knew them now.

She had wanted to trust him.

The implications stormed around her. If Petey was telling the truth, then someone at the office had called him off his shift the night of the robbery. Someone who was either involved or bought off. But who had contacted him? Who at Security Systems had been brought into a conspiracy? All the questions revolved like swirling water around the obvious answer: a number of people could be involved. Three, four, five? Locals, from the rez? Arapahos caught up in a plan to steal from their own people? But it wasn't locals who had conceived the plan. That had taken outsiders, people who knew how to make Indian artifacts disappear, and where to sell them for the most money.

And that kept leading back to Trevor Pratt, a man who had lived a double life, who still had contacts from that other life. A client she hadn't known or even suspected was anything other than on the level.

She had taken the turn into the reservation too fast, she realized as the Jeep swung into the oncoming lane. She fought to bring it back, tires howling on the asphalt. She tapped on the brake and kept the Jeep at forty past the small houses and wide stretches of pasture with ponies grazing lazily in the sun. She made another left, a comfortable speed this time, and drove through the shade of the cottonwood tunnel into St. Francis Mission. A few vehicles were parked around Circle Drive. A couple of Indians climbed down from an extended pickup and started across the drive and down the alley between the church and administration building, probably heading for some kind of meeting at Eagle Hall. She pulled into a parking space in front of the administration building and hurried up the concrete steps.

Inside her footsteps rang through the wide corridor. Even before she looked into John O'Malley's office on the right, she knew by the silent emptiness in the building that he wasn't there.

"Good afternoon."

The old man had stepped through the doorway at the far end and was walking toward her. Gray haired and pink faced with blue eyes that regarded her over the rimless eyeglasses slipping partway down his nose. For thirty years, John O'Malley had told her, Bishop Harry Coughlin had been in charge of the spiritual well-being, and at times the physical well-being, of thousands of Catholics surrounded by Muslims and Hindus of India. He moved with the poise and confidence of a man used to his own authority, yet the kindness in his gaze and the turn of his mouth suggested that the authority had been softened and tempered by time. He seemed perfectly at home on the rez, as much a part of the mission as the old building and the wide, creaky corridor and the cottonwood trees outside the windows.

"I was looking for . . . Father John." Vicky had stopped herself from calling him John.

"I believe you will find him at the museum." The bishop stopped a few feet from her, close enough that she could make out the web of tiny blue veins in his cheeks.

She thanked him and started toward the door, then turned back. "Any news about the director?"

"I'm afraid not," he said. His voice was etched with such a sense of dread and sadness, it sent a chill running through her.

25

The sign on the door said Closed. Vicky felt a jolt of surprise when the knob turned in her hand. She stepped into the dim coolness of the entry. Directly ahead, the exhibition hall floated in shadows, cut loose from its purpose. It should have been packed with tourists and school children and Arapahos learning about the lives of the ancestors, the "Show" Indians in strange lands, far from the plains, reliving their own lives. "John, are you here?" she called.

Father John emerged through the doorway down the corridor, smiled, and motioned her forward.

Even as she headed down the corridor, she could feel the ghosts of the place following at her heels. The Arapaho kids who had come to school here, riding ponies bareback across the plains, tiny bundles of belongings strapped to their backs. Her own ancestors had learned to read and write and speak English in the big, high-ceiling rooms that had been combined into the exhibition hall. She had gone to school here, before the school was closed for lack of teachers or money. She rounded the corner, past the sign that said Director.

John was on his feet behind the desk covered with stacks of papers and file folders. "I was just about to call you." He gestured with his head toward a folding chair, then dropped onto a swivel chair. "I've been trying to make sense out of the papers tossed about when they ransacked the office," he said. Vicky looked over at the filing cabinet next to the window. The top drawer hung out partway. Empty spaces gaped among the folders left in the drawer.

"What did they take?" he said. "What did they leave behind? I was hoping I might get an idea of what they were thinking."

"What were they thinking?"

"Looks like they were interested only in files in the top drawer. The other drawers weren't disturbed." John looked over at the cabinet a moment, as if he were wondering if that was really the case or if he had missed something. She doubted he had missed anything. "Financial records in the second drawer, receipts for purchases of artifacts, contracts with other museums for the loan of artifacts, that kind of thing. Nothing seems to have been disturbed. The other drawers are filled with miscellaneous research notes and clippings probably collected by directors over the last five years." He leaned forward and tapped the stack of empty file folders. A maze of freckles covered the top of his hand. "They knew what they were looking for," he said. "Everything is missing in the folders marked: 'Artifacts, Specialists.' 'Museums.' 'Experts.' 'Arapaho.' 'Cheyenne.' 'Sioux.' 'Apache.' 'Navajo.' 'Dealers.' 'Collectors.' Probably everything Eldon had printed off the internet."

"They're looking for a buyer." Vicky felt a surge of certainty. It was all becoming clear. "They killed Trevor and they're not sure how to dispose of the artifacts for the kind of money Trevor might have gotten."

"I think they took the entire file on Trevor." John thumped the top of the folders. "Otherwise the file folder would be here. They didn't take any chances of leaving behind something that might suggest Trevor was not who he said he was." He sat back and regarded her a moment. "I did some research on Trevor," he said.

"You mean, Thomas Plink," Vicky said.

John gave a little laugh. "Why am I not surprised you already knew that? Convicted thief," he went on, as if he were reading from a resume. "A year behind bars for illegally dealing in Indian artifacts. Eldon had been trying to track the artifacts on the internet," he continued. "He thought they might show up for sale. Maybe he was suspicious about Trevor, so he did some research and found Thomas Plink, convicted artifacts thief. Maybe Eldon tipped his hand, mentioned his suspicions to the wrong person."

"I spoke with Trevor's ex-wife," Vicky said.

"Let me guess. Julia Hyde? Former partner?"

Vicky smiled. "She owns a Victorian antiques shop in Dubois. She spoke fondly of Trevor. They remained friends, she said. She also claimed that Trevor had left the old life behind. He was an expert on Indian artifacts, so he manufactured an impressive resume and started a legitimate business. He dealt with museums and the type of collectors he would have avoided in the past. Legitimate collectors who wouldn't have recognized him."

John got to his feet, came around the desk and leaned against the edge, his forehead creased in the familiar way that she knew meant he was trying to bring opposing ideas together. "Trevor wanted to see Wild West artifacts returned to the Arapahos. He said they belonged here with the people. He had stolen artifacts from tribes in the past, and I think he was trying to make amends. He was looking for redemption."

Vicky jumped up and began trolling the center of the office: window, desk, chair, and back again. She could marshal her thoughts better when she was moving, as if the necessity to keep moving were part of her DNA, inherited from the ancestors. *We were traveling people*, her grandmother had told her. *We could think best when we traveled*. "It's possible Trevor changed his name, but nothing else," she said. Then she told him what Julia Hyde had said about the insurance scam her ex-husband had run in the past, and how Trevor might have set up the same kind of scam for the artifacts. She told him about the two men who had come to the ranch in Colorado looking for Trevor. "He kept in touch with the thieves he'd worked with," she said. "He was smart. He fooled everybody. He certainly fooled me." She stopped moving and locked eyes with John O'Malley for a long moment. There weren't many people who had fooled him; she couldn't think of any. She looked away. John had believed in the man. "The two men he stayed in touch with are most likely the white men in the car we saw racing away from Trevor's ranch," she said. "Hol Chambers and Raphael Luna. They had some kind of falling out . . ." She began circling again. "A falling out of thieves. They went to his ranch and killed him."

"We don't know that for certain."

She stopped and spun toward him. "Come on, John."

He looked past her toward the window and Vicky followed his gaze. Deep shadows of late afternoon fell through the cottonwood branches and lay like soft blankets over the mission grounds. It was peaceful at the mission. Almost impossible to imagine a man abducted from here, an office ransacked. John brought his eyes back to hers. "A couple of outsiders were at the Arapahoe powwow two weeks ago trying to buy regalia from the dancers," he said. "Could be the same men. They claimed they had collectors interested in Indian artifacts. Offered very little money." He shrugged, as if that were obvious. "If they are the same men, we know two things about them. They were looking for artifacts and they are dealers."

"Logical," Vicky said. He could be so infuriatingly logical. "Why isn't it just as logical to conclude that two men racing away from a murder scene had committed the murder?"

"Possible," he said.

Vicky went back to circling the office. "Who did they talk to at the powwow?"

John walked around the desk and sank back into the chair. "They tried to buy a vest from Cam Merryman," he said. "They were under the impression that Cam's ancestor, Sonny Yellow Robe, had worn the vest in the Wild West Show. Turns out it's a replica that Cam made from a photo. He has no intention of selling it. They also tried to buy a tanned hide dress from Wilma RunningFast that had belonged to her great-grandmother."

"So we know something else about them," Vicky said. "They're looking for artifacts with a history." Logical, she was thinking. All of it logical.

"You really believe Trevor was behind the theft?" John said. She could hear the doubt in his voice. He had sat back, elbows resting on the armrests, fingers tipied under his chin. "Working with partners from the past?"

"They couldn't have done it alone," Vicky said. "They needed insiders." She caught the flash of surprise in John O'Malley's eyes. Arapahos stealing their own artifacts? She had long ago given up the notion that all

302

crimes against her people were committed by outsiders. "Someone to notify them when the artifacts were moved to the warehouse," she said, pulling at her fingers. "Someone at the security company to call off the guard. Someone who knew the security code to open the warehouse door."

He told her that the Riverton Police had obtained videos from the warehouse. "Three men in ski masks entered through the door, removed the artifacts, resealed the cartons, and disappeared."

Vicky could feel the smile creeping through her face. "What did I say? Trevor and his two old partners."

She perched onto the chair, feeling spent now, as if she had traveled a great distance across the plains. "I have a new client," she said. "Petey Many Horses. He was fired from Security Systems for not showing up for work the night the artifacts disappeared. The thing is, the office called him and told him not to come in. All part of a conspiracy planned by a smart, experienced thief, Trevor Pratt. A man with connections. A man who knew everything about Indian artifacts, according to his ex-wife. What they were worth, who would buy them without asking questions. A man who could play both sides of the game. Sell the artifacts and collect the insurance." She waved a hand to forestall any objection. "I'm guessing Trevor might have run into trouble moving the artifacts as fast as he had planned. His partners probably thought he was holding out on them. Perfect motive for murder."

John didn't say anything.

Vicky could feel the quiet settling over the office like a physical object, broken by the sound of water gurgling in a pipe somewhere and the distant yawning and stretching of the old building. After a moment, she went on. "They wanted to make sure Eldon couldn't take his suspicions to Gianelli. If they've killed once . . ." She stopped, letting the words hang in the air between them a moment. "Trevor had the connections. They could be having trouble selling the artifacts. They could still be in the area, and someone on the rez might know where they're hiding." Vicky shifted in her chair until she faced the desk. "Do you know a Rap, early twenties, I'd say, named Jason?"

"Jason Gains?" John said. "Played first base for the Eagles a couple of seasons nine or ten years ago."

That was when she told him that Jason Gains worked for Security Systems. She could see the young man, as if the image were burned onto her retinas: loping over to the counter, checking something on the lower shelves, cocking his head in her direction, ears practically sticking out like antennas. "I think he may have placed the call to Petey and told him not to come to work." She took a breath and hurried on. "We should tell Gianelli what we know."

"What do we know?" John said. "All we have are theories. No connections, no evidence." He seemed to consider the consequences of this for a moment. "Let me talk to Jason," he said, and the way in which he said it gave her a rush of shame. A white man who knew that the police or the fed interviewing an Arapaho about theft, murder, abduction would get Jason Gains fired and make it difficult for him to find another job off the rez. John O'Malley was right, she could feel the truth in her bones. She didn't even know if the record from the cell company would prove the call had come from Security Systems, as Petey claimed. Before they talked to Gianelli, they had to have facts.

26

The sun blazed over the high, jagged peaks of the Wind River range and sent orange and magenta flames swirling across the sky. Miranda Lambert on the CD. Vicky stared at Rendezvous Road loping over the plains ahead and tried to tamp down the sense of unease that had come over her. There were no other vehicles in sight, nothing but the red-tinged brush and wild grasses doing a slow dance in the fields outside the windows. She tried to make herself relax, but her muscles felt as if they were glued together. A cacophony of thoughts banged in her head, like instruments playing different melodies. Somehow they had to be welded together into one harmonious piece, but she couldn't figure out how to do that. A man named Thomas Plink who had become Trevor Pratt, shot in the chest in a horse stall; Eldon White Elk, abducted from the museum. God, let him be alive. White

Elk knew the artifacts business, he knew how to use the internet. Maybe he could even figure out how to find buyers. They would keep him alive, those two white men, as long as they thought he might be of help.

There were other thoughts: Petey Many Horses, fired for following orders, and Jason Gains, slouching at the end of the counter, eavesdropping on her conversation with the receptionist. Jason Gains, the guy who had called off Petey? Well, John would talk to him and in five minutes have a good idea of whether he was involved.

What if he were involved? That brought up a whole other range of possibilities. Jason didn't get the idea on his own to call the security guard and tell him not to come to work. Someone had given the instruction. Trevor? That made sense, she thought, tapping her nails against the edge of the steering wheel. The big man, pulling the strings. But how did he know Jason Gains? What made him think Jason would go along? She jammed a fist against the wheel.

Her cell was ringing, a Willie Nelson song that broke through "The House that Built Me" on the radio. Vicky held the wheel with one hand and jammed the Bluetooth in her ear. Slowing for a rabbit that scooted across the road, she said, "Vicky Holden, here."

"Cell phone company just faxed the record for Petey Many Horses." Annie's voice, professional with a barely submerged hint of curiosity.

"Read me the calls for last Monday."

"Looks like he got a call from Mary Many Horses at 1:00 p.m. Another call from Mary at 1:54 p.m."

At least that tallied, Vicky was thinking.

"Let's see," Annie was saying. "Another call came in at 6:01 p.m. from Security Systems."

Vicky exhaled a long, slow breath. "Thanks," she said. She ended the call, picked up the phone, and scrolled to Petey's number.

There was a buzzing noise, followed by Petey's voice, tentative and scared. "Hello?"

"You can relax," Vicky said. "The cell phone records confirm you got a call from the office."

"I told you . . ."

Vicky cut in: "I spoke with your boss."

"Old boss," Petey said.

"Who do you know in the office?"

"What?" Petey said, then he blurted out: "Nobody. Mr. Ritter, that's all."

"None of the clerks in the front office?"

"I never went there."

"What about a Rap named Jason Gains."

"Oh, yeah. I heard a Rap started working there couple months ago."

"Did you ever talk to him?"

"What about? I told you I don't know him." Vicky heard the shushing noise at the other end, as if the young man were sucking in breath through a straw. "Wait a minute," he said. "You think he was the one that called?"

"Would you recognize the voice if you heard it again?" In the rearview mirror, Vicky saw the dark sedan coming out of the reddish sunset, coming on fast.

Petey made another shushing noise. "I'd recognize it."

Vicky told him she'd stay in touch and ended the call, watching the sedan gaining on her. Traveling too fast for the road that bent into a curve ahead. She could see the cowboy hats bobbing in the windshield. The sedan couldn't have been more than fifty feet behind her now. Over Miranda Lambert's voice, she heard the sedan's engine revving and straining, or was she imagining it? A hard knot tightened in her stomach as she pressed down on the accelerator, trying to put as much distance as possible between the Jeep and the two men in the dark sedan.

The first collision came at seventy miles an hour. The Jeep jumped ahead as Vicky pressed down on the gas pedal. She watched the road, the speedometer, the dark sedan coming after her all at once, feeling disembodied, like one of the spirits able to see everything. Another crash. The Jeep shimmied over the road. The CD jumped to another track. She gripped the steering wheel hard to right the Jeep and stomped on the gas. Eighty miles per hour, eighty-five, and still the sedan stayed behind her, a horrible appendage she couldn't cut loose. Her heart jumped in her chest. She was barely aware of the sun glinting on the roofs of Arapahoe outside the passenger window. There was no one else on the road. She had the sense of galloping through space, the Jeep growling around her, music sputtering somewhere.

The next collision sent the Jeep hurtling toward the borrow ditch, rocking back and forth, plowing into the ditch, as if it were a living creature, a giant horse huffing and snorting as it attempted to right itself. She eased on the brake, but the Jeep was flying and she was flying inside it, held down by the seat belt that dug into her chest, gripping the wheel to keep from being flung out into space. The Jeep came down hard on the right wheels, teetered sideways, and went into a crazy half spin before it plopped onto its side. Glass shattered, brittle, sharp pellets spraying her face and neck and biting into her arms. The loud whooshing noise careened around her. Something gray and hard had burst from the steering wheel and pinned her against the seat. Strange, she thought. She was hanging above the passenger window, strapped against the seat, the huge gray air bag pressed against her windpipe. Past the gray bag, through the fractured windshield, she watched fragments of orange and red clouds twirling past one another. The music had stopped, leaving the eerie silence broken by the noise of glass plinking onto hard surfaces.

Footsteps came running across hard-packed dirt. The two men, coming for her! Vicky tried to find the seat belt release, but the bag was in the way and her fingers gripped air. The hot flash of panic rose inside her. The footsteps were close, like a gust of wind about to smash against her. Her fingers brushed the plastic button. Clenching her muscles for strength, she rammed the button down into the metal holder. The pressure in her chest and across her ribs released, but now the only thing holding her in place was the gray bag. She was on a horse rearing upward, the passenger seat and dashboard falling away. The footsteps slid to a stop, something knocked against the door. Pain seared her chest as she tried to twist past the bag to see who was outside. She would look them in the eye, yes, she would look the two white men in the eye before they killed her.

"Are you hurt?" It was a woman's voice that echoed the panic banging like drums inside her.

"Don't try to move," a man said. "We've called 911. An ambulance is on the way."

"Who are you?" Vicky heard herself ask. Her larynx felt tight; it was hard to catch a breath.

"We saw everything," the woman said. "We turned out of Arapahoe when we saw that car speeding past. We saw it run you off the road."

"Don't move," the man commanded, and Vicky realized she was still struggling to get free. Odd, she thought. Without the bag pushing against her, she would fall facedown into the glass pellets. From the distance came the wail of a siren, joined after a moment by the long lament of another siren. She fought for another breath as she felt her muscles relax against the seat. The gray bag, the outlines of the inside of the Jeep, and the pulsing colors of the sky closed down around her into a pinprick of light;

312

then were lost in darkness. From far away she heard the man say, "Hold on. Hold on. Help is on the way."

Father John left the papers and stack of folders on the desk — Eldon would return them to their rightful places. Dear Lord, let the man be alive. He turned off the light and started down the corridor. At the junction with the back hall, he switched on the overhead light and walked toward the back door that Leonard Bizzel had installed this morning. Leonard had taken care of the mission buildings for at least thirty years, making sure everything worked — faucets and drains, eaves and locks. A heart attack had slowed him down a year ago, but he still insisted that Father John call when he needed help, and Father John suspected that Leonard found it hard to accept the idea of another handyman doing his work.

The lock had been thrown, the door held fast when Father John tried the knob. A solid-core door, Leonard had told him. Not likely any burglar would break through. Father John retraced his steps down the hallway and was about to switch off the light when the front door opened. A dark figure, lit from behind by the orange light outside, stepped into the corridor.

Father John didn't move; his fists clenched.

"Hey, Father. It's Robert." A nervous twang to the voice, as if Robert Running-Fast had sensed Father John's tenseness. The man moved past the shadows and into the light. "I stopped at the office. Nobody there, so I come over here. Got a minute?"

"Sure," Father John said, starting back to the office. He'd gone a few steps when he realized the man wasn't with him and turned around. Robert stood in the doorway to the exhibition hall.

"Lot of old stuff here," he said, glancing around.

"Would you like to see it?"

"Nah." He was shaking his head, but he hadn't moved from the doorway. "What the hell. Go to a museum, you might as well see what they got." He stepped forward into the shadowy hall. Father John followed and flipped the light switch. Ceiling lights stuttered into life, then the hall seemed to break free and fill up the entire museum.

Robert had walked over and was standing in front of the poster of Buffalo Bill. "Grandmother says he liked Indians," he said. "You ask me, he wouldn't have had much of a show without them. Looks like he knew what he was doing. You want people to come see your show, you have Indians and cowboys shooting each other."

"There was more to the Wild West Show than that," Father John said. He was about to launch into an explanation about how Buffalo Bill had wanted to educate audiences about life in the old West, the clash of civilizations as settlers threw themselves across the plains, into the wilderness. He stopped himself. The young man had moved on to the glass case exhibiting a beaded vest posed over beaded, high-top moccasins.

"1880s, 1890s," Father John said. "Probably similar to the artifacts that were in the show."

"Arapaho stuff was gonna go here?" Robert moved to the opposite wall and planted himself in front of three cases that had an unfinished look, with posters splashed on the walls and clear plastic glass holders and blocks arranged around the photos and programs on the floor.

Then Robert's gaze seemed to land on something that pulled him sideways. He stopped in front of the portrait of Chief Black Heart.

"The artifacts that were stolen belonged to him." Father John walked over. "Bernard Tallman's great-grandfather."

"Looks like him," Robert said. "Yeah, I

can see a real family resemblance. Who's this?" He leaned forward and squinted at the typed plaque next to the photo of Sonny Yellow Robe.

"The chief's adopted son," Father John said.

"The Rap that stole the artifacts in the first place."

"That's not what his descendants think. Chief Black Heart didn't believe it either."

Robert shrugged. "Look at it," he said, waving into the center of the gallery. "Nothing but old stuff. Who cares about hundred-year-old stuff?"

"Your grandmother cares."

"She's stuck in the past, like a lot of Raps. Where's that gonna get you? Me? I'm looking at the future."

"Would Wilma like me to put her grandmother's dress in our vault?" Father John said, searching for a reason for the visit.

Robert threw his gaze around the hall again. "She already found a hiding place. You ask me, she heard the museum got broken into and the director got kidnapped. She had me take the dress out to my uncle's ranch. He's got a storage shed that's so jammed full, he puts the dress in there nobody'll ever find it."

Father John didn't say anything. A new

thought had begun taking shape. He wondered how many other Arapahos might decide against allowing any of their precious old things to be exhibited in a museum that didn't have enough security to prevent a burglary. They would have to increase the security; a solid-core door with a bolt wasn't enough.

Robert had gone back to studying the photo of the chief. "So that's what got stolen," he said. "Eagle feathered headdress, vest, wrist cuffs. Even that flag shirt. Stuff he wore in the show?"

"Black Heart's father also wore the items in battles," Father John said. "He wore the headdress at the Battle of the Little Big Horn. They weren't just show costumes."

Robert didn't move his gaze from the photo, as if it held some fascination. "Black Heart and Yellow Robe. Buffalo Bill himself. They're all dead now."

"They were alive once. Could be the items they wore are a witness to their lives."

Robert jerked his eyes away from the photo, as if he were flinching from an electric shock. He walked over to a case in the middle of the room and stared down at the belt buckles, lariats, and hand-tooled boots, some of the items worn by Buffalo Bill himself. Father John looked past the young man at the unfinished cases, a quality of waiting about them. What an exhibit it would have been!

Robert rapped a knuckle against the edge of a case and turned toward him. "Can I talk to you?" he said.

27

Robert's knuckle tapping the glass case sounded like a metronome.

Father John studied the young man. Round shouldered, slouched against the case as if it would hold him up, eyes shadowed in concern, Adam's apple jumping up and down. He hadn't come to the mission to tell him his grandmother didn't trust the museum for her ancestor's dress. That was an excuse.

"What is it?" Father John tried to keep his voice steady, the voice he hoped imparted confidence. In his head, he heard Vicky: *They couldn't have done it alone. They needed insiders.*

"How can I help you?" He made another effort.

"Look," Robert said, throwing out both hands like a kid protesting innocence to whatever misdeed he might be suspected of. "I needed the money. I want to go back to school. I been working hard, living with grandmother and trying to get enough money together . . ."

"Let's start at the beginning," Father John said. "Who offered you money? What did they expect in return?"

"Okay. Okay." Now both hands were thrown in the air, as if the young man had surrendered to some inevitability. "I got a call from some guy. Don't ask me, 'cause I don't know. He said I didn't need to know. He said there was a thousand dollars for me to do a couple things. Nothing would be traced to me, so I had nothing to worry about."

Father John waited a moment before he said, "You were to call him when the artifacts were delivered to the warehouse?"

Robert nodded. His gaze stayed on the floor.

"You said a couple of things. What else?"

"He needed the security code for the door pad."

"You knew he intended to steal Arapaho artifacts."

"I didn't *know*. It wasn't my business what he wanted to do. I figured he'd sneak into the warehouse, take one or two artifacts. I never thought he'd clean out the cartons. I mean, the fed and cops would come after him like he was a wild grizzly gone crazy. One or two things, maybe nobody would've noticed. The collector that bought the stuff might holler, but that'd be the end of it. Besides . . ." A tremor came into his voice. He shifted his gaze toward the photo of Black Heart. "It's nothing but a lot of old stuff."

"A man was murdered," Father John said. "Another man's life is in danger."

"I never thought that was gonna happen, I swear. I never would've gotten mixed up in murder. You gotta believe me, Father."

"Do you have any idea who might have called you?"

Robert shook his head so hard, his whole body was shaking.

"How did he pay you?"

"After I took the stuff to the warehouse, I called the number he gave me. He told me to be on Blue Sky Highway just north of Seventeen-Mile Road at 2:00 a.m., park on the side and wait. I waited fifteen minutes. I was about to give up, figuring I'd been played, when I seen headlights. A car slowed down and the driver tossed an envelope out the window. It sped up and was gone. I picked up the envelope, got back inside my pickup, and counted out ten big ones."

"What number did he give you?"

"I flushed the paper I wrote it on down the toilet. I didn't want anything linking me to whatever was going down at the warehouse."

"You have to talk to the fed," Father John said.

"No way." Robert backed into the edge of the adjoining case. "The guy on the phone said something I didn't tell you. If I snitch, I'm dead."

"A man's life is at stake," Father John said.

"I don't know anything else. I can't help him."

"Why have you told me?"

"You're a priest, right? You're supposed to forgive people."

"This isn't confession," Father John said. Robert was squinting with such desperation that he tried to soften the rest of it. "Confession means you would have to make amends, Robert. Do what you can to set things right. It's not just getting things off your chest. If you want me to hear your confession, you're going to have to tell Gianelli everything so he can find Eldon White Elk."

Robert swallowed hard, his Adam's apple bobbing. He seemed to make an effort to steady his gaze, but his eyes kept darting between the photo and the floor. When he didn't say anything, Father John said, "You could be dragged into this, Robert. You could be charged with conspiracy to commit murder, as well as theft. Abduction. Burglary. Good Lord, man, if you won't help Eldon, at least help yourself."

"You're not gonna talk to the fed." Robert straightened his shoulders, as if a steel rod had just been jammed into his spine.

"You aren't leaving me a choice." Only the two of them in the gallery, he was thinking, and Robert RunningFast had twenty years on him and probably a lot more street experience. He could attack and leave with nothing more than a few bruised knuckles. But Father John had Commonwealth Ave. Nights walking home from late baseball practice, street lights glowing and neighborhood bullies lurking on the stoops he'd passed. He'd learned to defend himself. There were times when they had outweighed him and outnumbered him, four or five to one, but he had learned to outsmart them.

"It wouldn't be a good idea," Robert said.

"You said your grandmother only cares about the past," Father John said. "You're wrong about that."

"What are you talking about?"

"She cares about the future. Your future,

323

Robert. She wants to see you back in college. There's no reason you couldn't graduate. Things will go easier for you if you go to the fed. You might get off with a misdemeanor charge that won't hurt your future."

Robert's shoulders sank again; he dropped his head. "Jesus," he said under his breath.

"I can go with you. We can call the fed now."

The young man threw up one hand and began backing toward the door. "I gotta think about it."

"Listen to me," Father John said, but he realized he was talking to an empty hall. Robert's boots clicked across the corridor, the outside door slammed shut. It looked like the photo of Black Heart wobbled a little, but Father John couldn't be sure.

He turned off the light, let himself out the front door, shook the key free from the other keys on the ring, and locked up. The sky was alive in the sunset, the clouds glowing red, gold, and orange, lit from within. He took the steps two at a time, his thoughts on Vicky; they had never left his head. He started around Circle Drive, realizing she had been in his head the entire time he'd talked to Robert. Pushed to the edge of his mind, lingering like an old melody. He smiled, seeing again the way she carved out a circle around the office floor, like she always did when she was upset or trying to work out some thorny problem. So many years they had worked together; he had memorized the little idiosyncrasies that might escape a casual observer. He had learned to trust her instincts, the way she had of leaping toward the truth, while he plodded on, testing the logic of each hypothesis, inching forward.

And yet, it was difficult to reconcile what they both knew about Trevor Pratt — that he had changed his name, that he was a convicted thief — with the man who had sat in his office. Like a penitent, when he thought about it now. Head bowed, tone somber and serious, as if he were pulling the words from the deepest part of himself. *So many tribes have lost parts of their heritage. I want to give back.*

He should have pushed the man. Good Lord, what had he been thinking? He'd counseled all kinds of people. Years of unhappy marriages and relationships, troubled kids, alcohol and drug problems. He knew the questions to ask, and yet he hadn't asked Trevor Pratt the simplest question. Why? Why was he so keen to give back?

He wondered now if Trevor would have

opened up and told him. It was possible. He could see the man slumped forward in the chair, chin resting in the cup of his hand. Yes, he thought. Trevor might have wanted to tell someone, to unburden himself. He had needed forgiveness. Everything he had done — purchasing the Arapaho artifacts, arranging to donate them to the museum — had been a cry for forgiveness. God help me, Father John said to himself. He had missed it.

His thoughts swam back to Vicky, her voice drumming inside his head. Trevor hadn't changed. All her instincts told her that Trevor Pratt was still a thief. In a flash, he saw that what he believed about Trevor was also based on instinct. No logic or accumulation of facts. Just an instinct that the man had wanted to make amends. That's how it was with instincts: they could be wrong as often as they were right.

He hurried up the steps to the administration building, intending to check the phone messages, return calls, and spend a little time working on the budget, which didn't seem to change no matter how he arranged the numbers. Each bill had to work its way up the to-be-paid pile, a slow process that depended on the rate at which donations arrived. There was some consolation in the thought that the donations always arrived. He let himself into the old building and headed into his own office.

"John!" The bishop sounded agitated. A sense of urgency in the flap of his elbows as he came down the corridor.

"What is it?" Father John turned and faced the old man who had arrived in the doorway and was gripping the frame to steady himself. "A terrible accident," he said.

Father John felt his breath stop in his throat. He knew it was Vicky even before the bishop said, "Vicky's Jeep turned over on Rendezvous Road. I just got off the phone with the police."

"Is she okay?" Father John said. His mouth was dry, the words felt like pebbles he was spitting out.

"She's at Riverton Memorial."

Father John didn't know when the bishop had stepped out of the doorway. He had no recollection of retracing his route into the corridor and down the steps. He was in the Toyota pickup, the gas pedal pressed down, flying through the cottonwood tunnel and out onto Seventeen-Mile Road. Ten minutes later he pulled into a spot marked Clergy and ran for the entrance.

28

Berlin
July 23, 1890

The evening was warm, a slight breeze ruf-
fling the tipi flaps. Lamplights glowing in
the canvas created cones of light up and
down the grassy path and cast a dim twilight
over the camp. A few Indians were walking
ahead, but most had already retired. Sonny
kept his eyes on the shadows as he walked
with Chief Black Heart toward his tipi. Herman Marks dwelled in the shadows. Hushed
voices from inside the tipis drifted in the
breeze as they passed. A baby wailed somewhere. Every few seconds, Sonny glanced
over his shoulder. The flap of the big tipi
had been thrown open. He could see the
tall figure of Buffalo Bill pacing back and
forth inside, lamplights bouncing off his
white shirt and trousers.

Before they left, Sonny had told Buffalo
Bill about Marks. The big man's face had

remained as rigid as a mask, but Sonny had seen the anger flare in his blue eyes like tiny fireworks. He had treated the Show Indians like men and women, paid them a fair wage, saw they had the same food as everyone else, the same accommodations. Sonny respected and admired the man for that. Buffalo Bill would put a stop to Marks harassing the people, he was certain.

It had been a ungrateful Indian, White Horse, who started all the trouble. Told lies about how the Show Indians were mistreated. Lies, all of it. Now the commissioner of Indian affairs in Washington could refuse permission for the Indians to be in the show, even if the Indians wanted to be here. Sonny gave a snort of contempt that some white man they had never met held such power over their lives.

"What bothers you?" Black Heart said, and Sonny realized he had probably been mumbling and snorting under his breath, his thoughts galloping ahead down the path.

"The idea all of this could be over for our people," Sonny said.

"We'll go to Washington and speak to the commissioner. We'll tell the truth." Black Heart stopped and laid a hand on Sonny's shoulder. His grip was that of a man who had tamed and ridden mustangs, and roped

329

and branded cattle. A man who had fought in battles and could drive an arrow through a tree. "Are you certain you want to go?" he said. "You could stay here and finish the tour. The money will help you get your own spread when you go back to the reservation."

Something seemed to move in the alley of shadows between two tipis. Sonny felt his stomach jump into his chest. Marks could pounce out of the shadows like a grizzly and claw and club at his prey, rip the regalia off Black Heart's back. A dog trotted out from between the tipis, its muzzle searching the ground.

Sonny realized Black Heart was still waiting for his answer. "I go with you, Father," he said. "We can speak the truth in their own language. This is good," he said, nodding around the camp. "Indians making more money than we knew existed. We've crossed the waters, come to strange places and met all kinds of strange people. French and Spanish and Italian and German. They meet us and see that we're people, too. They learn our ways, how our ancestors lived in the time that is now past. And we remember how we were once free." He cleared his throat, forced a smile, and tried for a lighter tone. "Besides, two Indians are better than one."

Black Heart tossed his head back and laughed. Then he said, "White people that call themselves reformers don't like us acting like Indians. They say it's not good for Indians to relive the old ways when we're supposed to become civilized." He laughed again, a low, rumbling noise in his chest.

They walked past the dining tent at the edge of the Indian camp. The dark cone of Black Heart's tipi was ahead. Sonny turned partway and let his eyes scour the area behind them. Buffalo Bill still pacing, a smaller figure now, taking up less space than usual. "How can there be a Wild West Show without Indians?" Sonny said. "We are the Wild West."

"The commissioner will understand." Black Heart spoke softly, as if he wanted to reassure himself. They had reached the chief's tipi, and Sonny opened the flap. He stepped inside the cool, quiet space, found a box of matches and lit two oil lamps that faced each other across the center. The chief pulled out the large black leather satchel from its place next to the wall and opened the lid. Then he removed the beaded wrist cuffs and laid them in tissue paper at the bottom of the case.

"I believe Buffalo Bill will fire Marks tonight," Sonny said.

"One last night to keep my ancestor's things safe." Black Heart took off his vest and laid it inside the bag. "I will keep the bag here tonight. I will stay awake and guard it. You can stay, too, if you like. We could take turns."

An image flashed in front of Sonny, like a vision after long days and nights of fasting and praying. A vision must always be respected. *This is the way you must go.* He saw Marks slinking past the flap. He would use a club or a knife, a silent weapon. Black Heart's head would be bashed in and so would his. Or their throats cut. It would happen in a few seconds. No one would hear anything. Marks would take the black satchel, and he and Black Heart would never speak to the commissioner. The Wild West Show would no longer exist.

"One last night," Sonny repeated the chief's words. "Marks will hear that we leave tomorrow, and he will know I'm the one who told Buffalo Bill about him. He is desperate for your regalia, like a wild beast that won't be satisfied until he devours his prey. You must stay the night at another tipi," he said. All the other Arapahos would be honored to share their hospitality with the chief. "I will take the regalia to a safe place."

"Marks will come to your tipi."

"There is another place," Sonny said. "A secret place he knows nothing about."

Sonny waited until Black Heart had disappeared inside a tipi partway down the path, then he extinguished the lamps in Black Heart's tipi and went outside to stand guard in the shadows. A warrior in the Old Time, making certain the enemy was nowhere about. The glow of a tipi here and there broke the silent darkness. A field of stars shone against the black sky. Sonny felt a pang of homesickness. The night sky over the reservation was as black as coal, the stars full and bright, twinkling like living beings. It would be good to go home. He would take the money he kept in the pouch strapped to his chest and go to the Wind River Reservation, where his sister lived with her new husband. He would use the money to get a little ranch, a few head of cattle. He would find a beautiful Arapaho girl and marry her and they would have many children. He smiled at the thought. He would miss the reservation in Oklahoma and Black Heart, but things were changing there. White settlers moving onto Indian lands. It was as if the land itself had begun folding around the Indians, leaving them in a smaller and smaller place. There was still open space in Wyoming, and he would bring his family to visit Black Heart as often as the government agent gave him permission to leave.

He went back into the tipi, hoisted the black satchel onto his shoulders, and slipped outside. He crossed the midway fast before plunging into the shadows. The bag scraped at his shoulders. It felt light and precious. He started through the field of brush and grasses behind the camp. The Wild West train stood on tracks across the field, the metal wheels shining in the starlight. Clusters of ancient stone buildings stood in front of the train, abandoned warehouses and other railroad buildings, ghosts from another time when the railroad spur had been part of the main line.

Last night, after he confronted Marks in Black Heart's tipi, he had determined to find another hiding place. The old buildings beside the track had reached out to him. This morning, he had walked through them, knocking at the walls, checking on the soundness and tightness. They were older than any buildings he had ever entered. The floors creaked and shook under his boots.

The building closest to the train was stone, walls two feet thick and rooms filled with the dry smell of dust. He had kicked up little swirls of dust as he'd walked about. He had stumbled upon a wooden staircase and clumped downward into the basement. A dim remembrance of daylight had worked past the small, dirty windows near the ceiling.

He had found the perfect place: a large vault with even thicker walls, located across from the stairs. He had only found the vault because the door had been left open, the metal key dangling from the lock concealed in what was meant to look like molding. When he closed the door, the vault became part of the wall. Nearly invisible.

An abandoned building, a vault no one knew about in the basement, and he would have the only key.

Now he made his way around to the back of the old building, glancing about as he went, still expecting Marks to jump from the shadows. A strip of gravel ran alongside the train tracks and butted into the wild grass. He stayed on the grass, footsteps as silent as if he were tracking an enemy on the plains. Odors of coal ash hung in the air. Sonny rebalanced the satchel on his shoulders, holding it with one hand while he opened the back door. He had to turn sideways to step into the small porchlike room that funneled into a corridor with doors hanging open on either side. He closed the back door, set the satchel on the plank floor, and moved toward the narrow, rectangular window. Standing to the side, he cleared a small space on the smudged glass and stared out into the night under the canopy of stars. Nothing moved. From the distance came the nighttime noise of the camp, a muffled cough, a child's cry, the whinnying of a horse.

He let several minutes go by — five, ten — before he lifted the satchel and headed down the corridor to the first door on the right. His own body blocked the dim starlight filtering through the window, and he had to feel his way along the corridor, one boot forward, then the other. Turning sideways again, he started down the dark steps into a well of shadows bisected by dim strips of light flowing past the windows. Still feeling his way, he moved toward the vault, focused on a single necessity: Black Heart's regalia must be safe. The chief must return to Oklahoma with the precious regalia that had been touched by the ancestors, that had covered their bodies. A reminder for the people of who they were, where they had come from, and what the ancestors had believed in.

He set the satchel inside the vault next to the right wall, away from any light that might throw itself across the floor should anyone manage to locate the vault and open the door. Then he stepped out, slid the door into place and turned the key. The bolt clicked into place. He tucked the key next to the money he had saved inside the tanned pouch around his neck, and headed back across the basement in the direction of the stairs, running his fingers along the cold stone wall to guide himself.

He stopped. A noise outside, like a twig snapping under a boot. He stayed very still; he could blend into the stone wall, he was thinking, like the vault. He held his breath and listened. Another sound, so small and muffled that he wondered if he heard it or only imagined it. Then he saw the trouser legs moving past the window in slow motion, as if the man were walking through water. Lift one boot, set it down. Lift the other boot, set it down. There was a remnant of sound, a faint disturbance in the air. The trouser legs disappeared, but only for a brief moment. They were back, patrolling past the window toward the back door. He could barely hear the whispered voices, the short, strained commands. Marks was here, but he wasn't alone. Sonny heard the back door creak open.

He took two steps around the side of the stairs, keeping his footsteps light, as if he were floating on air. In the corridor upstairs, the muffled clack of boots. The door to the basement snapped back against the wall, followed by the kind of stillness that comes when everyone stops and holds their breath. A sudden burst of light flooded the stairs and shot across the basement floor toward the vault. Someone whispered, "Basement's a good hiding place."

"Take a look." Another whisper.

Sonny folded himself against the wall underneath the stairs. Overhead, the first step groaned and shifted. Through the space between the steps, he could see the gas lamp swinging from a large, mottled hand. Smells of perspiration and tobacco and gas floated toward him. A band of light worked past the stairs and crossed his face. He could hear his heart beating like a drum in his ears.

The key! He had to hide the key. He managed to pull the pouch out from inside his shirt and grip the key between his thumb and index finger. His hand was shaking. The next step shifted under the weight of the man with the lantern. A puff of dust drifted downward. Sonny held his breath and waited until his hand was steady. Gripping the key in his fist, as if he were gripping his own life, he ran his other hand over the stones in the wall until the tips of his fingers slid into a tiny notch.

Big enough! He turned his shoulders sideways and pushed the key into the notch, holding it in place for a moment until he was sure it wouldn't fall out.

The man was on the next to the last step now, the smell of perspiration so strong that Sonny had to clamp his lips tight to stifle a cough. The long dark shadow fell backward over the steps, the lamp swung out ahead. Light flooded across the basement floor and walls, like a river overflowing its banks.

"See anything?" The whisper came from the top of the stairs.

The man with the lamp took the last step and planted both boots on the basement floor, swaying as he swung the lamp from side to side. Then he turned back toward the steps. Sonny could feel the instinct that had turned the man around, as if he had sensed Sonny's eyes on his back. He pressed himself against the wall and watched Herman Marks lower the lamp until light penetrated the spaces between the steps. He could feel the strips of light splayed over his body.

"Well, well," Marks said. "What have we here?"

29

The emergency waiting room was empty. Across from the entrance were the metal doors that led into a corridor flanked by examining rooms. A row of plastic chairs with scooped seats lined the wall opposite the counter. There was no one behind the window with the metal intercom inserted in the center. Father John pounded the bell on the counter. "Hello!" he shouted. "Anybody here?"

God, where was everybody? He pushed on the bell again — once, twice. The high, shrill noise bounced around the waiting room. He was about to crash a fist into the ringer again when a gray-haired, middle-aged woman with slumped shoulders and an irritated expression emerged from beyond a side door.

"This is a hospital . . ." She sucked in a breath. "Oh, Father, I didn't know it was you."

"Vicky Holden," he said. "Where do I find her?"

"I'll call the nurse." The woman stretched a hand toward a phone below the window.

Father John swung about and strode toward the metal doors. He knew the emergency room by heart; how many times had he been called here? More than he wanted to think about. Arapahos with heart attacks and strokes. Arapahos in car wrecks and fist-fights, bucked off horses or fallen off tractors out on a ranch, all rushed to the hospital in an ambulance.

That was how Vicky would have come.

"Father! One moment . . ."

He pushed through the doors that banged behind him as he strode down the corridor. The door to the first examining room stood open, the room vacant, a white strip of paper pulled over the examining table. The next door was closed. He could hear the muffled sounds of voices inside as he knocked. The door swung back a few inches, and an anxious-looking nurse with blond hair and green scrubs peered out. "Father John!" she said, yanking the door back. "You're looking for Vicky Holden. I'll take you." She stepped out and closed the door behind her, but not before he caught a glimpse of a bulky figure under the white sheet and the strands of red hair spread over the white pillow.

The nurse hurried ahead. "She's in here," she said, nudging open the door to the next examining room.

There was no one on the table. Then he saw her by the window on the left side of the tiny cubicle. She turned toward him and crossed the space between them. In a second, he pulled her toward him and held her. She was trembling with shock.

"Are you hurt?" he said, still holding her close, as if he could protect her. How ridiculous. He could never protect her.

"They tried to kill me." Her voice was muffled against his shirt.

"Vicky," he said. "Are you all right?" God, let her be all right. It was all he wanted, he thought. It was everything.

She pulled away. Her eyes wide with astonishment, as if she just realized she had been in his arms. "A little stiff and sore," she said. "The doctor's reading my X-rays now, but I think I'm okay."

"Shouldn't you be resting . . ." He nodded toward the ruffled white sheets on the examining table.

"Rest?" she said. "How can I rest? The bastards are still out there."

"The two men in the sedan?" They came

and went like gusts of wind, touching down one place, then another. Taking Trevor Pratt's life. Abducting Eldon White Elk. And now Vicky. My God, where will it stop?

"I've been going over everything in my mind," Vicky said. "I keep coming back to Jason Gains. He has to be the one who called Petey from the Security Systems office to make sure there was no security guard near the warehouse. He has to be involved with those two white men. I think he must have told them I was catching on. They wanted me dead."

Dead. The word hit Father John with the force of an arrow. He wanted to erase the pain and fear in her expression. He had to stop himself from reaching for her again.

"I'll talk to Jason tonight," he said.

"I think he might work the late shift, since he called Petey about six. He's probably still at the office. I'll go with you."

"Only place you should go is home." A tall, athletic-looking man in trousers and short-sleeved white shirt came through the door and walked over to the X-ray screen on the wall. "How you doing, Father?" He was Doctor Larry Harris, an old acquaintance from other trips to the emergency room. Obviously not expecting an answer, Doctor Harris plastered a large black film

344

against the screen and flipped on a light. "You're lucky." He threw a sideways glance at Vicky. "Cervical discs look normal. No sign of rupture or bulging. That doesn't mean you won't develop symptoms later, such as headaches or fatigue. With some accidents, it can take time for injuries to manifest themselves. But at this point, it looks as if your biggest worry will be stiffness and soreness. You should rest for the next couple of days."

He switched off the light and faced them. "I'll give you a prescription to help you relax and sleep. Questions?"

"Thanks," Vicky said. Father John could hear the denial in her tone. She had no intention of taking the prescription. She had no intention of relaxing or sleeping until two murderers were in custody.

The doctor nodded in a way that said he also caught the meaning in her tone. He opened the door. On the other side was the nurse in green scrubs, Adam Lone Eagle beside her. The doctor brushed past them, and Adam stepped inside and closed the door.

"I came as soon as I heard." He kept his eyes on Vicky. "News about the accident is all over the moccasin telegraph." He drew in a deep breath and ran a hand through his black, gray-streaked hair. "I've been crazy with worry."

Vicky seemed to need a moment before she reached out and placed a hand on Adam's arm. "I'm okay," she said. "The two men in the dark sedan ran me off the road."

"Do the police know?"

"Police cars, ambulance, they all showed up." Vicky pulled her hand away. Father John could see she was trembling. "I told them what I had seen. Dark sedan, two white men. They ran up on me and crashed into the tailgate, then came alongside at a curve and pushed me off the road."

Adam did a little half turn, as if he had to look away from what might have happened, then he pivoted back to Vicky. "A couple of white men on the rez can't hide forever. The cops will get them."

Hundreds of miles of empty roads, Father John was thinking. And in Riverton, obscure motels that blended in with the strip malls and warehouses. Anybody could disappear in the area for a long time.

He tried to focus on what Adam was saying. Something about Petey Many Horses and the accident.

"This wouldn't have happened if I hadn't asked you to talk to Petey," Adam said. "Mary told me you talked to his boss this afternoon."

"What else did Mary tell you?" Vicky said.

"Come on, Vicky." A sharp note of irritation punctuated the Lakota's voice. "We talked about Petey. She said you were trying to get his job back. I could never forgive myself if . . ." He sucked in the rest of it. "I should never have gotten you involved." He moved forward and placed his arms around her. "Why didn't you call me right away? I see you called your friend."

Father John could feel the laser heat of the glance the man shot him.

"I came as soon as I heard," Father John said, but he doubted the words had registered with Adam Lone Eagle. Everything about the man was focused on Vicky, the way he stood, holding her like a fragile and breakable sculpture. He was in love with her. And now he was back.

"I'm going to take you home," Adam said.

"I'm not ready to go home just yet." Vicky pulled away, scooped a black bag off the only chair in the room, and fidgeted with the strap on her shoulder, avoiding Adam's eyes, Father John thought. Then she shouldered past him, flung open the door and walked into the corridor.

Father John started after her, but the Lakota caught up and pushed past. He took hold of Vicky's arm and swung her toward him. "You've been in a serious accident. You might have been killed. The Jeep's probably totaled. Let me take you home, Vicky. Let me take care of you."

Vicky had started backing up, shrugging out of his grasp. "Two men tried to kill me," she said. "When they failed, they would have come back if a couple hadn't come along when they did. I could be dead. Don't you get it? I have to know why."

The evening was warm with the smells of sage and dust that blew past the opened windows of the Toyota pickup. Vicky sat huddled in the passenger seat, arms wrapped around her black bag, eyes fixed ahead. "Adam and the doctor are both right," Father John told her as he'd driven out of the hospital parking lot. He had offered to take her home, but she had given him such a look of determination that he knew, even if he took her to her apartment, she would find a way to get to Security Systems and talk to Jason. He had pressed the play button on the CD player, and now "Ch'ella mi creda" drifted beneath the wind.

He turned onto Federal. The traffic light, a few SUVs and pickups crawling along, the red stop lights taking forever to change. "Robert RunningFast came to see me earlier." He tapped the steering wheel. Then he told her how Robert worked unloading cargo at the airport and how, for a thousand dollars, he had agreed to call a certain number and report the time the artifacts were placed in the warehouse.

"A thousand dollars," Vicky said slowly, as if she were trying to fit this new information into its proper place. "How much did the white men pay Jason to call off the security guard?"

"We don't know it was Jason," Father John said. But someone at Security Systems had no doubt made the call, and whoever it was had also alerted the two white men that Vicky was close to the truth. He could feel a rash of anger moving into his neck and face. Jason — or someone — it hardly mattered who. All that mattered was that the person had to be held accountable.

"A perfect setup," Vicky said. "Trevor tracked the shipment, so he knew when the artifacts arrived. He had Eldon contact the shipping company, change the delivery until the next morning and make arrangements for the artifacts to spend the night at the warehouse where they would be safe." She laughed, but Father John glanced over to see if she was crying. "How many others are involved?" she said after a moment. "Robert, Jason, even Petey, although he didn't know he was being set up. You have to hand it to them," she hurried on. "A couple of strangers on the rez, flashing money around, pretending they wanted to buy artifacts. What they wanted was to get close to people who could help them steal the most valuable artifacts."

Father John waited for the SUV in the oncoming lane to pass, then took a left down a wide, dimly lit street with darkened commercial buildings — a mixture of metal structures and garages, flat concrete aprons in front, a graveyard of vehicles spread over the lots. Ahead, a circle of light flared from the pole next to another concrete apron. He turned under the light and parked in front of a slope-roofed, brick building with slats of light that glowed through the blinds at the front windows. He got out and started around the pickup to open the passenger door, but Vicky was already marching across the sidewalk.

30

The reception area was all plastic and vinyl under stuttering, buzzing fluorescent lights. Father John followed Vicky across the vinyl floor to a counter that divided the area from rows of desks stretching toward the back wall. Most of the desks had been cleared, chairs pushed in, computer monitors blank. Two women sat at the front desks. Jason hunched over a monitor in the back. The tap of computer keys pierced the quiet. No one moved.

"Hello," Father John said.

A moment passed before a gray-haired woman swung around and gave them a flat, appraising look, as if they had materialized out of nowhere. "Help you?" she said, without getting up. Then she pointed a finger at Vicky. "You were here this afternoon. Mr. Ritter's gone home. You can try to catch him tomorrow, but I doubt he'll want to talk to you again. From what he told me, Petey Many Horses is not coming back."

Jason was on his feet, hurrying up the aisle. "I'll handle this," he said out of the corner of his mouth as he passed the woman's desk. "What do you want, Father?" He clasped his hands on the counter. His hands were shaking.

"This is Vicky Holden," Father John said.

"I know who she is."

"Can we talk privately?"

"Go away, okay? You're gonna get me fired." He squared his shoulders toward Vicky. "You think you're helping Petey, coming around here and threatening the boss? Well, you're not. I heard him say he's sorry he ever got involved with Indians. That means I'm next to go."

"Is that what you're worried about?" Father John said. Jason was gripping his hands as if he were afraid they might detach themselves and fly away. "We had better talk."

Jason glanced over his shoulder. Both women were watching, elbows on desks, heads bent toward the counter, a mixture of curiosity and boredom in their expressions. "I'm gonna take a smoke break," he said. Then he came along the counter, lifted the gate, and headed toward the door.

Outside, Jason flicked a cigarette out of the package he'd slipped from his shirt pocket and fumbled with a lighter he'd produced from a trousers pocket. His hands were still shaking, and his thumb kept slipping off the switch. The cigarette between his lips bobbed up and down.

Father John took the lighter, flipped it, and held the tiny flame to the cigarette until Jason managed to suck in enough air that the end glowed red. "Why are you here?" he said, drawing down the smoke. The man's chest rose and fell.

"Your friends tried to kill me a couple of hours ago," Vicky said.

"What?" Jason belched the word around the cigarette dangling from the side of his mouth. "What friends? What are you talking about?"

"Listen to me," Father John said, crowding the Arapaho. "You could be in a lot of trouble. Conspiracy to commit theft and abduction. Murder. You could be looking at the rest of your life in prison."

"I don't know what you're talking about." Jason had gone back to sucking on the cigarette. Smoke trailed out of his nostrils. He held the cigarette with one hand; the other hand banged against his thigh.

"Trevor Pratt was murdered," Father John

said. "The museum director has been abducted. Vicky was nearly killed."

"I didn't have nothing to do with any of it, I swear." The man might have been standing in a fierce wind, he was shaking so hard. He dropped the cigarette and ground it into the concrete with the heel of his boot.

"We know the call to Petey came from this office," Vicky said. "It's only a matter of time before the fed proves it came from your desk phone."

"A slam dunk," Father John said. Not quite true, he was thinking. Even if the call was traced to a specific extension, there was no proof Jason had made the call. All they had was a theory. And a young man, blanched and wide-eyed and shaking.

"I'm swearing to you, Father." The man ignored Vicky and stared at Father John as if he hoped he would throw him a lifeline. "On the graves of my ancestors. I didn't know anybody was gonna get killed. I never been in trouble . . ."

"I know that," Father John said. The counselor's tone again: he was on Jason's side; he and Vicky were here to help him. "I think you trusted somebody who betrayed you. I think you called them after Vicky left the office this afternoon. Was it a couple of white men? Strangers asking around the rez about artifacts?"

Jason stepped back and tilted his face toward the sky a moment.

"How much did they pay you?" Father John pushed on.

"Pay me?" The astonishment in Jason's voice was so palpable, Father John felt as if he could reach out and grab hold of it. "What are you talking about?"

"At least one other Arapaho took money in exchange for information," Vicky said. "The Riverton police and fed are tracking all of it. We can't help you unless you trust us. Who told you to call Petey? Who did you call today?"

"Oh, God." Jason dropped his face into his hands. Deep sounds of grief and fright rumbled in his chest. He started sobbing, and moisture leaked around his fingers.

Father John placed a hand on the young man's shoulder. "What is it you know?" he said.

"She asked me to tell Petey his shift was changed," he managed, his voice shaking. "It was no big deal. Some guys she knew were gonna help themselves to one of the artifacts. There were a lot, she said, so nobody would notice one was missing."

"She?" Vicky said.

"I loved her more than anything," Jason

said. He peeled his hands from his face and stared down at the concrete. "She was my whole life. When she found some other guy and broke up with me, I came close to driving my car off a cliff. I didn't want to live. Then she called and said she missed me. Missed me! God, I was over the moon. We should get back together, she said. But we'd take it slow this time. I'd keep staying at my mom's; no moving in right away like last time. She needed a favor. I'd do anything, I told her. Just ask."

Father John had to step away. He looked out across the dark street toward the row of buildings swallowed in the shadows, and the lights of Riverton twinkling beyond. A haze of stars glowed overhead. God, he should have seen it. Everything was starting to come into focus. The young woman at the center of it all. Plans to donate Arapaho artifacts to the museum. Plans to hijack them from the warehouse. Plans to sell them on the illegal market. He wondered how Trevor Pratt had drawn her in. What had he promised? How much money from the artifacts would be hers? What happened when she found herself involved in murder? She had seemed so innocent, ambitious, eager to learn the museum business. And yet, even after Trevor's murder, she had stayed involved with his partners. Even today she had warned them about Vicky.

"Sandra Dorris," he said, turning to face the red-rimmed eyes of the Indian.

"She didn't do anything," Jason said. He looked as if he might start sobbing again. "You gotta keep her out of this."

"Keep her out?" Vicky shouted. "She's in this up to her eyebrows. She's working with two men that killed Trevor and tried to kill me."

Father John cut in. "Eldon White Elk might still be alive." He took a moment and said another silent prayer. "They won't hesitate to kill him when he isn't any use to them. Sandra may know where they're holding him. You've got to tell us, Jason. Where's Sandra now?"

The trace of light around the window curtains suggested someone was inside. Father John parked near the front stoop and slammed the door against the quiet that gripped the night. From far away came the faintest sounds of a barking dog, the noise of an engine gearing down out on the road. A steady wind swept over the fields around the house. Jason had balked at saying anything more about Sandra, except that he loved her and they were back together.

Sandra couldn't have anything to do with theft or murder or kidnapping. He had swiped his hands at the air, as though he could erase the words written on a chalk board. If Father John or Vicky said anything to the law, he would deny he had ever talked to them.

Father John had taken Vicky's arm and guided her back to the pickup. She had resisted at first. She would have stayed outside in front of Security Systems cross-examining a man who was like a mule that couldn't be led any farther, even if he stood in the path of a tornado. Father John had seen that kind of bulwark rise up in counseling sessions. There was no point in continuing. The man needed time to regain his balance and begin the slow, painful move away from denial. Finally Vicky had seemed to realize the same thing, because she had matched her step to his.

"I take it you know where she lives," she said when they had gotten into the pickup.

Father John shook his head. "I know where to start looking."

Now Vicky knocked on the door as he came up the three concrete steps. Whoever was inside would have heard the pickup arrive. Sandra? Her mother? Neither would want to talk to them. He looked around at the brush and grass moving like gray ghosts in the wind. Another moment passed before the door creaked open. Peering around the edge, Barbara Dorris took them in with a frightened, lingering look. Then the door sprung open and she beckoned them inside.

"She's dead, isn't she?" The woman backed into a chair and dropped onto the seat. "You come to tell me my girl's been in an accident or got shot or something."

Father John walked over and set his hand on the woman's shoulder. "We thought she'd be here. We came to talk to her."

The woman stared at him out of big, uncomprehending eyes. "You mean Sandra's okay?"

"I don't know," Father John said. "What would make you think she's dead."

"She's gotten herself into trouble, hasn't she? That's why you brought a lawyer." She nodded at Vicky.

"She's going to need help," Vicky said.

"I knew it." The woman flattened the palm of her hand against her mouth. "I knew something was going on by the way she moped around here, watching TV, acting real calm. But she was nervous as a cat every time the phone rang or somebody come to the door. She wouldn't tell me anything. Kept saying everything was fine.

Those outsiders she started hanging around with, they're the ones got her into trouble."

"What outsiders?" Father John said.

"Couple white guys. One of 'em might be Mexican. I don't know their names. They come around looking for her once. I didn't like the looks of them, didn't trust them. They looked creepy, like they crawled out of a ditch. I told them to go away, leave my daughter alone."

"What makes you think Sandra was hanging with them?" Vicky said.

"I knew, oh, I knew," she said. "Sandra came home after those artifacts got stolen. She was real shook up." She stopped, as if she had stumbled onto a bed of glass shards. "I'm not saying she had anything to do with that. She had been working on the exhibit, so naturally she was upset the Arapaho stuff got stolen. But I could tell she was scared, like maybe she knew something about it. Those men — they took the artifacts, you ask me — then they took the museum director. I think she suspected them. She laid low here the last couple days 'cause she was scared."

"What about Jason Gains?" Father John said. He wondered how much Jason had left out in his eagerness to protect Sandra. "Did he come around?"

"Jason?" The woman shrugged. "That's been over for a while."

"Jason says they're back together," Vicky said.

"What? She never told me that. Oh, God . . ." Barbara sank back against the chair and wiped at her eyes. "I don't know what Sandra's been up to."

"Listen to me," Father John said, then he stopped. He was about to tell the girl's mother that her daughter could be involved in serious crimes. There was no point; the woman was worried enough. "We have to talk to Sandra," he said. "When do you expect her home?"

The woman looked up at him and shook her head. "She went back to that basement apartment in an old house in town. She calls that home now."

31

"I'll take you home first," Father John said.

"I'm going with you." Vicky rubbed at her neck in a futile attempt to rub out the kinks that gripped her muscles. She should have taken the prescription, she was thinking. She probably wouldn't get much sleep tonight. The headlights searched the road ahead and illuminated a coyote that darted across and disappeared into the darkness. "Sandra's at the center of this," she said. "She must have gotten involved with Trevor. There's no other explanation, although it's hard to imagine she would go for an older man. But he had money."

John O'Malley didn't say anything. From the set of his jaw, she understood he was still trying to reconcile the Trevor Pratt he had known with everything they knew now.

"Ambitious, smart, successful." Vicky tried for a little laugh. "Hard combination for an ambitious girl to resist."

"He may have paid her."

"She fell for him, John. Jason said she broke up with him because she had met someone else. When Trevor found out her ex-boyfriend worked at Security Systems, he must have convinced her to let Jason think she wanted to get back with him. She used that poor guy." Vicky turned sideways a little and watched the profile of the man behind the steering wheel, shadowed in the lights of the dashboard. He glanced over and caught her eye, then went back to staring at the road. "Even after those white men killed Trevor, she kept working with them. She's looking for the big payoff."

Seventeen-Mile Road butted into Highway 749, and Father John turned left toward Riverton. The headlights of cars in the oncoming lane threw new patterns of shadow and light over his face. She would go anywhere with this man, she thought, and forced herself to look away. The scrub brush and grasses passed outside in dark smudges; the black expanses of land stretched away from the highway.

In Riverton, the streetlights drifted over vehicles moving past the quiet, nighttime shuttered buildings. Father John stayed on Federal for several blocks, then made a couple of left turns into a neighborhood of bungalows, lights glowing in the windows and cars parked in the driveways. Sandra's mother had given them the address, and Vicky had written it in a small notepad. The notepad was in her bag. She had memorized the address. "Should be up ahead," she said, trying to catch the numbers over the front porches.

He slowed toward a small rectangle of a house. No lights glowing in the windows, no cars around, no sign of life. The dark hulk of a shed stood at the end of the driveway on one side. An overhang roof jutted toward the driveway. Beneath the overhang, Vicky could make out a partly submerged door to the basement. Headlights flashed across the window in the door as John pulled into the graveled driveway.

The pickup was still rolling to a stop when Vicky swung open the door and got out. Pushing through the stiffness and soreness, she headed around the pickup to the top of the concrete steps. In the shadows below was a landing covered with leaves. The pickup door slammed behind her and John O'Malley's footsteps scraped the gravel. She started down the steps and was about to knock when his arm brushed past her. He rapped hard on the door.

No answer. The entire house was as still

as a vault.

John knocked again, and she stared through the window into what might have been a dark cave. "Nobody's here," she said.

Then he moved around her and reached for the doorknob. There was a tiny squeal, like that of a mouse, as the door inched open. "Sandra?" he called into the dark interior. "It's Father John and Vicky Holden. Anybody here?"

Vicky realized she was holding her breath, half expecting someone to jump out of the darkness. The two white men had killed before. They would kill again. She grabbed hold of John O'Malley's shirt as he stepped inside, an instinctive move, she realized, as if she could pull him back from danger. He must have found a wall switch, because a dim light flickered into life over a small living room, littered with things that had been left behind. Remnants of clothing — sweatshirt, crumpled blue jeans, tee shirts, newspapers, cardboard pizza boxes, and Styrofoam containers crusted with old food. The black futon sofa against the left wall listed to one side. A sleeping bag lay crumpled on top. Scattered about the debris were two metal chairs and a wooden stool. Another sleeping bag had been tossed into a corner.

"Sandra?" Father John called again.

Across the room was an alcove that served as a kitchen: sink, cooktop above a miniature refrigerator. A closed door on the left probably led to the bedroom and bath. "So this is where the men were hiding." Vicky sliced a hand toward the sleeping bag on the futon and the other bag in the corner. "Perfect. Nobody would look for them in a basement apartment in Riverton. They must have kept the sedan in the shed in back. God, John. Sandra had no idea the type of people she'd gotten mixed up with. What have they done with her?"

He was already crossing the room. He flung open the door, and Vicky followed him into a short hallway. She waited as his hand swept along the wall. The click of a switch, but nothing changed. Then he pushed open a door and reached inside. A ceiling light came on, and a rectangle of light spilled out. "Sandra?" he said, his voice soft.

Clothes, towels, papers, and what looked like textbooks, tossed about the floor. The bed, a tangle of sheets and blankets. At the headboard were two pillows, worn and thin looking and crushed in the middle with head prints. "Jason wanted us to think he wasn't staying here with Sandra," Vicky said, nodding toward the pillows. "What a cozy love nest. A couple of killers in the living room."

John didn't say anything. He backed into the corridor, and she heard another door open. Vicky went after him and peered past his arm into a bathroom so small she wondered how anyone could turn around inside with the door closed. A few raglike towels thrown into the corner shower stall. On the glass shelf above the sink sat a can of shaving cream and an electric shaver, still plugged into the wall socket.

"We're too late," Father John said. "They've taken off."

"What about Jason?"

"I think he loved Sandra, so he helped her. Probably called her tonight."

Vicky went back into the living room and glanced about — looking for what? A master plan? A map with directions to where they were going? "They could be halfway to the state line," she said as Father John walked over to the front door. She turned in a half circle, still surveying the room. "Where did they keep the artifacts? In a corner? Out in the shed? And what about Eldon White Elk? Where was he held? He must have been constrained, or he would have found a way to escape." She pulled in her lower lip, not wanting to utter the words. Eldon could be dead.

John had pulled his cell out of the case on his belt and was punching the keys. Then, staring at the monitor, he said, "Ted, it's John O'Malley. Vicky and I are at Sandra Dorris's apartment in Riverton." He rattled off the address and said the apartment was in the basement. "It looks like the two white men might have been hiding here. We talked to Jason Gains," he said, then he told the fed that Sandra had asked Jason to call off the security guard Monday night. "Looks like they've abandoned the apartment," he said. "They must have the artifacts, and I hope . . ." He hesitated. "Vicky and I are hoping they have Eldon and he's still alive." He pressed another key and slipped the cell back into place.

"I'll take you home," he said.

"It's hard to imagine Sandra didn't know what she was getting into," Vicky said. They had retraced the route across town and were on Seventeen-Mile Road. The billboard next to the mission entrance loomed against the star-speckled sky, like a dark, giant sentry. "St. Francis Mission," painted in white, shone through the darkness as they passed. He had asked her if she liked Puccini and turned on the CD player in the middle of the seat. A haunting, lilting melody filled the cab. *Girl of the Golden West*, he'd told her.

"I think you called it right," John said. "She was an ambitious girl."

"But the murder of a man she'd gotten involved with? That should have scared her silly. The abduction of her boss? What did she think when those two men brought Eldon to her apartment?"

"They may not have kept him there."

"Still she knew who was responsible for the abduction." Vicky was quiet a moment. "It's hard to imagine what greed can make people do."

"You're a lawyer, Vicky. You've seen this before."

Vicky looked sideways at the man behind the wheel. "I keep forgetting," she said. "I always want to forget."

"Gianelli will put out an alert, and every law enforcement organization in Wyoming will be looking for a dark sedan with two white men, an Indian girl, and an Indian man."

Which sounded hopeful, Vicky was thinking, yet she couldn't shake the disturbing feeling that had come over her in the apartment, as if everything was too pat, too logical. Sandra and the killers had realized things were starting to close in and fled the area. But they could have left yesterday, or the day before. They could have left after they killed Trevor. They had stayed, even though the longer they remained, the greater the chance they would be discovered. They must have been having difficulty selling the artifacts, and Eldon White Elk was their best hope. An expert on Indian artifacts, connected to museums and legitimate dealers but also — certainly — aware of a shadowy underworld.

Another piece of the logic snapped into place. For a while, it had been safer to stay than to flee with a hostage and a million dollars worth of artifacts in a sedan every cop and deputy in the state was looking for.

"They'll be picked up before morning," John was saying, and in the strained reach for hope in his voice, she heard the echoes of the uneasiness nipping at her. "How are you feeling?"

"Stiff and sore." Vicky tried to shift her thoughts away from the men in the sedan. It seemed natural to be here, driving down Rendezvous Road now, past Arapahoe, lights twinkling in the windows of the box-shaped houses, around the curve where the white men had run her off the road. No sign of the accident. Even skid marks were lost under the faint layer of dust. The Jeep had been towed. "My motto for a while," she said, massaging her fingers into her neck. She tried for a smile.

"What about Adam?"

"Adam?" The question had hurtled toward her like a comet out of nowhere. "What about him?"

"He's in love with you."

Vicky took a moment, watching the scene of the three of them in the hospital examining room unfold across her retinas. She and John O'Malley and Adam Lone Eagle, and Adam going on about how he wanted to take care of her. "I suppose he is," she said. "In his own way."

Vicky waited for the next question: how do you feel about him? She stared across the hood into the headlights streaming ahead. They had passed Hudson and were rounding the big curve toward Lander. A haze of lights glimmered on the dark horizon.

The question didn't come, and finally, Vicky said, "Adam has opened his own office in town. He'll continue to specialize in natural resources law. He's helped a lot of tribes. Secured rights to water, oil, gas, coal, methane. He's good at what he does."

"So are you," John said. "You've helped a lot of your people."

And we'll go on, she was thinking. As before, each of us, including John O'Malley, doing what we're good at doing.

It was getting late. Only a few vehicles moved slowly on Main Street. The sidewalks were empty, the windows of the shops and restaurants dark. In the flare of the street-lamps, she tried to make out the time on her watch. Ten minutes to ten.

John made a right and drove down a side street, past houses lost in the shadows beyond the front lawns, past the dark shapes of trees and cars at the curbs. The three-story brick building loomed against the sky ahead, lights glowing in the glass-walled entry. John slowed the pickup for the turn into the parking lot and pulled into the empty space with Reserved written in black letters on the concrete curb.

Vicky followed him with her eyes as he got out and came around the front of the pickup. The opera was still playing, a soprano singing in Italian. She had no idea what the song was about. The door opened. "I'll see you in," he said. Still it took a moment before she managed to swing her legs out of the pickup and get to her feet, a sense of loss sweeping over her like a blunt and unforgiving gust of wind. Don't hurry, she told herself. No reason to hurry away.

Under the ceiling light in the entry, he reached past her and pressed the elevator button. From somewhere in the building came the cranking noise of cables shaking themselves into action, followed by the dull buzzing sound of a large object dropping through space. It was then Vicky felt John O'Malley's arms around her, reining her to him until he was kissing her.

The elevator door opened and she found herself stepping inside. "Do you want to come up?" she said, one foot placed against the weight of the door as it tried to close.

Without responding, John O'Malley turned and started for the door. She caught a glimpse of him walking past the wall of windows as the door folded shut.

32

This was the life he had chosen. The words circled through Father John's mind like a CD stuck in a track as he retraced their route through Lander, out onto the highway, down Rendezvous Road. He had chosen to be a priest, with all the rules and regulations that came with the vocation. A calling, he had always thought of his decision. What else could it have been? Growing up, he had never imagined he might become a priest. High school, college, studying American history, playing baseball, dating girls. Beautiful girls who went on — where did they go? Into their own futures. Marriages, children, homes, careers. He had always thought he would marry. Have some kids and a home, teach about the American Revolution and the Civil War in a New England college. It was the path he had been on, but then something had started to pull him in another direction, interrupting his dreams at night. *Who will I send?* The same question every night until finally something inside him had begun to respond, like Isaiah: "Send me, Lord."

The lights of St. Francis Mission flickered through the cottonwood branches. The heartbreaking melody of "Ch'ella mi creda" soared out of the CD player.

God, help me. Oh, he had counseled many people who had been caught up in something stronger than they were, carried down a crashing river, unable to get their bearings, work their way back to the hard surface of the real and necessary. It happened; it was human. He had to laugh at that. What a great excuse. He'd had no right to draw her toward him, no right to kiss her. Vicky had her own life, a man who loved her, a future waiting for her. No right. No right. The thought pounded like a metronome in his head. A jumble of thoughts swirling about now: he had come so close to losing her; she might have died in the accident. But there was nothing — nothing — a priest could offer her.

The soft noise of the wind blew through the cab, muffling the sounds of Puccini. He felt as if the pickup and its noises were moving through a fog of silence that engulfed the rez. He tried to force his thoughts to what they had found in the girl's apartment — he and Vicky. So many cases they had worked together, trying to help some Arapaho accused of some heinous crime. Always digging down, down, down to the truth. The truth in other people's lives. He laughed out loud at the thought. What was the truth in his own?

The apartment. He had to stay with the apartment because that other train of thought was not one he could follow.

Sandra Dorris harboring two killers in her apartment, going along as they threatened Eldon White Elk, hoping he could lead them to collectors with a lot of money who didn't care where the Wild West artifacts came from. Maybe even helping them keep Eldon White Elk locked up somewhere. Fleeing through the night now.

He had misjudged the girl, just as he had misjudged Trevor Pratt. He was losing his edge, accepting people at face value, believing they were who they seemed. Except that most people were who they seemed. It was only the few who weren't, the practiced liars and actors and charlatans, but in the past, he had seen into them, *felt* something untrue and unsteady about them. When had that changed? When had it become possible that a man like Trevor Pratt could fool him completely? And yet, even now it was hard to believe that Trevor had planned the theft. Oh, he was one of the best. He had lived a whole different life and kept it secret.

But the girl? She was new at the game of deceit, inexperienced. He should have spotted something off about her. Taking up with a man twice her age because of what she might get out of it? He had heard enough confessions to know it happened. He pounded on the steering wheel. Why hadn't he seen it?

He slowed past the billboard for St. Francis Mission, turned right and drove through the cottonwood tunnel, shadows of branches swaying in the headlights. His thoughts on their own path now. Cam Merryman, convicted felon, who had sensed the danger in the white men's proposal and backed away. Robert RunningFast, like Sandra, falling for the lure of money. And Jason? Jason had believed in Sandra. He had done what she asked. They were a couple again, Jason had said, but taking it slow this time.

I'd keep staying at my mom's. The words started like a drumroll in his head.

Father John cleared the tunnel and drove onto Circle Drive. Lights burst from Eagle Hall, but he could see that the men's committee meeting was breaking up. Groups of men wandered down the dirt road that ran between the hall and the church. Others stood about talking and smoking, flicking red ashes onto the dirt. Pickups and sedans lined both sides of the drive and spilled into the field of wild grasses. He slowed past several men and waved, his thoughts fastened now onto Jason Gains. Staying at his Mom's. A new thought hit him, like a fastball in the stomach that he should have seen coming. It wasn't the imprint of Jason's head on one of the pillows in the bedroom.

He felt as if a lock had snapped into place, and everything else tightened around it. There was so much more he hadn't seen, even while it had played out in front of him like the action on a big screen, images clear and, when he thought about it now, obvious. Sandra Dorris working in Eldon's office, her laptop opened at the side of his desk, the sad regret in her eyes when she left the office, the reluctance in the sound of her footsteps in the corridor. All of it clear, but he had missed it. Not wanting to see, not wanting to believe. And the artifacts themselves? The words he'd read on the internet flashed before him: *It appears the regalia had been hidden in a concrete vault deep in the basement of a condemned building.*

He knew now with a cold certainty where the thieves had hidden the regalia. Before they left the area, they would come for them.

He waited until the driver of a pickup vacated a spot at the curb halfway between the church and the museum, then pulled in. In the side view mirror, he spotted Bishop Harry and a couple of men crossing the drive. He got out and headed for the museum, walking fast, running. "John!" the bishop shouted behind him, but he kept going. Taking the wooden steps in front of the museum two at a time, crossing the narrow porch, yanking his keys out of his blue jeans pocket.

"John!" The bishop's voice again, shaded with bewilderment. Father John was about to insert the key into the lock when he heard the sound of his cell ringing. Oh, God. If they were inside, they would hear the phone. He unsnapped the leather pouch on his belt, found the Off button with the tip of his finger and pressed it hard. Then he inserted the key, stepped into the entry, and closed the door. A stream of headlights swept across the corridor, and lights from the streetlamps blinked in the front windows. He ran his hand along the wall for the switch, then stopped. If they were still here, he didn't want to give them any warning.

He stayed close to the wall as he went down the corridor. The old floor was tighter against the wall joists, the creaks softer. The exhibition hall lay in the building's shadows. The door to the office stood open, but the lights were off. As he turned down the back hallway, his breath caught in his throat and his heart leaped against his ribs. The back door that Leonard had just fixed hung open on its hinges. In the dim light, he could see crowbar marks along the edge. The frame was splintered. He forced himself to walk slowly toward the faint trace of light that flowed up the basement steps and out into the hallway through the opened door. As he started down the stairs, he could see the source: a pencil of light lay along the base of the door that led into the museum vault.

Vicky sat on the bench in front of the window, knees pulled to her chin. She sipped at the hot tea she had brewed and stared outside, trying to make sense out of what happened. What kind of line had they crossed, she and John O'Malley? She had let herself inside the apartment in a daze. In a daze listened to the telephone message: Annie's voice, raspy with worry. Are you okay? What can I do to help? Call me as soon as you get in. I'm with Roger.

With Roger. The words uncurled like a rope in her head. Everybody was with someone.

She felt adrift, floating over the roofs of Lander, dodging the streetlamps that poked through the treetops. This was not what she wanted, this confusion, and yet, it was what she had wanted for a very long time. Now that it was here, that John O'Malley had allowed some part of his own feelings to break through the carefully controlled and logical exterior, she felt lost. Before this evening, there had been no possibilities, no different scenarios. Now everything seemed possible. She took a small drink of tea, then ran her hand over her cheeks. The moisture clung to her palm. She had never liked uncertainty; she had planned and worked hard for so many years. She had known exactly where she was going.

She closed her eyes and watched John O'Malley turn away again and cross the entry to the door. She saw him hurry past the window, and with the image came an understanding that brought such a wave of sadness she had to grab the edge of the bench to steady herself. Gradually, she began to recapture the sense of being anchored in her own world. This was not something they would ever mention. This was something to forget.

She forced her thoughts to Sandra Dorris, falling in love with Trevor Pratt and going out on a limb for him, agreeing to the whole outrageous plan of stealing valuable Arapaho artifacts. What had she dreamed about? That she and Trevor would leave together, go where no one would think to look for them? Or would they stay here, living on his ranch, confident no one would ever connect them to the theft? Is that what she had thought? Incredible. Such a terrible risk, and yet, love was a terrible risk.

Except that Sandra was resilient. How quickly she had rebounded! She envied the girl her uncanny ability to forget, to put the past behind and move forward after Trevor was murdered. She had held onto part of her dream. She had kept working with the two white men, intent on getting what she thought was coming to her. She had even taken Jason back. Keeping him close, beside her in bed, his head on the pillow next to hers, telling him she loved him, and Jason, believing all of it. She could almost feel the hunger in his eyes when he talked about Sandra. They were getting back together, he said. Taking it slow, but together.

Vicky uncurled her legs and slammed her feet against the floor. She jumped up and started circling the small dining area. From the counter that divided off the kitchen, around the dining table to the window, back to the counter. She made the loop again, trying to pull it all together. Four people had been sharing the apartment, the two white men in sleeping bags on the living room floor; Sandra and Jason in the bedroom. Where was Eldon? Handcuffed and gagged out in the shed? Possibly, and yet something wasn't right; she was missing something. She circled again, once, twice.

What else had Jason said? *Staying at my mom's.*

She stood still and gripped the hard edge of the counter, the realization hitting her like a meteor, threatening to drive her into the ground. They had been wrong, she and John O'Malley. They had grabbed onto what seemed logical, what made sense, even though it didn't make sense. And he had realized it didn't make sense. It wasn't like the Trevor he knew. Yet John O'Malley had gone along — with her.

She knew the rest of it in an instant, as if the bits and pieces of images had formed themselves into a photograph. The artifacts were stored at the Arapaho Museum. No other place would have been as safe. No one would look for them there. And the thieves would retrieve them before they left the area.

The last piece of the photograph snapped into place. John O'Malley driving into the mission, noticing something at the museum — a light flickering — and walking in on two killers.

She threw herself across the counter, grabbed the phone, and punched in the number for his cell. The sporadic ringing noise buzzed in her ear.

"Pick up," she shouted, as if her voice might carry all the way to the mission. "Pick up!" The buzzing cut off, and John O'Malley's voice was telling her to leave her name and number and he would return the call as soon as he could.

She jammed her finger on the end key, then called the number for the mission. A louder buzzing noise sounded this time, more confident. For a moment, she had the sense that he was at his desk, reaching for the phone. Then his voice again, the same instructions.

God. God. God. It was evening at the mission, meetings going on, the bishop probably in Eagle Hall, and nobody noticing the museum. Except for John, who would spot something unusual and would go to check. She tried his cell again, but there was no buzzing noise this time, just the disembodied message.

She punched in the number for Roger Hurst. Annie picked up on the first ring, as if she had been waiting for the call. "Vicky? Are you okay? Oh, my God, we heard about the accident. You could've been killed."

"Listen, Annie," Vicky said. "I have to borrow your car."

"My car? Are you sure you're okay to drive? I mean, I heard the ambulance took you to the hospital. Roger and I were on our way to Riverton when we got the news you were released, so I've been waiting until you called. I can't tell you how worried . . ."

"Annie, I need you and Roger to bring me your car right away. Mine was totaled."

"But should you . . ."

"Yes, I should," Vicky said.

33

The stairs creaked under his boots. He kept an eye on the door to the vault, expecting it to fling open, but it stayed shut. The pencil of light flickered. He reached the bottom of the stairs and started across the concrete floor. For the first time, he could hear the whispered voices, like the wind knocking against branches. A hurried note in the voices, a mixture of fear and elation. He waited for a moment at the side of the door, stung by the sense of violation. The mission was a place of peace and hope. They had turned it into a den of thieves. A hot flush of anger moved through him. He reached around, grabbed the knob, and threw the door open.

Three men stood frozen on the far side of the small room. A few feet away was Sandra Dorris, half hunched over a closed carton, a package of strapping tape in one hand. Flashlights arranged around the floor flared upward over their faces, like stage lights. Shock and surprise registered in their eyes; their mouths hung open. The opened cardboard cartons at their feet were leaking Styrofoam. One of the white men must have been in his fifties, six feet tall with curly steel gray hair, thick shoulders, and thick fingers that gripped the edge of a feathered headdress. Beside him, a thin man, younger, with brown hair and wild eyes and roped muscles that popped in his arms, was holding open the flaps on a large carton. He let the flaps drop and stepped back.

The other man, black haired and Arapaho, came forward, as if he had been in charge of the operation and would now take charge of the interruption.

"Hello, Eldon," Father John said.

"Who's this guy?" The big white man with shaggy gray hair dropped the headdress. Long black and white feathers fluttered over the top of a carton. The other man moved behind him, as if he were searching the shadows. Hol Chambers and Raphael Luna.

"The pastor," Eldon said. "Let me handle this." He locked eyes with Father John. "You shouldn't have come here. Now we'll have to take you with us." From somewhere he had produced a small, black revolver, which he leveled at Father John. "Sit on the floor over there until we finish," he said, gesturing with his head toward the concrete wall. The gun remained steady in his hand.

"You won't get off the rez," Father John said. He moved sideways to the wall and began sliding down. "Every cop in the county is looking for you."

"We'll see." Eldon motioned to the others to resume packing the artifacts. Across from him, in piles along the wall, Father John could make out the beaded vest and wrist guards; the red, white, and blue flag shirt; the tanned and beaded leggings and moccasins. An aura about them, he thought, of age and history, of old battles and Wild West Shows and cheering crowds.

"You surprise me," he said to Eldon. The gun looked like a bazooka. He was thinking that he had missed seeing into Eldon. So many signs, yet he hadn't seen them. "I never expected a man with your credentials to steal Indian artifacts."

"My credentials?" The Arapaho gave a shout of laughter, and the gun jumped in his hand. "Where'd my credentials get me? A series of dead-end jobs in third-rate museums! Hell, with my credentials, I can work twenty-four-seven the rest of my life and still not have anything. Take Trevor Pratt. He had everything except the credentials. But he made himself an expert. He knew how to buy and sell Indian artifacts, and that made him rich."

"He didn't want to hijack any more artifacts. Isn't that what happened?" Father John said. He sat on his haunches next to the wall, keeping his eye on the gun. Chambers and Luna moved quickly stashing the artifacts into small cartons. Sandra moved behind them, turning down the flaps and slapping on the tape.

"Trevor was a fool!" Eldon started coughing, then he gathered some phlegm and spit it sideways. It wiggled and glistened on the concrete floor. "Playing the high and mighty authority on Indian artifacts, holed up at his ranch like a king. Well, I found out he wasn't all that great. He got his start stealing artifacts and selling them to rich people all over the world. That was the man you thought so much of. Too high and mighty to go along with his old buddies here . . ." He tossed his head toward the other men. "He made his stash. Didn't give a damn about anybody else getting a chance."

"Shut up." Chambers straightened himself over one of the cartons and waved a thick hand at Eldon. "You talk too much."

"What difference does it make? Father

389

here is not gonna be talking to anybody else."

"So Trevor turned down his old friends, and they came to you and formed a new partnership." Father John hurried on, not waiting for a reply. He could read the truth of it in the way Eldon's eyes flashed between the other men. "Problem was, Trevor threatened to go to the fed, and his old partners couldn't have that. Didn't it make you wonder who you were mixed up with, when they killed him?"

"Hold on!" Chambers booted a carton out of his way and moved toward Father John. "You got it all wrong, Padre. Maybe we've lifted some artifacts and dumped them on the black market, but we're not killers."

"I saw you and your friend here racing away from the ranch just after Trevor was killed," Father John said.

"Don't prove nothing. Trevor was our old buddy. Sure, he turned down the chance to make some big bucks on the Wild West artifacts, but that was no reason to kill him. He would never have turned us in. All he wanted was for us to return the artifacts. He wanted us to come to the ranch and talk it over. Trevor would've paid us for our trouble 'cause that's the kind of guy he was. Yeah, we drove up to the ranch, but Trevor was already dead."

Sandra dropped the plastic container of strapping tape. It clanked and rolled across the floor. She reached over and grabbed Eldon's arm. "You filthy liar," she screamed. "Filthy, filthy liar! You told me they killed Trevor. All we had to do was get our money, then we'd cut them loose. Never see them again. You! You killed that nice man! What did Trevor ever do to you?"

"Stop it!" Eldon flung his hand at the girl, but she dodged the blow.

Both white men started moving toward Eldon, as if they were stalking a wild animal. Except that the animal had the gun. "Back off," he said, waving the gun from one to the other. "Let's just get on with it here. Load the cartons into the car, take them to Santa Fe like we agreed. We'll collect our money from the buyer that, let me remind you, I found. We'll go our separate ways. What's done is done."

"You sonofabitch!" Chambers bent his massive head toward Eldon. "You swore you had nothing to do with Trevor getting murdered. You said he'd had trouble with some rancher, and that's who killed him."

"He was gonna blow everything," Eldon said.

Luna's mouth hung open in an O of

shock. "He wanted the artifacts. He would've paid us."

"Paid us? Don't make me laugh. He offered peanuts. We're the ones took the risk, everything going just like we planned. It was my chance. My ticket out of nowheresville. What right did he have to blow it? I offered to cut him in, but he wouldn't listen. He came at me with a club! What choice did I have?"

Sandra was bent over herself, shoulders shaking. The sound of moaning expanded into a long wailing noise that filled the small room. "I didn't have anything to do with this," she screamed. She flung her arms about, wild-eyed, on the edge of hysterics. Then she locked eyes with Father John and seemed to steady herself. "I don't know anything about murder," she said. "You gotta believe me, Father. I didn't want to steal the artifacts. Eldon said he'd see that I never worked at another museum if I didn't go along. He made me do it. You gotta help me. You gotta tell the cops I'm innocent."

"I told you to shut up!" Eldon said, swinging the gun toward the girl.

In that split second, that half breath, Father John threw himself upward and lunged for Eldon's arm. He knocked the arm sideways and clamped his fingers over the man's wrist, trying to dislodge the gun. A gunshot splintered the air. A patch of concrete wall exploded. Little pieces of concrete trickled onto the floor. Father John twisted Eldon's hand, but this time, he realized he wasn't the only one trying to make the man drop the gun. Chambers' burly arms locked across Eldon's neck, yanking his head backward. Eldon's eyes bulged; he was gasping for breath. Still he held on to the gun until Father John grabbed his hand, pried open his fingers, and pulled the gun away.

In another second, Chambers drove a boot into the back of Eldon's knees, and Eldon crumbled onto the floor. "I told you, we aren't murderers," the big man said. "We're thieves." He grabbed something from behind his back, then spun toward Father John. The silver revolver glistened in the dim light. He took a step closer. "Drop the gun, Padre, before you get a bullet in the knee. Drop it, I said!"

Father John let the gun slip out of his hand. It banged against the floor, and Luna swept it up. "Okay, this is how it's gonna go," Chambers said. "Raphael and me are gonna load the cartons into the sedan outside and drive out of here. We're gonna leave you with Eldon and this crazy girl locked inside the vault until somebody misses you and comes looking. Could be awhile." He chuckled at this scenario. "On the floor, Padre," he said, gesturing with the gun. "You, too." He nodded at Sandra. The girl started whimpering as she folded herself downward.

"You won't get off the rez," Father John said.

"Do it!" he shouted.

Out of the corner of his eye, Father John saw Sandra throw out her arms and dive downward next to Eldon. As Father John dropped to his knees and started to stretch onto the floor, he saw the shadowy motion on the stairway.

"Don't move." It was Curtis Soldier Wolf, one of the men he'd seen talking to the bishop outside, and cradled in both hands was a shotgun pointed at Chambers' heart. Filing down the stairs behind him was Lucky Talkman, and behind him, Bishop Harry. "You're gonna hand over the guns real peaceful like, or you're gonna get shot," Curtis said.

The big man seemed to hesitate. He glanced at Luna who stood motionless, looking befuddled and scared, as if he had wandered into a battle he didn't want to fight.

"I suggest you do as you were told," the bishop said. "These men are very upset at your attempt to steal their heritage. I'm afraid neither Father John nor I have any control over what they might do."

Chambers took hold of the muzzle of the gun with his other hand and held it out to the bishop, grip first. Luna did the same. "We aren't killers," Chambers said.

"I've called the police," the bishop said. "We'll wait until they arrive."

"Father John was on his feet again. Through the thick, old walls of the museum, he could hear the faint sounds of commotion — people milling about outside, voices muttering, feet stomping about. Beyond the sounds came the high-pitched, mournful wail of sirens somewhere out on Seventeen-Mile Road.

Vicky pushed the gas pedal into the floor as she came out of the curve on Rendezvous Road. The road was empty, flanked by the winking lights of Arapahoe to the west and St. Francis Mission to the east. She tried to hold the steering wheel steady, but the car had a way of jumping about. She was going too fast, she knew, and yet she was unable to ease up on the pedal, as if every muscle in her body propelled her forward, faster and faster. She had called Gianelli again before she was out of Lander and left another message. Shouting over the noise of the engine. He had to get to the museum. John O'Malley was in danger. Then she had called 911. She remembered telling the dispatcher to get the police to the mission, that killers and thieves were there, that they could kill Father John.

She managed to slow down and roll through the stop sign at Seventeen-Mile Road, then sped up again until the billboard loomed ahead. She took her foot off the gas and made a wide, shaky turn into the tunnel of cottonwoods. Flickering in the branches were the red, blue, and yellow lights of police cars. As she emerged onto Circle Drive, she saw the ambulance parked between the cars and Gianelli's white SUV. Other cars lined the curbs and were parked here and there in the field. Groups of people stood about, huddled near the porch of the museum as if they were at a wake. It was that thought that made her start shaking. She gripped the wheel hard, trying to control the spasms that moved up and down her arms and legs. Her stomach was lurching, and for a moment, she was sure she would be sick.

She stopped the car alongside an SUV at

the curb and slid out. "What happened?" She was shouting into the night, to the people huddled about, to no one in particular.

"Looks like burglars in the museum," somebody said.

"There was a gunshot." A man's voice this time.

Vicky dodged past the bystanders and ran for the porch, gasping for air. Her lungs burned as she ran up the steps. A uniformed officer at the door held up a hand. "No one allowed inside," he said.

"You know who I am," she shouted. "My client is in there."

He stepped back, reluctance written in the shadows of his face. "Who's your client?"

She had already run past him down the corridor and was in the back hall, following the sounds that the old building gave up and the dim light that ran up the basement stairs. She had been right. The killers and Eldon were here for the artifacts. The answer to the cop's questions pounded in her head. John O'Malley was her client. He was always her client. And now, oh, God, he could be dead.

She threw herself into the stairwell and started down the steps. Lights flickered below, then the blinding light from overhead bulbs burst over the stairs and the basement, the walls lined with stacks of cartons and shelves filled with dark objects. Sounds of voices and scraping footsteps rose toward her, like a wall of noise thrust up from the depths of the earth. At the bottom she spotted the door hanging open to a small room. The muffled sounds came from the room.

Just as she started across the basement, Gianelli walked out, one hand gripping the shoulder of Eldon White Elk whose arms were pulled back. He walked with his head down, as if he were picking his way over the potholes of a battlefield. Vicky stood still and watched the rest of the parade file out of the room. Four uniformed officers, two men in handcuffs, and Sandra Dorris. The girl walked ahead of the last officer, throwing her eyes about as if she might grasp the chance to make a run for it. When Vicky saw Bishop Harry emerge at the end of the line, she felt as if the muscles in her legs would melt into liquid. She reached for the rough concrete wall to support herself.

"Father John?" she managed as Gianelli came close. "Is he . . ."

"He's back there," Gianelli said.

Vicky waited until the last officer had started up the stairs before she walked over to the room. A vault, she realized now, with a heavy steel door that hung open. She stood in the doorway a moment and watched John O'Malley lift an eagle-feathered headdress, examine it, run his fingers along the woven edges of the headband.

"Are you okay?" she said.

He swung around. "How did you get here?"

She smiled. "I was afraid you would walk in on Eldon and the others."

"So you figured it out." He spoke with certitude, as if he were stating the obvious, and she knew that he knew she had also called Gianelli and the police. "All the artifacts are here and in good shape," he said.

She felt the smile freeze on her face. It was as it should be, she thought. John O'Malley at St. Francis Mission, where he belonged.

34

The church was jammed, rows of brown faces, gratitude and sorrow mingling in black eyes. Hard-worked, knobby hands thumbing daily missals and fingering rosary beads. Everyone had heard about the recovery of the Wild West artifacts last night and the arrest of the museum director, the two outsiders, and Sandra Dorris, one of their own. Father John tried to imagine how the news had passed so quickly. Cell phones, text messages, internet. And yet, the moccasin telegraph had been carrying messages with lightning speed as long as anyone could remember, even in the Old Time.

He was nearing the end of the Mass now. *Go in peace, to love and serve the Lord.*

Thanks be to God.

He was sure he had come to himself again, as if he'd been lost on the plains and found his way back to the sanctuary of the mission. Nodding to his parishioners as he walked down the center aisle. This was what he had been called to do. He stood out in front and shook hands with the usual old men and the old women who attended daily Mass, as well as the younger generation who were here this morning.

Bernard Tallman held onto his hand for a long moment. "Black Heart's things will be with us, just like he wanted," the old man said.

"As soon as possible," Father John said. Two Riverton police officers had pulled into the mission last night after everyone else had left and taken the artifacts to a secure place — they had given their word — as evidence. Eldon would be charged with first-degree homicide along with larceny and conspiracy and other crimes that the county attorney would decide. As accomplices, Chambers and Luna and Sandra were also looking at felony charges of murder, larceny, and conspiracy. After the trials, the artifacts would come home. It would take time. "We'll have a big celebration," he told the old man. "We'll give the artifacts a place of honor in the Wild West exhibition, just as we'd planned. We'll have cake and lemonade." The old man's eyes filled with tears. "Everyone on the rez will come," Father John said.

Lord, let it be, he prayed silently. He would have to find a replacement for Eldon, someone who loved small museums and the chance to bring the history of the people to life.

Bernard squeezed his hand with the strength of a man half his age. "Thank you, Father," he said.

He was in the office by eight o'clock, after a quick breakfast of oatmeal, toast, and coffee, and a torrent of questions from both Elena and the bishop, who had demanded a play-by-play account of everything that happened last night. How had he figured out Eldon was involved? Nice enough man, smart, too, Elena had said. Well, maybe she could picture him wanting to steal the artifacts. But murder? She had swung back to the stove, shaking her head. She never would have pictured him as a murderer.

Father John had exchanged a quick glance with the bishop. There was nothing they hadn't heard in the confessional, nothing that either one couldn't picture. So many terrible acts that only God himself could forgive. He had excused himself and headed over to the administration building, stopping along the way to throw a Frisbee for Walks-On. Seven or eight tosses, and still the dog wanted more, trotting back with the Frisbee between his jaws, eyes cocked with the eternal look of hope. "Later," Father John promised, then he had climbed the steps and let himself through the heavy, old wooden door. Sun rays danced down the corridor in the floating moats of dust.

He had slept badly. A deep tiredness and sense of futility dogged his footsteps. He crossed the office and sank into the old leather chair that probably bore permanent imprints of his body. Most of the night he had spent sipping coffee in his study, looking out over the shadows and moonlight rolling across the mission grounds. An endless sea of bright stars shone against the black sky. His thoughts had catapulted about. Crazy thoughts about other paths, other possibilities, and at the center, Vicky, as real as if she were in the study with him. Finally he had dragged himself upstairs and dropped off into a series of dreams that made no sense, grasping hands, jumbled voices calling his name, and Vicky, always moving away, walking into the distances where he couldn't reach her. He had awakened with a start, surprised at the dawn and the deep magentas and oranges underlining the massive white clouds. He had to let all thoughts of her go, he told himself.

For her sake.

The laptop whirred into life when he switched it on. He kept his eyes on the blue screen, peopling itself with small, colorful icons, and tried to bring into focus a thought that had followed him from the day Trevor Pratt walked into his office. He typed in a search for "Indian regalia, Buffalo Bill's Wild West Show" and ran his eyes down the materializing Web sites. Halfway down the screen was a link to a *New York Times* article. Black headline blazed across the top when he clicked on it. "Swiss Museum Returns Artifacts." He read through the text. *A museum in Geneva has arranged to return Sioux artifacts to the Pine Ridge Reservation in South Dakota. The artifacts consist of numerous headdresses and items of clothing worn by members of the tribe during European performances of Buffalo Bill's Wild West. All of the items had been purchased by the museum from Herman Marks, an interpreter with the show who used his position to acquire many unusual pieces. "We learned recently that Colonel Cody had terminated Marks' employment after it came to his attention that Marks had pressured Show Indians to sell their regalia," said Martin Grublitz, museum curator. "Given the conditions under which Marks may have come by these items, we decided they should be returned to the tribe.*"

Father John pulled out a notepad and wrote: *Herman Marks, interpreter. Fired by Buffalo Bill.*

He started another search, this time typing "Chief Black Heart, Wild West Show." Web sites jumped onto the page. He scanned the list, then moved to the next page and clicked on the second site. A familiar photo: Chief Black Heart dressed in the red, white, and blue shirt and beaded vest, eagle-feathered headdress crowning his head. In another photo, the chief galloping through the sunshine, Indians galloping behind, clouds of dust bursting from the ground. The caption read: "The crowd cheers at the spectacle of Chief Black Heart leading Arapaho warriors into the Berlin arena, July 23, 1890."

He scrolled down until he came to another newspaper article with the headline: "Arapaho chief praises Buffalo Bill." In the photo, Black Heart, dark shirt and bolo tie, as stern and solemn as the old Jesuits in the photos out in the corridor. The chief sat behind a table, hands clasped on the top. Father John read down the column of tiny type:

In a hearing before the commissioner of

Indian affairs yesterday, Arapaho Chief
Black Heart, who had traveled with Buffalo
Bill's Wild West for eighteen months, said
that Buffalo Bill had always treated the
Show Indians fairly. "We were raised on
horseback," the chief said, referring to
himself and other Show Indians. "That is
the way we had to work. Buffalo Bill fur-
nished us the same work we were raised
to; that is the reason we want to work for
him." He said that Buffalo Bill also encour-
aged the Indian women to make beaded
items and sell them to the visitors in the
Indian camp. The money Indian families
made, the chief said, was a big help when
they returned to the reservations.

Father John moved to a second article,
published several days later, under the
headline: "Show will go on!"

After listening to the testimony of Chief
Black Heart, who recently returned after
performing in the Wild West, the commissioner of Indian affairs granted Colonel
William F. Cody, known as Buffalo Bill,
permission to continue taking Indians on
tour with the show. The ruling ensures the
Wild West will continue, despite the claim
of reformers that the show encourages

Indian savagery at a time when government agents on the reservations are trying
to civilize the Indians.

Father John sat back and stared at the
lines of black type. When Black Heart testi-
fied before the commissioner, he didn't
know that his regalia had been hidden in a
basement vault. Vaults meant safety, security, which was why Eldon had placed the
stolen artifacts in the museum vault. But
who had put the artifacts in the Berlin
vault? Not Black Heart. The chief had
grieved over the loss of his regalia. He had
claimed his adopted son, Sonny Yellow
Robe, kept the regalia safe and would bring
it home when he came.

Father John pulled the notepad over and
ran a black line under the name Herman
Marks. Dealer in Indian artifacts. A man
who put pressure on Show Indians to sell
precious belongings, most likely for pennies. And Sonny Yellow Robe, who protected
Black Heart's regalia.

Hiding it in a vault that Marks had never
found.

Father John moved the cursor back to the
search box. A hunch now. He typed in:
"Unidentified human remains found in
Berlin." Dozens of Web sites came up. It

was impossible. Two wars, the city nearly destroyed twice. Probably thousands of unidentified remains uncovered since 1890. It would take all day to read through the sites, and none of the remains might be that of an American Indian. And yet, he knew from researching an obscure fact in the days when he taught American history that the truth had its own way of filling in the spaces between the known facts, of reaching out and taking hold. The truth could not be shaken off.

He pushed back from the desk, went down the corridor, and told the bishop he'd be out for a while. Someone he wanted to visit. The bishop had looked up from the book flattened in front of him and assured Father John that he would man the phones and greet the visitors.

35

Cam Merryman walked out of the barn, rubbing an oil-spotted rag between his hands. He stopped, eyes narrowed against the bright morning sunshine, as Father John pulled in close to the fence. Then he started moving fast, one hand lifted in greeting. "Hey, Father," he called.

By the time Father John got out of the pickup, Cam was beside him. "Heard Black Heart's stuff was found," he said.

"Eventually, it will be in the museum." Father John slammed the door. The hard thump cut through the sound of the wind steering across the pasture, raising little dust balls on the driveway. The sun seared the back of his neck, and yet, the hint of cooler days was in the air. He explained how the artifacts would be held as evidence until after the trials for Eldon and the others. Then he said, "Your ancestor didn't steal the artifacts."

Cam gave a resigned nod, as if he wished that were true.

"I think he was killed trying to save them. That's why he never came home. He would have returned had he been alive."

Cam seemed to consider this a moment before he said, "The Tallman clan has been saying he took off with the chief's things and lived high in Europe."

"It was Sonny who hid them to keep them safe," Father John said. "The past keeps its secrets, and we can't always know the exact truth. But we can look at what we do know and figure out what must have happened." He took a moment, marshaling his thoughts into a logical order. Then he explained how Buffalo Bill had fired a man named Herman Marks for pressuring Show Indians to sell their regalia. "The vault where Black Heart's regalia was found was in the basement of an old building close to the Wild West arena. Black Heart always said that his adopted son had protected his regalia. I think Sonny hid it in the vault."

"Hid it for himself," Cam said.

Father John shook his head. "Herman Marks was after the regalia. I think he tried to get Sonny to tell him where it was and killed him when he wouldn't talk. He probably buried his body somewhere in the area."

Moisture had started to pool and glisten in the Arapaho's black eyes. He looked away and swiped at his cheeks a moment. Still staring across the pasture, he said, "All this time, the Tallman clan's been accusing Sonny of stealing. Made it look like all his descendants was a no good bunch of thieves. I wanted to believe Sonny was a good man, but I guess I bought into what they kept saying."

"Black Heart believed he was good man," Father John said.

"You think the Tallman clan's gonna buy this? It's not like you got any evidence."

"There's evidence," Father John said. The evidence of logic, he was thinking. He told Cam about the museum in Geneva that had purchased regalia from Marks and, after learning how Marks had pressured the Show Indians, had decided to return the regalia to the Lakotas. "No doubt Marks could have sold Black Heart's regalia for a lot of money. If Sonny had taken the regalia, he had a willing buyer in Herman Marks. But Sonny had died protecting it."

"You gonna try telling that to the Tall-mans? The old man and Mickey?"

411

"I'm going to do my best," Father John said.

There was a moment, at the end of the driveway, when Father John hesitated. He thought about turning right and driving to Lander. Vicky would be at the office, but maybe she'd have time for coffee and he could tell her what he'd learned on the internet. It wasn't a new impulse, he realized. It was an excuse. In the side view mirror, he could see Cam watching, as if he wondered which turn Father John might take.

He turned left and drove toward the Tallman's house.

AUTHOR'S NOTE

While I have tried to paint an accurate portrait of the experience of Arapaho Show Indians in Buffalo Bill's Wild West, I have taken liberties with a few historical facts. It is true that Black Heart traveled through England with the Wild West in 1887 and returned to the show as leader of about one hundred Arapahos for the European tour in 1889–90. And it is also true that, at that time, so-called "reformers" mounted a vigorous campaign with the Department of Interior and the commissioner of Indian affairs to prohibit Indians from performing in Western shows, such as the Wild West. In the reformers' view, the Western shows glorified "savage" Indians at the very time reservations were trying to "civilize" them. Reformers also raised the red flag that Buffalo Bill mistreated the Indians, parading them around like monkeys. To the reformers, it was a far better thing to subject

413

Indians to the poverty, hunger, joblessness, and depression on reservations than to allow them to enrich their lives through travel and exposure to other cultures, and to support their families with the much-needed money they earned.

By mid-1890, it looked as if the reformers would win the day and the commissioner would forbid Indians to take part in any further tours of the Wild West, which, as Buffalo Bill knew, would mean the end of the Wild West. How could the West be portrayed without Indians? In November, Buffalo Bill brought the Indians home. Seventy-nine Indians traveled to Washington and met alone with acting commissioner Robert V. Belt. Through an interpreter, they spoke eloquently of the fair and generous treatment they had received and assured the commissioner they had never been mistreated in any way. They wanted to continue being part of the Wild West. Black Heart spoke passionately for the right of Indians to work at jobs they knew how to do, an opportunity that Buffalo Bill had given them.

While Black Heart is a historical figure, Sonny Yellow Robe is a figment of my imagination. For the purposes of the story, I had Black Heart leave the show in July and go to Washington to speak to the commissioner. There is a photo that shows him in his beautiful regalia, which — unlike in the story — he brought home with him. Also, there is no evidence that Black Heart's father had fought at the Battle of the Little Big Horn, but there is also no evidence to disprove the possibility.

I am indebted to many people for guiding me through the intricacies of the world of the Wild West. Special thanks to Steve Friesen, director of the Buffalo Bill Museum and Grave atop Lookout Mountain in Golden, Colorado. Under Steve's leadership, the museum was named the Western Museum of 2011 by *True West* magazine. It was in the museum's archives, which Steve kindly made available, that I discovered Chief Black Heart and the role he played in speaking up for Buffalo Bill, the idea that grew into my story. Steve also took the time to advise me about various Wild West artifacts, and his excellent book, *Buffalo Bill: Scout, Showman, Visionary*, filled with beautiful photographs, was at my right hand while working on this story.

Other books I found helpful are: *The Lives and Legends of Buffalo Bill*, Don Russell; *Wild West Shows and the Images of American Indians*, L.G. Moses; *Buffalo Bill, Last of the*

Great Scouts, Helen Cody Wetmore; *Four Years in Europe with Buffalo Bill*, Charles Eldridge Griffin; *Buffalo Bill's Wild West, An American Legend*, R.L. Wilson with Greg Martin.

I'm also grateful to the Buffalo Bill Historical Center in Cody, Wyoming (itself worth a trip to Wyoming!) for the hours I spent touring the exhibits, lost in the magical world of Buffalo Bill and the Wild West.

As for guiding me through the intricacies of federal criminal laws, I am again indebted to Todd Dawson, special agent, FBI, and to Ray Brown, special agent, U.S. Fish and Wildlife Service, Office of Law Enforcement, both of Lander, Wyoming.

Thanks also to my keen-eyed friends who read the manuscript and suggested some excellent changes: Virginia Sutter and Jim Sutter, Wind River Reservation; Karen Gilleland; Carl Schneider; Beverly Carrigan; Sheila Carrigan; and my husband and first reader, George Coel. And to my always perceptive editor, Tom Colgan, and agent, Rich Henshaw.

And a special thank you to Merle Haas for the gift of her story about her great-great-grandfather Chief Yellow Calf's reluctance to travel across the "trackless" waters.

My heartfelt thanks to them all.